MARSHALS STORM

GLEN W. CHRISTEN

Green Ivy Publishing
1 Lincoln Centre
18W140 Butterfield Road
Suite 1500
Oakbrook Terrace IL 60181-4843
www.greenivybooks.com

ISBN: 978-1-944680-12-1

PROLOGUE

Before dawn began to show in the sky, Sue and Ted were safely concealed in the shelter of a row of boulders at the canyon's mouth. Less than a hundred yards away, four sleeping figures were clustered on a bare patch of ground around the campfire's remnants.

Ted whispered, "Can they escape up the canyon?"

"Not on horses. They might be able to on foot if they were to get away from us," she whispered. "There's a cave off to the left that would hold them all. I'm surprised they aren't using it."

Dawn broke before the first of the outlaws stirred. His hand moved to his gun as his eyes swept the campsite. He kicked a sleeping companion and snarled, "Go check on Harry. He was supposed to wake us up a long time ago. If he's asleep, shoot the bastard."

The victim of the kick growled, picked up his rifle, and started walking toward Harry.

Just a few seconds later, Ted bellowed, "Drop your guns! You're under arrest!"

Pandemonium erupted as the other outlaws dove for cover. The erstwhile guard's relief whipped up his rifle with his snapshot going wild as two rifles smashed him down. The return fire splattered against the boulders that were protecting them.

There was a moment of silence when Sue heard Ted swearing under his breath.

"They have some protection from that dip I couldn't see in the dark. They can't run, but we can't either. Stalemate," Ted said bitterly.

They traded sporadic shots through the sunrise. Sue's sharp eyes detected a flicker of movement near the campfire site, and she centered her aim, slowly squeezing off a round. The bullet burned a furrow across the back of a rustler. He leaped to his feet, cursing as he raced for shelter. A bullet from Ted's rifle brought him down, but they both ducked instinctively when return fire ricocheted in all directions.

Silence descended momentarily before it was broken by a rifle shot that came from behind them. Ted pitched forward, blood streaming from his head, and Sue started to swing her rifle around.

A surly voice rang out, "Freeze, bitch! I'd like nothing better than to kill you."

She froze when she recognized the voice of Weasel Wilson.

"Now, drop your gun."

The rifle dropped from her numb fingers.

"Mel! It's me, Weasel. Keep her covered. I'll come around to meet you. The other bastard is dead," he lowered his voice before turning to Sue.

"Get out from behind those rocks where they can see you."

Turning her head, she spotted his rifle, which was covering her from point-blank range. Her heart thumped in her throat.

He sneered. "Now, it's your turn."

She stood up slowly, and at a wave from his gun barrel moved out from behind the protecting boulders. Rising from their shelter, two figures moved toward her with guns in hand while they covered her.

Weasel sidled around her to meet them, crowing, "I saved your hides. Mel, you can have her too. But I get her first. She's even wearing a tin star you can use for target practice."

The marshal smiled coldly. Unable to fathom that any woman might be dangerous, both older men turned away from Sue to face Weasel. "Sure, kid. You can have her, but Snake Carson always gets first choice."

Stunned, Weasel stopped. He paled in horror and gasped in disbelief, "Snake Carson!" He began backpedaling as the two men moved closer, feeling his dreams of a life of crime and riches vanish.

Snake laughed with insane delight at the naked fear. Shifting his aim from Sue, he fired once. Weasel buckled at the knees and collapsed.

With Snake's attention diverted for a second, Sue's hand flashed down and back up, driven by desperation— she would live or die by her skill with a gun. The instant it cleared leather and came level she triggered six shots in a continuous flash of fire. Two guns roared in return while she staggered in piercing pain that stabbed her side.

TABLE OF CONTENTS

CHAPTER 1

Spring came late to the Rocky Mountains of Colorado after an unusually severe winter. The drip of melting snow from the rocks and trees got lost in the thunder of streams and rivers engorged by snowmelt. Flocks of birds wheeled joyously in the sky above, welcoming their release from the prison of winter's blasts.

Sue Mason stood in front of her barn next to her dog, Mutt, and watched the water converging into larger streams in every direction. She smiled delightedly and felt like singing in spite of being muddy to the knees. The end of three long months of being snowbound and isolated in her mountain home had arrived. The mountain peaks towering above her were accentuated by the early morning sun. Although they were covered in deep snow that would take many days to melt, her heart fluttered in anticipation.

Leaving the barn and the chores she had just completed, she slogged her way across the yard to the ranch house with Mutt trailing her. He curled up next to the doorway as she sat down on the top step of the front porch. Wiping the mud off her high-heeled rider's boots with an old rag, she stripped them off and carried them into the house. At six feet and two inches in bare feet, she had to duck at the doorway but her Stetson still caught the doorframe. She backed up and ducked lower to make it safely inside.

She dropped her boots in their usual spot next to the back door before hanging her coat, vest, and hat on pegs. After she stripped off her gun belt with its holstered Colt 45 and hung it on another peg, she stoked the coals in the kitchen stove and added more wood. The pantry's shelves were distressingly bare. A deer, occasional rabbits, and other small game had provided meat during her long confinement, but the end of winter and her food supplies were in a dead heat. Only a single row with a meager number of cans remained on the otherwise bare shelf. She felt distressed, knowing she still had to ration herself and couldn't travel to town for more supplies for days.

The impending arrival of spring made her giddy. For no reason, she laughed to herself while she put a tin boiler on the stove and partially filled it with water. Any outdoor chore was made more difficult because of the mud, so today was a day for indoor work. After breakfast, she planned to attack her pile of laundry with soap, hot water, a washboard, and elbow grease. She stripped off her man's jeans and chambray work shirt, added them to the pile, and slipped into a worn-out robe. She heated up one of the few remaining cans of stew, eating slowly, savoring the stew and the moment of respite from her routine of morning chores.

Eating with her right hand, she flipped through the pages of an opened book with her left. Confused for a moment, she turned back a page, re-reading it to clarify one of the principles of law the writer was attempting to explain. When she was done eating, she returned the textbook to its spot among the many on the shelves her father had left her. When she was done washing the dishes in the dishpan, she turned to the basket of laundry waiting for her attention.

***

Four days later, the warm weather had transformed her world as the predawn sky began to lighten. The snow was virtually gone from her yard and the surrounding area at her elevation, but the mud and running water remained.

It was still early, so the sun had not yet shown above the mountains in the distance as she saddled her gelding in the shelter of the barn. When the saddle was snug to her satisfaction, she put a pack saddle on her favorite pack horse, which was an old mare she could count on to follow her anywhere without need of a lead rope.

Sue hummed as she rode out of the ranch with Mutt trotting along and headed for town where she could restock her depleted supplies. Her face displayed a wide grin while she enjoyed the weather that was warm enough for a light jacket instead of a heavy sheepskin coat that had been necessary. Many times during the winter, she had ridden out to check on her scattered herds and returned half-frozen with hands and feet numbed from the unrelenting cold. Today's weather was heavenly in comparison.

She turned aside from the main trail to check her herds penned in canyons, which formed natural corrals. The first she rode into held her brood cows that looked as wide as they were long with shaggy winter coats that made them appear even larger. A few had already dropped calves that were eagerly nursing.

When she started to sing aloud, the cows within earshot were so startled she had to quit and began to laugh. Even Mutt turned to her and tilted his head as if he were astonished. Despite the unusually severe winter, her animals were in good condition and that made her simply delighted. She continued on to the natural corrals with her spirits high.

When Sue rounded the last canyon wall that concealed the gate to the corral for her yearling stock, her spirits crashed and shattered into tiny pieces. She gasped, horrified. The split-rails that formed the gate across the mouth of the canyon corral were tossed carelessly aside. Immediately, she urged her horse into a trot, feeling a cold knot settling in her belly. Mutt raced ahead.

The mouth of the canyon was aligned with the prevailing winter winds and was always swept clear of snow. The bare soil was covered with the tracks of many cattle and numerous horses' hooves, which all led outward from her canyon corral. Cursing under her breath, Sue drew her Winchester from the scabbard and levered a round into the chamber. She balanced it across the pommel with one hand and rode into the canyon mouth.

A half-hour search confirmed her worst fears. Not a single animal remained to be found. Many horses' tracks were the mute evidence to a systematic sweep by more than one rider. Heartbroken and furious, she considered following the rustlers alone for a split second. However, her better sense overruled the urge when she realized she'd be badly outnumbered. Bitterly, she turned her horses toward the Marshal's office in town. Her morning's joy was gone, replaced by a bleak and dreary mood.

Two hours later, she drew rein on a ridge that gave her an unobstructed view of the entire town of Wilford. The town was nestled against the flank of a mountain on a small plateau with the far side sloping to the west. The near side sloped down to the east in the direction of a rushing river of snowmelt. The business district, which was only a few hundred yards long, was clustered next to two lines of steel rail. Several saloons were scattered at one end of town, near the bank of the swollen creek that tumbled toward the river far below.

The town marshal's office was located in the middle of the business district between the bank and an empty store. Sue urged her horses onward and a few minutes later arrived at Doc Madison's home, which was a white, two-story house. There were no horses tied in the front, so she assumed there were no patients in his office. Mutt curled up by her horse as she dismounted stiffly and dashed up the steps to the porch. Before she even touched the knob, the door swung open.

Doc's eyes widened at her drawn, haggard face and skinny frame. "Good God, girl! You look terrible! What's the matter?"

"The rustlers." She flailed her hands. "They cleaned out my entire herd of yearlings!"

He pulled her in for a quick hug, having known her all her life and how fiercely independent she was. "We'll try to figure out what to do over dinner. You look hungry. I've got a hot meal on the stove."

Sue sat down at the table. He ladled food onto her plate, heaping it high. She tried to protest but he retorted. "You're so thin it's obvious you haven't eaten enough this winter. What did you do? Run out of food?"

She grinned in spite of how she was feeling. "Almost. I only have enough for less than a week. It was a near thing."

He filled his own plate and sat down. "Now, tell me what happened."

Being around him eased her panic. She ate slowly while she told him of her daily struggles to keep her corralled livestock alive despite constant blizzards and biting cold. "Then spring finally came. Thought I was sitting pretty, until today. Until I found all my yearlings missing," she sniffled, lost in bitterness. "By the way, what is today's date anyway?"

"Thursday, May the tenth." His hand gently enveloped hers, resting on the table. "Next week is your eighteenth birthday."

She shook her head, and her brown eyes met his light green eyes. "Right now, I don't know how I'm going to handle the rustlers…but that reminds me. I do need to thank you for volunteering to be my legal guardian when Pa died. Without you cosigning the papers, I wouldn't have had any options at all back then…"

He smiled at her fondly. "Whatever you decide, I'll back you. But you need to know that Marshal Logan died several weeks ago. We have a new Marshal named Mel Victor," he sighed.

The tone of his words warned her of his poor opinion of the man. "I suppose I'd better go see what, if anything, he can do. Have you heard of anyone else getting hit by rustlers?"

He shook his head and rubbed the back of his neck. "No, but there were a lot of other ranchers that have been snowbound this winter like you were. More than usual. They haven't been in town for months either. They'll probably start showing up in the next few days like you did."

"I'd better go see the marshal. I just hope he can do something." She stood up, towering over him. He grinned up at her in encouragement, his white shirt and black coat a sharp contrast to her faded jeans and shirt when so close together.

Settling her Stetson on her shoulder-length, brown hair, unkempt and uncut all winter long, she shrugged. She fiddled with her gun belt, shifting it to a better position on her hips before hugging him again. "I'll see you before I leave town unless you're out on a call."

Gently, he hugged her and patted her on the back in goodbye.

Sue decided to leave her horses at the livery by the railway depot at the end of the street... they needed to be fed hay and the rare treat of oats regardless of the cost. Mutt stayed in a pile of hay next to his friends to await her return. Her next stop was Horwick's General Store that was a door down, where she gave her long list of needed supplies to Darol, the proprietor.

"Good to see you survived the winter," he greeted her. "How did your livestock fare?"

She scowled. "They did real well until rustlers drove off all my yearlings."

Startled, he turned to face her. "You're the first to report having lost any. 'Course, a lot of your neighbors haven't been to town yet. They may have lost some."

"And I don't know of anyone else who had 'em all corralled in one spot. I'm probably the only one who'd know for sure if I lost cattle until roundup."

After a moment's reflection, he spoke, "That's true. I'd suggest you talk to the new marshal."

"That's where I'm headed next."

CHAPTER 2

It was just a short walk up the street. Sue scowled in disgust even before she entered the Marshal's Office because her nose was assaulted by the sour stink of an unwashed body. A man was standing behind a side window, and when he turned to face her, a marshal's star was on his vest. Her previous opinion, based solely on the conversation with Doc Madison, plummeted even further at the sight of his dirty, stained clothing and his greasy, stringy hair. Her skin crawled as he leered.

His eyes moved over her body, probably undressing her as they went. He averted his eyes in a tardy display of respect. "I'm Marshal Victor. What can I do for you, ma'am?"

"Rustlers just cleaned me out, and I'd like to know what you're going to do about it."

A gleam of interest showed in his eyes. "First of all, who's your husband? What's your name?"

She seethed at his casual dismissal. "Sue Mason. I'm not married."

"What brand?" His eyes shifted below her neck as he added condescendingly, "Or did you even brand them?"

"They were all branded with the double M," she snapped. "Do you want me to draw you a picture?"

He flushed at her unbridled sarcasm. "Ahem… How many head did you lose?"

"Almost two hundred."

His grin was oily. "How many do you have left?"

"About the same number of cows. They've just started to calve, but I don't know exactly how many have dropped."

He chuckled sardonically, "No woman can run a ranch alone. Why don't you marry me and let me take the worry off your shoulders?"

Sue choked in revulsion and spun on her heel, stumbling blindly through the door. She was almost to the street when another figure blocked her way. Seething in rage at the Marshal's casual dismissal, she focused on the newcomer's face before her eyes dropped to the Deputy Marshal star pinned to his vest.

She snapped as her foul mood enhanced her distaste for the man, "What do you want?"

Weasel Wilson pretended to be hurt. "You promised me last fall you'd go to a dance with me."

"I wouldn't be caught dead with you even if you were the last man on Earth!" Her angry voice carried above the street noise, causing people to stare.

Weasel turned red and grabbed her arm. She slapped him away with her left hand while her right flashed to her gun. When it cleared the holster, she triggered a round. The muzzle flash and unburned powder scorched his legs. He froze, staring at a bullet hole neatly drilled in the dirt between his boots.

Startled onlookers from all over the street turned to them.

"If you ever touch me again, I'll put the next bullet in your belly!"

Looking down at the revolver inches from his gun belt, he tried to stare her down but blinked first. Humiliated, he turned on his heel and stomped away in a fit of rage.

She watched until he was out of sight before turning to the marshal, who was standing on the porch behind her, drawn by the gunshot.

"Keep your trained monkey out of my sight, or I'll put a bullet in him." She gritted her teeth. "That goes for you too."

The onlookers gasped as she stalked off, ignoring their stares.

***

Sue ate at the boarding house before returning home. An unnatural silence filling the dining room was broken by the friendly voice of Mrs. Manlick. Only the fact she had eaten nothing but her own cooking for so many months made her tolerate the silent chill. She was unwilling to tell anyone of the humiliation that she suffered from the Marshal's marriage proposal and refused to explain. As a result, the rumor mill painted her in the worst possible light.

***

Mutt trotted ahead as Sue rode into her ranch yard late in the afternoon. Her heart felt as heavy as the load on her pack horse. The trails were muddy and still covered in un-melted snow in many sections. As a result, her clothes were soaked through and she was shivering violently in the evening chill.

She unloaded the pack on the porch before leading her horses into the shelter of the barn where she unsaddled and fed them. A brisk rubdown of both horses brought a grateful twitch of their ears that helped to warm her as well.

Starting a fire in the kitchen stove, she treated Mutt to a rare can of stew in his bowl. She put away her stockpile of groceries in the pantry while she waited for the fire to build enough to heat her own meal and the kitchen. After eating, she hung her damp clothes near the stove and lit a lamp.

Laying a ragged piece of cloth on the table, she disassembled her Winchester for cleaning and inspection. She gave her rifle a light oiling, reassembled it, and dry-fired it several times. Satisfied, she laid it aside before she did the same with her Colt. Only then, physically and emotionally exhausted by the day's events, did she stumble off to bed where she instantly fell asleep.

The next morning, she rode out shortly after sunrise, feeling thankful for her dog's companionship and the warmth of her coat. The extra ammunition in each pocket added its own comfort. She took to high ground, carefully keeping in cover and away from the skyline so she wouldn't be easily spotted.

Relying heavily on Mutt's superior senses, she tied her horse to a stand of trees some distance from the gate to her canyon corral and crept forward. She scanned every inch of the canyon floor in all directions but saw nothing out of the ordinary. Even her tracks from the day before were still visible from this distance, which were outlined by the early-morning sunshine. Satisfied, she returned to her horse and picked her way down an almost invisible trail to the canyon floor below.

The rest of the morning was spent on surveying her natural corral, counting the cows with calves and the cows about to give birth. She found the bones of three that had died during the winter, counting herself lucky to have lost so few.

"Now, if the rustlers leave me alone, I should have a decent herd next year."

Her mount's ears perked up at the sound of her voice as Mutt turned to eye her as well.

Closing the gate behind her, she swept the ground clear with a switch of grass. She levered a cartridge into the chamber of her rifle, and with it near at hand, she rode on toward the empty canyon. She dismounted some distance from the open gate and inched forward, hugging the deep shadows at the base of the solid wall of rock that towered above her.

The silence was undisturbed except for the distant call of birds and the squeak of a startled rodent. Her previous tracks were disturbed only by a wisp of wind-blown sand. Sue squatted on her heels to examine those left by the rustlers, sifting through the mass of tracks. She saw two that were memorable: a right hind shoe that had a distinctive notch in one side and a right front with a half-moon dimple on the front edge.

"I hope those tracks hang you," she muttered.

She spent most of the rest of the afternoon searching this canyon as well, hoping against hope to find more clues or even a few head the rustlers might have missed. When neither materialized as the shadows lengthened, she was bitterly disappointed and turned toward home.

Again, Sue rode back the next morning to check on her herd of cows. Mutt ranged ahead with ears high and tail wagging. She found the gate still closed, but ice settled in her belly when she spotted another mass of tracks showing where more cattle had been driven away. She drew her rifle as she dismounted and bent to examine the tracks where a distinctive notch stood out vividly. Angrily, she remounted, did another thorough sweep, and tallied another twenty head missing.

Sue rode home, furious at the arrogance of the rustlers and the loss of her cattle. They had made no effort to hide their tracks as if they wanted her to know what they'd done. She flopped dejectedly into her father's rocking chair while her mind coldly rejected one plan of action after another. Mutt had been curled around her feet but jumped away startled when she suddenly jumped to her feet in excitement.

The dog's ears came erect as she chortled, "You and I are going to show them a thing or two. We'll teach them a lesson they'll never forget!"

He eyed her warily, watching her pick up the can of kerosene from the corner and fill the lamp on the mantle. Mutt followed as Sue grabbed her rifle, a handful of cartridges, and rushed out the back door. She stopped long enough by the back door to select several tin cans from the handy waste barrel.

She hurried to the foot of the steep slope and set the cans up in a row before eying a spot about a hundred and fifty yards uphill. She climbed to her chosen spot where she made herself comfortable and aimed her rifle downward. Twenty rounds later, she sighed in satisfaction because her sights were adjusted for a grouping that a hand could cover with ease.

Sue ate a light meal, made other last-minute preparations, and rode out. The last afterglow of sunset had faded before she was back at the canyon entrance with a lamp in hand. Mutt's ears lay flat against his head, dimly visible in the faint glow of starlight. Satisfied there was no one nearby, she lit the lamp. Lowering the chimney, she turned the wick down and set it on a flat rock near one side of the gate.

A short time later, she peered down on the gate from an overlook some distance away and a hundred feet higher. She positioned several rocks to give her protection and to rest her rifle. Feeling secure, Sue cleared the rocks from a small area and lay down on the sandy soil with her rifle stretched out in front of her. Mutt snuggled against her, the warmth of his body welcome against the chill of the night. She pulled a bedroll blanket over both of them.

After drifting off into sleep, she was awakened by Mutt's soft growl next to her ear, which alerted her instantly. She laid a hand on his shoulder to quiet him before flipping the blanket to one side. The position of the stars meant many hours had passed and dawn was not far away.

The night was silent except for very faint noises of moving horses slowly approaching in the darkness. There was no moonlight, but the stars were so bright she could see darker shadows outlined against the pale stone of the canyon walls. She watched intently while the shadows slowly materialized into five riders. She could hear coarse laughter of the riders approaching the gate.

One voice carried clearly across the intervening distance. "Stupid bitch! Thinks a little light will scare us off. Let's clean her out instead of just taking a few and wasting another trip."

Her whole body shivered. *They know who I am!*

One of the riders dismounted and strode to the gate. He jerked one of the split rails from its mounts and threw it aside.

Coldly, she thought. *I've set the trap but you didn't have to take the bait.* She whispered to Mutt, knowing his keen ears would hear clearly, "Sic 'em."

He vanished at a run, being silent as a ghost in the night. She focused on the figure illuminated by the faint glow of the lantern and slowly increased the pressure on her trigger finger.

The actual discharge came as a surprise—even to her. She levered in another cartridge, watching her first target crumple. Frozen in disbelief, the other riders failed to react until her second bullet hit one of them in the arm. They fired wildly in return, but their handguns were useless at that range. One rider grabbed the outstretched arm of the wounded man on the ground just as Mutt exploded in their midst. His savage howl spooked the horses as his fangs raked the shoulder of another rider.

Chaos exploded in their midst when they fired wildly at the phantom among them. One uninjured rider pitched forward, dead from a bullet in the head from a companion's gun. His horse raced away with the man's foot still caught in the stirrup and the body bouncing on the ground. Another collapsed over the saddle pommel, mortally wounded by another stray bullet from a companions' gun. The wounded man on the ground was safely out of the line of fire from the other riders' guns and was helped to another's saddle. The survivors spurred away, being chased by another bullet from Sue's rifle.

Her shill whistle recalled Mutt. She trembled in relief, listening to the retreating riders until they were out of her hearing range. When all was silent again, she rolled up the blanket and threw it over one shoulder before picking up her rifle. She slipped away from her hiding place and retreated to the copse of aspen where her horse was hidden.

She waited there in safety until dawn before leading her horse down the twisting trail to the canyon. Mutt ran ahead, quartering the entire canyon to the gate. The lantern was still burning but the fuel was almost gone. Another half hour, and it would've died. She lifted it from its perch and bent to the shadows in the sand where the light revealed a puddle of blood.

Unaware of the carnage inflicted by the outlaw's own gunfire, she said, "Well, Mutt. I winged one bad enough he's not going to be much good for a while." Blowing out the lamp, she replaced the split rail in the gate and headed home.

***

When she finished the morning chores and shuffled tiredly back to the ranch house, a cold breakfast waited for her and her dog. She gulped it down before staggering to her bedroom and plopping down on her bed. By the time she woke, the midday sun was streaming through the windows. Instead of banishing her fears, the bright sun intensified them. "They know who I am. That means they know where I live." She smiled in spite of her fears as Mutt growled in agreement. *But what do I do next?*

She stoked the fire and put the skillet on to heat while she ruthlessly examined her defenses in her mind. The ranch house is a trap, situated on open ground next to a bluff, and she couldn't defend it from more than one direction by herself. The barn had the same weakness, so only the surrounding timber would give her the freedom of movement to avoid being trapped if she were attacked.

Sue spent the rest of the day hiding food and ammunition in several safe locations she could easily locate during the day or night. She dispersed her horses as well, moving them to several hidden pastures that only she knew. She hoped.

With a line of retreat laid out, she began to place simple and reliable alarms in place. Tin cans filled with pebbles were placed in likely paths in all directions. Triggered by string or cord, they would make sounds if someone tried to sneak up on her. That would give her at least a few minutes warning.

CHAPTER 3

After a second night of sleeping under a massive fir, Sue was cold, tired, and furious. She flexed her stiff muscles as she got to her half-frozen feet, muttering under her breath. Mutt raced ahead to the ranch house. She stirred the leftover coals in the kitchen stove and the fireplace in the front room, coaxing small flames to life and adding kindling.

While the fires were building, she went to her father's empty bedroom and began to search through the trunk where she had left his treasures undisturbed since his death. After several minutes, she unwrapped the linen from a cylindrical object and exposed a spyglass to the morning sun. She slipped it into an inner pocket of her vest and returned to the kitchen. She dumped a share of her breakfast into a bowl on the floor for Mutt before heating her own. She ate silently, running her limited options through her mind.

I hate him, but he is the Law. Maybe he'll do something this time...

Sue went to the corral and saddled her favorite gelding. When she rode out, Mutt trotted ahead as she headed for Wilford. She had intimate knowledge of every inch of cover and every game trail that existed on the way. Still fearing an ambush of opportunity, she kept off the main trails. She halted at the edge of every open space or meadow, searching with sharp eyes and the spyglass. When it was possible, she followed the perimeter of every opening in the forest. Other times, she hastened as quickly as possible to the next cover.

When trails began to merge near Wilford, she moved even farther into cover. When Mutt growled at a flicker of movement in the distance, she was off the trail in seconds. She rode deep into the timber before she left her horse well hidden among the trees. With her Winchester from the saddle scabbard , she crept back toward the trail. She crouched behind a mass of shrubbery and pulled her spyglass from her pocket.

Sue was surprised to see Marshal Victor riding toward her. She almost called out but hesitated. The cold savagery in his eyes could be seen through the spyglass. She lowered it and hunkered down, turning her face away from the trail so he would not spot the white of her eyes or her face.

Sue waited until the hoof beats faded in the distance before she stepped out cautiously onto the trail and automatically looked down at his tracks. Her blood suddenly ran cold and her heart raced. The right front shoe of the marshal's mount had a half-moon notch she recognized. He was riding one of the rustler's horses! Rage and relief competed as she stared up the trail. He was involved in the thievery, but she hadn't told him about her defensive measures. *No wonder they knew who I was. He told them!*

Anger and determination fused as she hurried back into the underbrush to her horse. She led it back to the trail, quickly mounted, and urged her horse into motion. Mutt ran ahead. Sue followed cautiously, always being aware of every possible location where she could be spotted. At the first fork in the trail, he continued straight ahead, and at the second, his tracks veered off to the right.

She was grateful. *He's not headed directly for my ranch.*

The spacing of the fresh tracks showed that the marshal was moving at a brisk pace, but Sue took nothing for granted. She called Mutt back to run beside her as she resumed course. The trail began to climb, the soil turned from soft and sandy to dry gravel, and the tracks became less obvious.

Reaching the crest of the next rise, she dismounted and moved into cover. She walked the rest of the way to the summit with rifle in her hand. She scanned every bit of possible cover even though the tracks continued innocently down the middle of the trail.

He's acting like an honest man this close to town. No one else knows what a crook he is. He'll be more cautious when he gets farther from town.

She scanned the terrain ahead with her spyglass. A slight movement in the distance caught her eye, so she focused on it. As expected, he had turned to scan his back trail. She sighed with relief, thankful that she hadn't blundered on ahead.

Sue waited again before she pushed her horse into the timber, onto a well-hidden game trail. She followed its path higher, knowing the few locations where she might be visible through breaks in the screening vegetation. Hours later, she went forward on foot, crawling the last few yards through the drifted snow of high elevation. The cover continued all the way to the edge of a precipice and she knew that the slightest misstep would be fatal. Reluctantly, she left Mutt and her Stetson with her horse.

Far below, a vast bowl stretched for miles, ringed on three sides by mountains still draped in snow. The floor of the bowl was a jumble of canyons, brush, rock, creeks, and rivers tumbled together in a fantastic hodgepodge.

She was thankful for the spyglass that allowed her to systematically scan the trails that twisted and turned through the maelstrom of rock. She saw nothing at first, so she repeated her sweep until something caught her eye.

Aha! Sue zoomed in, recognizing the roan horse and the marshal. Even at this distance, she could see him turning in the saddle to scan the trail behind. *Glad I guessed right and didn't try to follow him.*

She scanned the land ahead, trying to anticipate his destination. She discounted several possibilities before she exclaimed, "Lost Hope Canyon! I bet that's where they are. It'd make a perfect corral." A mile long with generous water but limited feed, the canyon would hold a small herd for an extended period or a large herd for a short time.

The canyon mouth was wide, shallow, and at the limits of her spyglass. She braced her elbows and held her breath, slowly panning from side to side and front to back. The image of two tiny riders and blur of color that had to be cattle wavered before her. She drew a deep breath and held it, refocusing. *Definitely, at least two.* She relaxed and steadied her breathing, once again focusing on the marshal.

He was still riding steadily toward the canyon. She was cold and wet. The sun slid to the west when his image merged with the others. She waited and waited some more. When the marshal showed no signs of returning, she forced her half-frozen body backward on all fours. An inner glow of satisfaction warmed her spirit but failed to stop her shivering. She mounted, wrapped the blanket from her saddle roll around her, and turned toward home.

***

When Sue finally rode into the ranch yard, the sun was well below the horizon. The afternoon warmth had fled, the evening had cooled rapidly, and her damp clothes were stuck to her body. She penned her weary mount in the warm and snug confines of the barn before she stumbled to the house, keeping pace with a travel-worn Mutt.

Sue relit the fires in both the stove and the fireplace, stoking them heavily in anticipation of dispelling the clammy chill. After changing to dry clothes, she hung her damp ones near the stove to dry. She collapsed into a chair at the table, stretching aching muscles to relax.

After a moment, she muttered, "Mutt."

He was curled against the wall and merely opened one eye.

She smiled wryly. "You kept me sane this winter, but you're going to have to listen some more. We're outnumbered, and even if we weren't, I can't fight the law. He's crooked, but no one else knows. That means we're going to have to enlist some help."

He cocked his head, appearing curious.

Sue yawned. "You and I are going to ride to Long Gulch to mail a letter. If you think you were tired today, tomorrow will be worse," She laughed when she was answered by a rumbling snore from the sleeping dog.

When she finished washing the dishes, she sat down at the table and began to write. Several minutes later, she finished her letter to the United States Marshal in Denver.

To Whom It May Concern:

I have witnessed the town marshal of Wilford meeting with the rustlers who stole my entire herd. I can prove from the tracks that he was one of those responsible, which is why he has made no effort to recover my cattle.

The high passes will be free of snow in another week or two, so they and hundreds more can be driven to markets west of here and be lost forever. I live three hours west of Wilford, so meet me at the train station there on Friday. I'll find you.

S. Mason

Sue read the letter as she smiled sourly. *That should get a reaction. If they believe what I wrote. In the meantime, since the rustlers were still at the canyon when I left, I'll have a nap before I go outside.* Too tired to think clearly, she dropped her head on the table and fell asleep instantly.

She woke at the first light of dawn, feeling so stiff she thought she'd never be able to move again. She forced her aching body to the stove and stoked the coals into life.

Later, astride her horse once again, Sue scanned the clear sky before she checked one last time to make sure the letter was safely in her vest pocket. Clad in a light coat but with her sheep-skin coat tied to the saddle behind her, she headed out.

That morning's trek was some of the hardest riding she had ever undertaken, which included crossing the mountains through a steep, high pass. Midday found her almost at her destination, a mining town located, like Wilford, on the railroad to Denver. She found the post office in the general store, which was a pale imitation of Horwick's Mercantile.

She paid for a stamp and asked, "When will this be delivered to Denver?"

"Tomorrow. The train is due in ten minutes, and I was just sacking the mail."

She could see the curiosity evident on his face.

"Where you from, Lady?"

"Over the mountains, north. I was here once before when I was a kid." She deflected further questioning. "Where would I find a good place to eat something?"

"A good place? You're out of luck in this town." He grinned. "If you want to settle for something to fend off starvation, the Gold Mine has food."

"That bad, is it?"

He grimaced and nodded. "The best of a bad lot."

The steak was tough, the potatoes were half cooked, and they both sat like lead in her stomach hours later as she forced her way through drifts and blowing snow. Sue had hurried to leave town and now pushed her horse hard. The clouds began to gather, but the storm still caught them at the mouth of the pass. Retreat was not an option, so they pushed on—wet, cold, and miserable.

She never knew just how they got over the pass and off the heights. Unable to see more than a few feet, she loosened the reins and let her horse have its head. In spite of her Stetson, snow caked her eyes, so she had to keep brushing them clear. Only when she realized she could see Mutt ranging ahead did she give a sigh of relief, watching the storm end as abruptly as it began.

Again, full darkness had fallen before she reached the ranch. Too exhausted to pick up her saddle, she left it lying on the floor of the tack room after she turned her weary horse into its stall. The dog kept pace, curling up on the kitchen floor. Sue's tired feet tripped on the doorsill as she entered the house. Luckily, she recovered enough strength to throw wood on the fires before shuffling down the hall to her lonely room.

Collapsing onto her bed, she fell asleep before she could remove her wet clothes. She woke up once near dawn, dimly aware enough to strip them off. Then she crawled under the covers and fell asleep again.

It was close to midday when she woke up. The sun was high overhead and its rays warmed her room. She grimaced in pain as her entire body protested the slightest movement. She gritted her teeth, struggled to her feet, and began searching for clean clothes.

After a hot breakfast, Sue found the aches and pains had abated except for a headache. She did the dishes before she headed for the barn to tackle the chores she'd neglected for too long.

CHAPTER 4

Sue was in Wilford Friday morning, dismounting at Doc Madison's hitch rail. She was on the porch and about to reach the door when Mrs. Brown called to her from next door.

"Doc left early this morning for the T-bar-Two. Missus is having a difficult delivery, and he probably won't be back until tonight, if then."

"Thanks." She was bitterly disappointed at missing Doc but masked it. "I'll just leave him a note."

"Can I tell him anything?"

"No, thanks. I'll find something to write on at his desk."

Mrs. Brown waved and returned to her kitchen.

Opening the unlocked door, Sue walked through the parlor to Doc's office and found the paper and pencil on his desk. She paused momentarily, deciding what to write. Writing quickly she ended with a short note.

The marshal is supposed to be here today from Denver. I'm taking him to Lost Hope Canyon to get my cattle back. Talk to you when I get back to town. — Sue

The street was crowded with ranchers and their families who came to town for supplies and socializing after the long winter. She dismounted in front of the bank and was greeted warmly by a few and warily by many. She eyed the Marshal's Office across the street while she dropped the reins of her horse at the hitch rail, knowing that tying them was unnecessary. At that moment, she saw Weasel coming out of the door but he retreated as soon as their eyes met.

Sue turned away and entered the bank. Her heart sank because she knew what was coming. A few minutes later, Sue was sitting in the banker's office when Mr. Holtzman appeared.

He was cordial but blunt. "I heard your entire herd was rustled. That doesn't leave you very much, does it?"

"No," she sighed. "I still have most of my brood cows left although even some of those were rustled this week."

His eyes widened at the news of fresh disaster.

"If I have to, I'll sell what's left. Even if it leaves me nothing. Doc is not going to pay my way even if his name is on the loan." Her voice was cold and brittle. "I'll know in a week or so what I'm going to do." *Or I'll be dead.*

The banker eyed her for a moment. He had known her all her life, but she still seemed to baffle him. She was wise far beyond her years, radiating steely determination no one could judge. He cleared his throat, appearing a little intimidated, "That's okay with me. I can even wait a couple months if you need. You can make a decision then."

"Thank you." She shook his hand firmly and left his office.

Having regained some confidence, she stopped at the teller's window and withdrew a small amount of cash from her account. The teller showed her the balance that remained, which was a distressingly small sum. She nodded in gloomy acknowledgement before she walked outside into the bright sunshine.

Momentarily, she stood on the boardwalk, eyes sweeping the street. A train whistle sounded in the distance as she acknowledged a friendly greeting. She smiled and turned toward the depot.

Sue was only a short distance from the station when the train pulled in, rolling past her. A cloud of coal smoke and steam punctuated by the screech of brakes enveloped her. She waited in the shade of the canopy that protected the passengers in bad weather. Three men stepped off the train, two of whom hurried away. The third man approached the station agent.

After a moment's conversation, the station agent nodded in her direction. The stranger's eyes widened as he stood motionless for a moment, eyes meeting hers politely. She made a quick appraisal of her own, watching him approach her. She was favorably impressed but decided to withhold final judgment until later.

When he reached her, he tipped his Stetson politely. With a hint of amusement in his voice, he spoke. "I understand you are known as S Mason."

Nice timbre. He's trying not to laugh. "I'm Sue Mason, and you would be…?"

He glanced quickly around to make sure no one was within earshot. "United States Marshal. Ted Storm."

***

When the agent directed the marshal's attention to the waiting young woman, he silently whistled to himself. She appeared young, around 18 or 19, with a fantastic, slender figure. She was also exceptionally tall because her eyes were on the level with his own.

It was obvious he was making a swift examination with his eyes, taking in the man's clothing that emphasized her figure. The man's shirt clearly outlined firm breasts while her faded jeans clung to full hips. It was not uncommon for women to wear men's clothing as a practical necessity, but he had never seen a woman wearing a gun and gun belt. His eyes returned to hers. Watchful and wary, they held a quiet air of authority. This woman knew how to use her holstered weapon.

Meanwhile, Sue was doing her own visual investigation. He was a young man of about her own height of six feet-two. He was clean shaven and his face was heavily tanned from long exposure to the sun. Reddish-blonde hair of medium length showed from under the battered Stetson which framed his face. His clothing was much the same as hers: faded jeans and chambray work shirt, scuffed rider's boots, a well-worn gun belt, and a soft leather vest.

She asked softly, "Why no badge?"

"I thought it'd be best to scout the situation first. Is the marshal in town?"

"I wouldn't know," she snorted derisively. "I didn't go into his office to find out. I do know his deputy, Weasel Wilson, was there earlier. I think they both went into hiding when I showed up."

"Oh?" The question asked volumes.

"The marshal is as crooked as a snake's back. Not only has he not caught any rustlers, I saw him ride out to meet them. That was after I saw his horse's tracks among those that stole my entire herd of yearlings."

His gaze was cold. "Those are fighting words. Would you repeat your accusations to anyone else?"

"No." She scowled in frustration. "Not because I'm lying, but because no man save one takes much stock in anything I say." Her eyes were as cold as his when she returned stare for stare. "Give me a day or two and I'll prove it! I'll take you to the canyon where I saw him meet the rustlers. Then you can make up your own mind."

Silently, he met her eyes. "Fair enough. I'll let you do that."

Sue turned away abruptly. She spat, "Follow me. I have some evidence to show you."

He trailed as she led the way, looping behind the jail and past the marshal's stable. It was empty, but she pointed to the dimpled hoof print showing in the dirt.

"That print was among those that rustled my cattle. It hasn't rained since they made off with my cows, so the tracks will still be there. I'll show you when we get there."

The marshal's eyebrows rose as some of the doubt left his eyes. "Let's go eat somewhere. I'll buy."

She nodded curtly. When she turned away, he followed her to Manlick's Boarding House. It had a well-deserved reputation for good food and fast service, taking only moments for their order to be filled. They had barely been seated before they were served a heaping plate of the noon special: steak, potatoes, and gravy. While they ate, they kept their conversation to topics that would not reveal his true status as a U.S. Marshal.

Several people stopped to visit, trying without directly asking to ferret out her relationship with the stranger. Sue overheard other comments that made her face grow hot. She knew that her decision to call for outside help was the correct call instead of revealing to local ranchers what she had seen.

CHAPTER 5

After they finished eating, Sue went to the general store where she loaded another order of supplies. The marshal rented a horse from the livery and was waiting when she mounted her own. They rode out of town and were soon into the forest. The trail was wide enough to ride side by side. When they were far enough from town to be safe from being overheard, he finally opened up.

"You claim Marshal Victor is part of the gang because you've seen him talking to them. You'd better tell me the whole story because the Mel Victor I know by reputation would never do anything like that."

Sue whipped around to face him as her anger flared. "If you don't believe me, why did you ever bother to come here?"

He studied her angry eyes for a while. "I didn't say I didn't believe you. The main reason I was assigned was because no one in their right mind would waste a day's ride just to mail a letter if there was no truth in it."

Her resentment was due to the many put downs and snide dismissals she had suffered and was never far from the surface. The unexpectedly mild response defused her anger, making her a bit regretful.

"Sorry…" After a moment, she continued. "Maybe, we're talking about two different men. This marshal has greasy black hair, a scraggly beard, and you can smell him from a mile away upwind. Does that sound like the Mel Victor you know by reputation?"

"No." He frowned. "I've heard he's clean shaven and has red hair that's turning gray."

"It sounds as though we have an imposter," she said grimly. "That would suggest that the real Mel Victor is dead and buried somewhere."

The marshal's face turned somber. "That's certainly a possibility. Why don't you tell me the whole story from the beginning? After that, we'll decide on a plan of action." Ted glanced at her sharply before he continued, "Which I won't consider adopting until I see the evidence of rustled cattle."

Sue gently urged her horse into motion. "That's fair. Marshal Logan died several weeks ago. Nobody in town wanted the job, so the big ranchers and some of the businessmen decided to hire an outsider. Somebody in the group knew the reputation of this Mel Victor, and that he was available. They telegraphed him and asked him to come to Wilford, assuring him the job was his if he wanted it. They received an immediate reply that he was coming. A few days later, this marshal showed up. As I said, no one around here wanted the job, so they didn't ask too many questions and hired him on the man's reputation."

The marshal urged his own horse into motion.

"I stopped to talk to him about my rustled cattle the first week he was in town. I never had such an instant distrust for anyone as I did for him. He made me feel dirty, just by looking at me. He told me I should marry him and let him take care of my worries. I left in a hurry. On the way out, I ran into his deputy, a local I don't trust either. When he grabbed me, I put a bullet between his feet and faced him down. Neither of them like me any more than I like them because I told them both rather publicly I'd shoot them both if I met them again."

His eyes widened, and he grinned. "So they don't dare show their faces while you're in town. They have to either shoot or run. No wonder they weren't around this morning."

Sue was continuously scanning their surroundings. "I wrote that letter to the US Marshal's office in Denver after I spotted Victor riding out of town while I was headed in. I dcn't trust him, so I dodged into the timber and let him go by. *That* was when I found his tracks that matched the rustlers. I followed him from a distance for several miles." Sue turned to face the marshal as their horses continued at a steady pace. "Then I split off and went to a high overlook where I could follow him with my spyglass."

He nodded, watching her pat the pocket of her vest.

"He was headed for Lost Hope Canyon and at least two riders came out to meet him. There were a lot of cattle penned up there, but it was so far away they were mostly just a blur of color. They knew each other. I didn't want to get caught, so I got the hell out of there. As soon as I got home, I sent the letter. And I hope I never see another day like that one!" Sue sighed in sheer frustration before she continued, though less vehemently, "I didn't sign the letter with my full name because I doubted anyone in Denver would take the word of a woman any more seriously than they do around here. I didn't think anyone would bother to respond if they knew it was me reporting a crooked marshal."

Ted met her eyes when she turned to face him. "I'm afraid there is some truth in that. Some men would think that way. As I said, the deciding factor that got everyone's attention was the post mark on the envelope and the ride it signified. That's when the District Attorney assigned me to check it out as I'm the low man on the totem pole."

They halted at the foot of a long uphill slope to let the horses rest. Ted opened his vest and shifted his badge to the left lapel. When he raised his gaze to his immediate surroundings, he saw a mile-long meadow that climbed gently ahead of them. At the far end, the trail disappeared into a shallow draw cut into the exposed rock. Soon after, it reappeared for a short distance before disappearing once again into the timber.

Ted turned his head, his eyes sweeping past Sue to follow the edges of the meadow rising high on either side. "Sure is a pretty sight."

Sue wondered if he meant just the land.

He asked, "How many head have you lost?"

"I had about five hundred head total. Two hundred for sale this spring." She was still bitter and snarled in frustration, "They're all gone. The rustlers stole another twenty or so of my brood cows that I know of. They're so brazen. Right now, I don't know for sure if I have any left."

His face showed deep concern.

Sue elaborated about her first count and the later loss. "I baited a trap when they came back the second time and winged at least one. Possibly two."

He shook his head. "So you don't really know how many rustlers we're dealing with. At least three, but two might be wounded. Maybe two more at the canyon. Or the two might be included in the three. We have somewhere between three and a dozen outlaws. After you show me the canyon, I'll scout it before deciding if I need to bring in more help."

Sue exploded. "If you think I'm going to play the dainty lady and stay behind, you're crazy!" Her voice dropped, and her eyes became frigid. "I'm going to get my licks in at that crook one way or another. Don't you try to stop me! You can't hunt them down without me because you damn sure don't know the country!"

He recoiled from her vehemence.

She spat her words like bullets, "I'll make you a deal. I have a firing range set up at my ranch. I'll bet you I'm as good as or probably even better with a rifle than you are. Even as fast or faster on the draw. If I can't beat you, then I'll stay back." She glared at him with eyes like daggers.

Sue had offered him an out, but Ted knew he was trapped. He scowled. "You don't offer me much of an option. Okay. Show me how good you are when we get there."

They rode on in frigid silence until she suddenly turned aside and followed an almost invisible trail deep into the woods. "I have a meadow where I cached some of my horses when I thought the rustlers might come at night. We'll swap for fresh horses here even though it's less than a mile from home."

"Sounds like a good idea to me." When they broke out into the meadow and he saw her horses, Ted whistled in admiration, "You have some mighty fine horses!"

Sue thawed a fraction. "I train horses. I don't break them. You have to make them trust you to get the most out of them."

He smiled.

She selected two, and they swapped gear. "These aren't the fastest, but they're the sturdiest. Where we're going tonight, endurance will count more than speed."

He mounted as respect grew in his eyes. "Fast as a horse and sturdy as a mule?"

Sue thawed another fraction. "I guess you could say that."

Mutt trotted out to meet them when they rode into the ranch yard. She explained, "I left him home so he could get some rest. We'll need him as our scout tonight."

She dropped the reins of her horse next to the water trough and dismounted. Ted followed her lead when she loosened the saddle girth and pulled her rifle from the scabbard, leading off across the yard and around a corner of a bluff away from the ranch house. Mutt followed at a distance.

Ted found a firing range laid out against the mountain, and he turned to her.

"You can have five rounds to set your sights. The cans are at hundred-yard intervals out to four hundred."

He stared at her, feeling as if he were treading on thin ice. "What are your sights set for?"

Her reply was almost contemptuous. "Two hundred offhand. But I usually hit at least one of five at four hundred using a rest."

The ice parted, and he fell through. "If you can do that, we're wasting our time. I'm already outclassed. We'll see what I can do at two hundred." He levered a cartridge into his own Winchester and brought it to his shoulder. He used his allotted five rounds to set the sights before reloading.

Sue instructed, "Five rounds at two hundred. Five at four hundred. If necessary, I'll set up more and take my turn."

He nodded and deliberately squeezed off five rounds. Three cans went flying. He dropped to his belly, but five rounds later, not another can had moved.

Sue sniffed at him in mild contempt and stepped to the line. Fast and smooth, five cans went flying. She dropped to her belly, and three more cans flew.

Ted stared at her as she picked two cans from a pile off to one side and tossed him one. "Ladies first."

She smiled and turned down-range.

Ted threw the can as high as he could and turned to watch. The can was on its downward arc when she drew almost faster than his eye could follow. Six shots roared, each throwing the can ever higher.

Astounded, he stared at her and threw his hands up. "I still don't like it, but you've proved you're a far better shot than I am. I've never seen anyone as fast as you are." His admiration of her ability was plain to see.

Sue ignored the compliment and turned, her eyes finding her dog. She whistled several notes. His ears shot up when she called, "Fetch."

They watched as Mutt bounded away.

Ted stared at her in confusion for a moment before asking, "What was that all about?"

She grinned slyly. "Just wait. You'll see."

A few minutes later, the dog trotted into view with the reins of her horse in his mouth. Ted turned to her as his mouth fell open in astonishment.

"I told you that I train animals. I don't break them." There was no trace of smugness in her tone. "They learn faster and remember longer what you teach them if they enjoy it."

He stared at her, showing what she craved most... respect.

She suggested, "Why don't you go pick up the old cans and replace them with new? Then unsaddle the horses. I'll go fix us something to eat because it's going to be a long night."

Sue was in the kitchen stoking the fire in the stove when he entered the front door.

She called. "It's going to be a bit before everything's ready. Why don't you take a seat in the parlor?"

"Okay."

Several minutes later, Sue found him standing in the middle of the room, staring at the walls lined with books her father had left her.

He turned to meet her eyes. "I've never seen so many. Where did you get them?"

"My father left them to me."

He asked an innocent question, "Where did he get them?"

Sue's vision blurred, and tears ran down her cheeks. "I have no idea." Her face was suddenly bleak. "He refused to tell me anything about his life. Even where he was from or who his family was."

He was taken aback at her reaction.

"I asked him many times, but he wouldn't tell me." Her eyes suddenly blazed. "If he were alive today, I wouldn't take no for an answer again!"

Ted asked another innocent question, "How did you happen to become a rancher by yourself?"

The following silence lasted so long it seemed as if she were ignoring him or didn't hear him. When she finally did respond, it was in a flat, lifeless monotone. "My Ma died when I was a very little girl. My Pa died two years ago and left the ranch to me. I found out later that if Pa hadn't already paid off the bank, the banker would've sold me out because I wasn't of legal age. That was bad enough, but there were a lot of ranchers who tried to get me to sell out to them because *no woman can run a ranch right*, much less a sixteen-year-old girl. I was too damn stubborn to pay any attention."

"I've seen evidence to make me agree with that statement," Ted observed with a dry chuckle.

Sue smiled in acknowledgement. Her tone lightened, and with more life in her voice, she continued, "Ma died when I was about four, so I don't remember her real well. Pa told me when I was old enough to understand that he had no relatives to send me to, so he did the best he could."

He stood still, listening.

She lifted her head proudly and turned to face him. "I was his little girl, but he treated me as a son. I rode behind his saddle until I was old enough for my own and after that I rode alone. That's why I wear clothes like this. A dress just won't work astride a horse. He taught me about ranching and life. He loved to read, as you can see from this library. Books and authors most of the people around here have never heard about. He was killed when his horse stepped in a hole and threw him."

***

Sue was aghast that she'd reveal so much hurt to a total stranger as her memories of that bitter afternoon flooded back. They had been searching the canyons and hollows for strays from their scattered herd. She had covered her assigned area and corralled the small herd she had collected in a box canyon. When her Pa failed to show up, she rode back to the area where she knew he'd been working but found nothing.

Worried, Sue expanded her search until she heard the terrified whinnying of a horse and turned her own mount toward the sound. She came around a deadfall into a small draw and found her father's staggering mount holding a shattered foreleg as high as possible. Panic rose in her throat as she drew her Winchester from the scabbard. She drew aim on the head of the stricken animal, which collapsed into merciful silence at the crack of her rifle.

She spurred her own horse, moving back along the tracks of the other horse. It wasn't long until she saw the figure lying on the ground and drew her mount to a halt in a cloud of dust.

She hit the ground and raced to her father's prone figure. She kneeled fearfully as her hand flashed out to gently shake him. She froze... his neck was bent at an unnatural angle. She was crying before her hand felt the chill of his flesh.

Sue could never recall clearly much of the following hours. A slim, sixteen-year-old girl somehow loaded her father's body across her own saddle. She led her mount on weary feet the miles back home, walking into the gathering dusk, then in the full darkness of a moonless night. When she finally reached the ranch house, she somehow managed to move her father's body onto the sofa in the front room. She remounted her weary horse and rode in a daze of grief to her nearest neighbor, the B-bar-F, for help.

She dimly remembered the next few days like a bad dream—the funeral and the burial. Only habit and determination carried her through the following days, and her resentment of neighboring ranchers began to mount.

Harold West was only the first of many. He rode in as she was inspecting the fence around her horse pasture. "Morning, Sue." He offered his condolences and continued with small talk for a few minutes. He asked abruptly, "How much do you want for the ranch? A youngster like you can't run it alone, so I'd like to buy you out."

Sue was still numb with grief and was barely able to keep her words civil. "I'm not selling. Pa left it to me and I'm going to keep it."

He stared at her, seemingly unable to believe his ears. After a moment, he touched his hand to his Stetson. "When you change your mind, I'd still like to buy it."

She glared as he rode off.

Her encounter with Adam Brown was much worse. She had met him in Wilford a few times when he had business with her father. He rode in just before sunset when she was walking wearily toward the ranch house.

He tipped his hat with exaggerated politeness and announced without preamble. "Miss Mason, I'm here to ask you to marry me. No woman can live proper unless she has a man to care for her."

Sue's face went white, then a furious red before she exploded. "You fool! I'd never marry you if you were the last man on earth! If you wanted to court me, where were you before my father died? You don't want a wife! You want my ranch! Get your worthless carcass out of here!"

Shocked, he stared at her, fleeing when she advanced toward him with her left hand balled in a fist and her right on the butt of her revolver. She watched angrily as he galloped away, convulsing with sobs and choked laughter.

CHAPTER 6

Ted offered his own condolences but discovered he was talking to himself. Startled, he watched tears trickle down her cheeks and waited silently until her eyes regained focus. He placed his hand on her hand resting on the table between them. "Your father must've been an unusual man. Not many would've taught their daughters to shoot."

Sue slowly became aware of the hand covering hers but made no effort to break the contact. "I always thought he was afraid of someone or something. He started to teach me to use my Colt when I was just turning thirteen. I've practiced ever since. I wouldn't want to go up against any real gunslingers, but I have to admit I'm moderately fast."

Ted chucked.

She smiled. "Weasel Wilson was the only man I ever had to pull a gun on. He didn't think I was serious until I put a slug between his feet. He was trying to force me to go to a dance with him, and I didn't like his attention. That was when I told him and the marshal that I'd shoot them if I saw them again."

"I see." He reluctantly moved his hand from hers. "You can't possibly run this ranch entirely alone. How did you manage to get by if none of your neighboring ranchers were willing to help?"

"My neighbor to the north, Benjamin Franklin, helped. I once took care of his wife for a couple of weeks when she was very ill. Cathy always appreciated that. When I needed help, Ben either came himself or sent his hired hand. Usually it was Ben because not many men will hire out or take orders from a girl my age."

Sue stood up and went back to the kitchen where the stove was radiating heat in all directions. Ted followed and watched from the doorway as she put the skillet on the stove.

Her armor softened and she asked. "What about you?"

It took some time, but he began to explain, "I'm originally from Iowa. I always wanted adventure, so I just up and left when I was seventeen. My family didn't try to stop me because they knew my nature. They even encouraged me because they knew a neighbor who knew someone that needed help to move west. I stayed with that outfit until we got to Cheyenne, then moved south on foot. I was sleeping in the haymow of an abandoned barn one night when I heard some men below me talking about plans to hold up a bank. I kept real quiet until after they left the next day. I found the local sheriff and told him what I'd overheard. The sheriff passed the word and later offered me a job. That's how I got into the law. I learned even later the gang I overheard was supposed to be the Snake Carson Gang."

Sue shivered at the mention of one of the most vicious and murderous outlaws in the west. "Is he as bad as they say?"

"No matter what you've ever heard, he's worse."

The skillet started to smoke and her attention was diverted to her cooking. A few minutes later, she placed a heaping plate in front of him.

He said, "I saw a law textbook on the table. Have you been reading it?"

"Studying it. I read a lot during the winter but I decided to learn all I could from this one."

Ted's eyes widened as his curiosity ratcheted upward. He kept asking questions while they ate, probing her understanding of what she had learned. Long before they finished eating, new respect showed in his eyes.

When they were done eating, Sue said. "I'll do the dishes while you saddle the horses. We want to use what light we have to get at least partway to the canyon. The last few miles are going to be hard traveling even with a full moon. Which we don't have."

Ted nodded as if he reached a decision. "I'll get them. Then I have a question to ask before we leave."

"No! I'm not staying behind."

"That isn't the question." He grinned at her obvious confusion but refused to say more.

Sue was waiting on the porch when he returned. Her curiosity was evident.

"You have more book knowledge about the law than the vast majority of sworn lawmen. For the authority and what protection it affords, would you accept being sworn in as a United States Marshal?" He grinned. "You'll outrank Marshal Victor."

Her eyes widened in disbelief, and she stared at him before asking in a strangled voice, "Me? Marshal?"

He nodded soberly.

As she gazed into his eyes, suspicion showed in her own. She suddenly smiled in agreement, "Yes."

When they rode out into the gathering dusk, she repeatedly looked down in disbelief at the star pinned to her vest. *Me! A woman. The marshal! Whoever heard of such a thing?*

Mutt trotted ahead as their scout while they rode side by side into the deepening twilight. Their pace lessened as the light faded to starlight while Sue described the trails running through the bowl they were approaching. When she told him everything she could remember, she concentrated on an almost foot-by-foot layout of the most probable route to the mouth of Lost Hope Canyon.

Ted shot questions at her in a voice scarcely above a whisper, questions that often Sue could not answer and which threatened to weaken her steely resolve. He could hear her uncertainty and advised, "Try not to worry about it. No plan is ever perfect. We'll just have to make adjustments as we go."

The stars indicated it was almost midnight when they rode into the vast bowl. They were thankful for the moon as it began to edge above the horizon.

They rode in silence, often in single file with Sue in the lead.

Much later, she reined in her horse, and he pulled up beside her.

She whispered, "We're about a half mile from the canyon. Where do you want to leave the horses? If it were me, I'd leave them in that little washout over there."

His face was hidden in the shadow of his Stetson as he considered the question. "It would be best to have them closer if we have to escape in a hurry, but surprise is a deadlier weapon. I hate to leave them this far away but getting closer raises too many risks."

They dismounted, ground-reined their horses, and stuffed extra ammunition in their pockets before they continued on foot. Their rifles were loaded and ready. Mutt padded ahead as they followed silently, stopping to carefully examine shadows and possible shelter at a distance before they moved forward again.

Both froze when Mutt halted with a rumbling snarl so soft it barely reached their ears. Ted pointed silently at a shadow within a shadow—an outlaw was on guard. Nerves stretched to the breaking point. Barely breathing, they waited for the cry of discovery.

The tension eased slightly at the rumble of a snore. Ted silently handed her his rifle and drew his revolver before inching toward the sleeping figure over the yards of open ground. He was almost within arm's length when some sound woke the outlaw, who drew a breath to bellow an alarm but collapsed soundlessly when the descending gun barrel crashed into his head.

Sue was beside them a moment later as her eyes met Ted's in the moonlight. She crouched beside the still figure and pulled a greasy shirt tail out of his pants with her left hand. Drawing her knife from its belt sheath, she began slashing long strips of cloth from the shirt. Within a few minutes, he was trussed up tightly with a gag rammed in his mouth and tied with another strip.

They stashed his inert form behind a huge boulder.

Ted whispered softly with his lips close enough for his warm breath to touch her ear, "That was close. We owe our lives to your dog."

She nodded and stepped out with Mutt in the lead.

Sue left the dog in hiding not far from their target as she whispered in his ear, "Stay."

He lay down obediently as they crept onward in the inky black shadows cast by the sliver of moon.

Sue and Ted were safely concealed in the shelter of a row of boulders at the mouth of the canyon before dawn began to show in the sky. Less than a hundred yards away, four sleeping figures were clustered on a bare patch of ground around the remnants of a campfire.

Ted whispered, "Can they escape up the canyon?"

"Not on horses. They might be able to on foot if they were to get away from us." Her whisper was as soft, "There's a cave off to the left that would hold them all. I'm surprised they aren't using it."

Dawn broke before the first of the outlaws stirred. His hand moved to his gun as his eyes swept the campsite. He kicked a sleeping companion and snarled, "Go check on Harry. He was supposed to wake us up a long time ago. If he's asleep, shoot the bastard."

The victim of the kick growled, picked up his rifle, and started walking toward Harry.

Just a few seconds later, Ted bellowed, "Drop your guns! You're under arrest!"

Pandemonium erupted as the other outlaws dove for cover. The erstwhile guard's relief whipped up his rifle with his snapshot going wild as two rifles smashed him down. The return fire splattered against the boulders protecting them.

There was a moment of silence when Sue heard Ted swearing under his breath.

"They have some protection from that dip I couldn't see in the dark. They can't run, but we can't either. Stalemate," Ted said bitterly.

They traded sporadic shots through the sunrise. Sue's sharp eyes detected a flicker of movement near the campfire site and she centered her aim, slowly squeezing off a round. The bullet burned a furrow across the back of a rustler. He leaped to his feet, cursing as he raced for shelter. A bullet from Ted's rifle brought him down, but they both ducked instinctively when return fire ricocheted in all directions.

Silence descended momentarily before it was broken by a rifle shot from behind them. Ted pitched forward, blood streaming from his head, and Sue started to swing her rifle around.

A surly voice rang out, "Freeze, bitch! I'd like nothing better than to kill you." She froze when she recognized the voice of Weasel Wilson.

"Now, drop your gun."

The rifle dropped from her numb fingers.

"Mel! It's me, Weasel. Keep her covered. I'll come around to meet you. The other bastard is dead." He lowered his voice before turning to Sue. "Get out from behind those rocks where they can see you."

Turning her head, she spotted his rifle, which was covering her from point-blank range. Her heart thumped in her throat.

He sneered. "Now, it's your turn."

She stood up slowly, and at a wave from his gun barrel moved out from behind the protecting boulders. Rising from their shelter, two figures moved toward her with guns in hand while they covered her.

Weasel sidled around her to meet them, crowing, "I saved your hides. Mel, you can have her too. But I get her first. She's even wearing a tin star you can use for target practice."

The marshal's smile was cold. Unable to fathom that any woman might be dangerous, both older men turned away from Sue to face Weasel. "Sure, kid. You can have her, but Snake Carson always gets first choice."

Stunned, Weasel halted. He paled in horror and gasped in disbelief, "Snake Carson!" He began backpedaling as the two men moved closer, feeling his dreams of a life of crime and riches being dashed.

Snake laughed with insane delight at the naked fear. Shifting his aim from Sue, he fired once. Weasel buckled at the knees and collapsed.

With Snake's attention diverted for a second, Sue's hand flashed down and back up, driven by desperation...she would live or die by her skill with a gun. The instant it cleared leather and came leveled, she triggered six shots in a continuous flash of fire and gun smoke, shifting from one man to the other. Two guns roared in return, she staggered at the piercing pain in her side.

Sue turned away, feeling sickened by the carnage she had created. Ted staggered toward her as she gasped in joy and relief. Blood was running down the side of his face.

"You're alive! Weasel said you were dead."

"A chunk of rock hit me in the head and knocked me out. I guess the blood made him think I was dead."

He was clearly woozy. "When I came to, you were standing there and someone was backing away. I tried to get to my gun, but by then the shooting was over."

He slowly closed the distance between them, as unsteady on his feet as she was.

Her voice trembled. "We just wiped out the Snake Carson Gang. The man that bushwhacked you was Weasel Wilson, the marshal's deputy."

Ted halted for a moment in astonishment. He sprang to her side as she abruptly turned away from the bodies and threw up. He reached for her when she began to sink to the ground.

His hand slipped in the blood at her waist. "You've been shot!" He eased her to the ground on her back and pulled the tail of her shirt out of her waistband. Her right hip was covered with blood flowing from a deep bullet gouge just above the gun belt. He folded the shirt tail and pressed it hard against her side. "Hold that tight. It should stop the bleeding."

Sue started when Mutt pressed his cold nose against her. "I'd forgotten about you. I'm glad you didn't obey this time." She patted his head with her free hand. "Fetch!"

The dog stared at her for a few seconds and bounced away while they both watched. Ted shook his head in disbelief, instantly regretting the movement as dizziness almost overwhelmed him.

He said, "There has to be water somewhere around. I'll see if I can find something I can use for bandages. Even if your dog does bring your horse, I can't take the time to ride back to get the medical supplies in my own saddlebags."

While Ted was searching, Sue struggled to get to her hands and knees. She crawled to the shelter of the boulders and out of sight of the carnage she had created.

A few minutes later, he returned with two canteens, dropped to his knees beside her, and offered her one. "I washed these in the spring I found but there's nothing clean enough in their camp to use as a bandage. We'll have to cut up a shirt." He abruptly rose to his feet and drew his gun as both heard the rapidly approaching hoof beats of more than one horse.

Mutt trotted into view with the reins of both horses in his mouth. Stunned, Ted stared as the trio stopped a few paces away. After a moment of bemused wonder, he untied his blanket roll from the saddle and spread it on the ground beside Sue.

She crawled on to it and lay down on her uninjured side with a sigh of relief, her hand still pressing the wadded shirt against her wound.

He knelt beside her with a small satchel in his hand. "Better drink some of this," he said as he handed her a flask of whiskey. "I doubt you're accustomed to it but it'll help kill the pain."

Sue was soon flushed and shaking. She whimpered in pain despite the effects of the whiskey before he finished cleaning her wound.

Ted picked up the flask as her eyes met his. "I'm going to have to douse it with this, or it'll get infected for sure. Are you ready?"

She gave the tiniest nod. He flooded the wound, and she fainted in agony. *That was probably the best for her.* Now, he had to figure out how to get her back to town.

He left her lying on the blanket and went searching for horses. He found the gang's picketed a short distance from their camp. He saddled and bridled one for the trussed-up guard, and was leading it back to join their own when he heard the thunder of many hooves in the distance. Immediately, he broke into a run.

CHAPTER 7

Fred Edwards was only one of the many young cowboys who were planning to enjoy themselves in Wilford's several saloons, milling around in the street before they went inside. He and his companions gawked in disbelief when they spotted Doc Madison hurrying down the street with a revolver naked in his hand. An unnatural silence fell while they watched him storm into the marshal's office across the street.

Doc was back outside only seconds later. He bellowed, "I need volunteers for a posse!" His voice could be heard all over the town.

None of the observers had ever seen him that agitated. More onlookers flowed into the fading sunlight, blanketing the street. They milled about in confusion until someone yelled, "What's the trouble?"

Doc tempered his bellow slightly. "Sue Mason has gone after the gang of rustlers that stole her cattle, which includes our very own crooked marshal." He paused for a second, "Well, that is with the help of a U.S. Marshal. The little hothead is likely to get herself killed if we don't get to Lost Hope Canyon in time."

Fred listened in stunned amazement. He had known Sue from a distance all his life and though he would never admit it to another soul, he was a little afraid of her. She was totally different from any other girl that he knew of in his limited experience. She wore a gun and knew how to use it, refusing to fit into the mold the rest of society deemed suitable for its women in the late nineteenth century.

The crowd surged forward. Every man in town admired and respected Doc. No matter what the reason, if he wanted a posse, he would by God have a posse! In only a few minutes, a dozen men, including Fred, were mounted and waiting. Doc selected the best of the remaining horses tied at hitch rails along the street. Everyone knew its owner would have to wait until the posse returned or walk home, but not a man there would have hesitated for a second to allow Doc to borrow any horse of his choice. Doc mounted and seconds later the posse was riding hard out of town on his heels.

The posse rode at a furious pace until the last glow of sunset was almost gone. They continued at a walk until it was too dark to see more than a few yards. Doc called a halt, and they ate a cold meal from the supplies the proprietor of the general store had hastily prepared for them.

A few of the men slept fitfully while others stood watch, but Doc paced in frustration and fear. When a sliver of moon rose very late in the night, he roused the posse. Once again, they pressed ahead on foot...helped only slightly by its nebulous assistance.

When the faint glimmer of an approaching dawn began to lighten the sky, they mounted and increased their pace. The first rays of sunshine found them covering ground at the limit of their horses' endurance. Later, when they slowed to allow their horses rest, Doc let his have its head and pulled the owner's rifle from its scabbard. He checked the magazine, levered a cartridge into the chamber, and flicked off the safety. He laid the ready weapon across the pommel of his saddle, holding it with one hand.

Behind him, Fred and the others did likewise. None of the posse voiced any questions, but Fred appeared to be wondering if Doc had ever considered the possibility of an ambush. In spite of the danger, they raced onward with no attempt at concealment and with no scouts out ahead. Fred wilted with relief when a single figure stepped into the open some distance ahead with his hands held high. The sunlight reflected from the star pinned to his vest.

***

Ted ducked into cover behind the line of boulders when he heard the thunder of many hooves rapidly approaching. There was no chance of protecting an unconscious Sue while standing in the open and very little from cover if the riders were hostile.

Moments later, observing from the protection of the boulders, he saw a dozen or more riders come racing into view. They were all armed with rifles at the ready. The man who was leading wore a suit and tie, his coat flying in the wind. They looked like a posse. Ted raised his hands shoulder high and stepped into the open, facing the oncoming charge. He shivered in spite of himself when every rifle centered on him.

Doc Madison leaped from his mount a few feet away with his gun in hand. In one step, they were face to face. He demanded harshly, "Where is she?"

Ted gestured at the rocks where Sue was sheltered. "Under cover behind the boulders. She's unconscious."

His eyes became murderous. Doc dropped his rifle and went for Ted's throat with both hands. He bellowed, "Why didn't you keep her out of it? You should've known she'd get hurt!"

Ted had to use all his strength to keep from being throttled. He protested, "God knows I tried!"

Sanity returned to Doc's eyes in a moment, and he relaxed his grip. "She is a mite stubborn at times." The momentary madness vanished, and he was instantly serious. "How bad is she hurt?"

"A bullet gouge in the side just above the hip. She's lost a lot of blood."

The rest of the posse dismounted at a more leisurely pace. After a quick survey of the many bodies, one of them asked, "Who were they?"

"Snake Carson's gang. We killed some of them in a gun battle before I was bushwhacked and knocked unconscious. Sue outdrew both Snake and your fake marshal while I was knocked out." He grinned lopsidedly and dropped his bombshell. "That was after I had deputized her as a U. S. Marshal."

A stunned silence followed, unbroken except for the sound of Doc's boots in the sand as he hurried to the boulders.

The posse gawked at the marshal when he continued, "There's a big herd of rustled stock in the canyon. Why don't some of you check them out? Six of you can start cleaning up here. Two of you go bring in the guard we left tied up back down the trail. I'll tell you where to find him."

***

Sue woke to see Doc bending over her, showing his grim face.

He asked, "How are you feeling?"

She mumbled in a drunken stupor. "I hurt everywhere. I'm dizzy, and I have a headache."

"That's understandable." He scowled angrily. "Dammit girl! Why didn't you tell me?" He continued before she could respond, "I know, I know! You wanted to prove you could do it all by yourself. Just remember there are men out there who sometimes need help too."

Half-drunk from the combination of pain and the whiskey, she mumbled, "You're an old softie."

His grim expression softened, and he patted her hand before he turned to Ted. "The bandage looks good. What else have you done for her?"

Doc cleaned and applied a bandage to Ted's head wound while he explained what he had done to help Sue. They moved a short distance away from her, leaving an uneasy Mutt snuggled tightly against her left side.

Ted asked softly, "How bad is she?"

"She'll recover as long as her wound doesn't get infected." Doc grimaced. "I'll take her back to town, but it's going to be a rough trip and a long recovery for her. I know she's been underfed all winter. She's also in a state of exhaustion and has been soaked in melted snow several times during the last few days. And now, on top of all that, she's lost a lot of blood." His concern was evident on his face. "But she's always been as strong as a horse and stubborn as a mule. Both are factors working in her favor."

Ted observed dryly. "I've noticed both of those traits."

Doc smiled briefly.

"It'll only take another hour or two to search the camp. I have some whiskey left if you want to knock her out as much as possible. Hopefully, that'll keep her from feeling the pain on the ride back."

"We'll try that." Doc took the flask and hurried back to Sue.

***

An hour later, the posse gathered near Sue's temporary shelter. Six of them were staying behind to begin sorting the mixed herd, which they estimated at about 2,500. The other six were returning with Ted, Doc, and an unconscious Sue. They will also take the surly prisoner who was bound, gagged, and tied into his saddle. The bodies of five more outlaws were tied over the saddles of their horses, waiting for the group to move out.

Three of the posse had made a quick search of the canyon to the north but found nothing noteworthy. Three others had searched the cave a short distance from the rustlers' camp while the rest of the posse was scattered in search of the immediate area in Lost Hope Canyon.

The entire group was waiting to remount when Ted said. "Just so you all know. We found several saddlebags filled with currency and gold dust in the cave." His face had lost its color when he explained. "We also found a tally book Snake kept. He claimed to have killed thirty-eight white men plus some women. He also killed an unknown number from other races but didn't regard them as human and didn't keep count."

The group listened ashen-faced.

He waved at one of the other riders. "Wes found three more bodies buried under rocks down the trail toward town. Doc said from the condition and the wounds, they were probably killed the night the gang tried a second raid on Sue's herd." He grinned at the satisfaction that mirrored his own radiating from the other riders. "With Snake's gang dead, this state is a much safer place to live." Ted nodded to the men remaining behind. "We'll send everyone we can find in town to help you sort out that herd. There are a lot of brands mixed in that herd."

He mounted his horse and waited a minute while Doc and another man gently lifted the slack body of a semiconscious Sue up to him. He cradled her limp form across his saddle, holding her in his arms. Doc mounted and rode close enough to place a sling over Ted's neck and around Sue's head and neck to support them against his shoulder. Moments later, the reduced posse rode out... both of the superbly trained horses Sue had provided joined the line of riders without direction from rider or reins.

The mass of riders soon sorted itself into a single file, spread over some distance and moving at a moderate pace. Doc and Ted were leading at the head of the line, periodically changing places. During one of those exchanges, they rode together for a space.

Doc asked, "I know Sue can be stubborn, but why couldn't you keep her out the battle even if you had to hogtie her?"

"I gave her my word not to." Ted paused before explaining. "She was going after them with or without me. I tried to persuade her otherwise, but the only way to make her stay behind would've been to handcuff her to something. That would've probably been fatal for me because we both knew she could outshoot me. Besides, I never could've found this place without her guidance."

Doc grinned bitterly. "I'd call that blackmail. Very effective but still blackmail"

Ted smiled sardonically in return. "She's one of those young hotheads you older folks keep harping about. The ones who get things done but get into a lot of trouble because they haven't learned any sense." His smile was warm as he looked at the still form in his arms. "Truth to be told…I guess I'm one of those hotheads since I'm not much older than she is."

***

Wilford erupted when the posse rode into town just before sunset. Spectators rushed into the street from every business and tavern, staring at the mass of bodies and shouting questions at the returning riders.

Silence fell momentarily when Doc raised his hand. "United States Marshal Ted Storm deputized Sue Mason and they went after the rustlers."

A roar of astonishment blanketed his next words.

Doc repeated, "They cornered the entire Snake Carson Gang, save one. Some of them were killed in the shootout before Sue and Ted were bushwhacked from behind. Ted was knocked out. Sue outdrew both Snake and our late, unlamented fake marshal. She was seriously wounded in the gunfight."

The crowd noise grew in volume and excitement as Doc urged his horse through the mass of people. Ted followed with Sue in his arms. They dismounted a few minutes later at Doc's office and hustled her inside.

***

Sue woke some time later to brilliant sunshine. She found herself lying on her back and after a few moments realized her belly was empty and cramping with hunger.

A fuzzy figure sitting in a chair exclaimed, "I was beginning to wonder if I should wake you up, but you beat me to it."

Her befuddled mind slowly made sense of his words. She whispered, "I wouldn't want to spoil something for you, so I decided it was time to wake up. What time is it, anyway?" she mumbled.

"It's late Monday afternoon."

"I've been asleep for a day?" she asked, too dopey to care.

Doc grinned unrepentantly. "I slipped a little something in your drink last night to keep you asleep. You have a talent for getting into trouble, and I didn't want to take a chance on losing you."

She mumbled again. Her tongue was as sluggish as her mind. "I wouldn't want to spoil your record, you old reprobate."

"You're too weak and sick to be up and about for some time." He patted her hand lying on the blanket. "I know you're hungry so I'll see about getting something for you to eat. I'll send Emma Brown up. She's been keeping an eye on you for me when I'm out."

"The lawyer's wife?"

"She volunteered. Knows you don't have any family. She's done that often since my Mary died. Whenever I need someone to care for a patient while I'm gone."

Sue managed to stay awake for a short time but fell asleep before she was able to finish the meal that appeared at her bedside. Concerned, Emma cleared the dishes, carried them downstairs, and then reported to Doc.

"She fell asleep? Didn't even finish her meal?" He scowled, and his expression hardened with concern. "I'd better check on her again. Can you sit with her tonight?"

Sue never remembered much of the next several days. Instead of improving, her condition deteriorated for no reason Doc could determine or combat. He sat with her as much as possible, as did Missus Brown. When Sue continued to grow ever weaker, Ted volunteered to take a turn sitting with her during the night.

He found her on her back with her head slightly raised on a pillow when he arrived in her room. A light blanket was pulled up to her chin and her hands were across her chest. He winced at the sallow gray of her face—unsure whether she was asleep or unconscious.

He shook his head in dismay. Although they had actually spent only a short time together, he found himself drawn to his attractive companion. She was, at different times, strongly opinionated, irritating, and aggravating. But she also displayed an innocent vulnerability.

Ted moved a chair close to the bed so he could face her and settled himself. He'd been considering his approach ever since he first volunteered. Leaning toward her, he took her right hand in his. His words were soft but penetrating. "Damn it, young lady! You've already proved you have courage. Everyone knows you're no coward, so don't give up on me now!"

For a second, he thought her hand squeezed his but any movement was so fleeting he was uncertain it actually happened. He waited for a few moments, but there was no further indication of awareness. He sighed and began to talk to her as though she was awake.

Ted talked to her for hours: sometimes carrying on a normal conversation, sometimes telling stories, and even once singing a lullaby he dredged up from deep in his memory. Late in the night, he fell asleep as the kerosene lamp burned low.

Doc found Ted the next morning, asleep in his chair with his hand still clasping Sue's. A squeaky floor board woke him. Quickly, he moved aside to let Doc examine his patient.

"What did you do?" Doc whispered in awed wonder, "She's much better this morning!"

The two men's eyes met, and relief shone in both.

"I didn't do anything except talk to her and hold her hand."

"Whatever you did or didn't do, I'm not letting you out of here until she's even stronger." The smile engulfed his face. "Right now, I'd say you're the perfect medicine for her."

Sue's recovery was dramatic from that morning onward as her strength returned. Two days later, she was awake when Doc and the marshal came to visit her. They found her sitting up, wrapped in a cotton robe, and talking with Emma Brown. Both men were carrying portions of a substantial meal, which they set on the table next to her bed.

"Emma, I see you were persuaded to let her get up. Both of you can share this because there's plenty for both of you. Sue, I have to go on a house call at the Two Bar S. I'll let these two take care of you while I'm gone." He shook his finger at her and added sternly, "I know you want to get out of this room for a while. If you do go for a walk, keep it short! Pay attention to Emma, and whatever you do, don't overdo it! You're not going to be healthy enough to be up and around much for several more days." He glared at her until she meekly nodded her acceptance before he turned and left the room.

Sue ate slowly but steadily as her curiosity grew. She kept glancing at Ted, but he remained silent.

"A lot has happened while you've been recovering," he said, breaking his silence at last. "The posse that rescued us confirmed the estimate of about twenty-five hundred head of cattle from a dozen brands in the canyon. Every rancher in the area has sent hands to help sort them out. They'll move yours back to your ranch, and someone will ride herd for you until you're up and around."

"I'm glad…" she sighed in resignation. "I know I won't be doing much riding for a while."

They engaged in small talk while Sue enjoyed her first substantial meal in many days. When she downed the last of her drink, Ted glanced at Emma, who was sitting behind her.

'Should I tell her?' he mouthed.

Emma nodded.

Ted said, "Snake and his gang have already been buried. Since you've been here, we found three more bodies buried in the canyon. The survivor said one of them was the one you wounded at the gate."

She paled at his statement.

He continued, "He was moaning all the way back from the raid on you. Snake couldn't stand it, so he just shot him out of hand. The other two were killed by their own crossfire that same night. We also found a large stash of loot from a multitude of robberies. The money and the survivor have already been shipped back to Denver. We found your hunch about Mel Victor was correct. Snake met him on the trail and shot him down for no reason at all. He then found the telegram inviting him to Wilford in his pocket."

Sue just blinked, listening to his every word.

"But I digress. Harold Easton finished burying them several days ago in the cemetery across the creek. He said it wasn't Boot Hill, but there had been a couple of drifters buried along the back fence over the years. He put the graves in the same area."

"That was fast." Sue grimaced. "I'm glad it's over with and glad I didn't know anything about it."

"I thought you might, but there is something else you should know. The town council is meeting this afternoon to see about finding another marshal. The mayor asked me if I'd take the job. I told him no because I have to go back to Denver in a few days."

Sue's face fell at the news.

He asked, "Would you want the job if they offered it?"

"No. I don't think so." She was silent for several moments, thinking. "I would take it for a short time to help out, but they'd have to wait until Doc turns me loose."

He nodded. "Why don't we take a walk down to the jail? I know you want to get outside for a bit, and it isn't far."

Her face lit up.

He grinned. "I'll wait downstairs for you."

Emma was helping Sue get dressed when she stopped abruptly to stare at the shirt and vest hanging on the back of the door.

"What's this?"

"Old man Horwick gave you a new shirt and vest. Your old ones were so bloody and cut up they were useless. He said if you could get shot up that badly, the least he could do was replace them."

Sue flushed in embarrassment before she followed Emma down the stairs. Very weak from the loss of blood and in near starvation, her pace was barely a shuffle as she steadied herself with a hand on the banister until she reached the first floor.

Ted gave her his arm for stability when they stepped outside. Her pace was still only a shuffle. She had to stop frequently because everyone on the street wanted to congratulate her. The looks of disbelief at the marshal's star pinned to her vest, which matched the one on Ted's, were poorly concealed. He was hard-pressed to keep a broad grin at bay.

They'd just reached the steps up to the porch of the marshal's office when they were hailed by a cheerful bellow from across the street. "Just a minute, you two."

Sue turned to see a bear of a man lumbering toward them through the watchers on the street, clutching a box camera and tripod in his arms. She waited until he was much closer before she introduced him. "Ted, this is Harold Easton. He's Wilford's cabinet maker, undertaker, and photographer."

He grinned. "I've already met Mister Easton."

She paled slightly, realizing that as the undertaker he would've been called to take care of the bodies of Snake and his gang. "I suppose you did."

Harold interrupted her, his face wreathed in a smile and his voice rumbling with enthusiasm. "I want to get some pictures of the first woman marshal in Colorado. Then the two of you together."

Sue started to decline, but Ted overruled her protest. "Sure. Go ahead." He ignored her glare with a smile.

The picture taking took time. The photographer was slow and deliberate as he posed them. They were dressed identically in faded jeans, chambray shirt, faded Stetson, and drooping gun belt. The crowd watched, fascinated, as he checked the focus, tripped the shutter, exchanged glass plates, and repeated the process. He took several exposures, thanked them profusely, gathered his equipment, and lumbered back down the street to his business.

CHAPTER 8

The day Sue had dreaded dawned with a rare heavy overcast that threatened rain. Dark and dreary, the weather mirrored her spirits as she slipped into her clothes, wincing at the slightest pressure on her dressing. Her gun belt was a notch looser on her gaunt frame, hanging lower than normal and away from the wound above her hip.

She walked to the boarding house for breakfast and was warmly welcomed on what was only her second excursion from Doc's care since the shootout. Rain began to fall while she was eating. A youngster eagerly volunteered to go to the livery and bring back the slicker on her saddle roll.

Listlessly, she picked at her meal until she could stall no longer. With help from another diner, she donned her slicker and splashed off down the street. She found Ted at the marshal's office, talking with a rancher whose back was turned toward her. Ted grinned and quickly rose to his feet.

"It looks like Doc finally let you loose. At least somewhat."

"He did." She scowled. "And scolded me until I agreed to stay in town a bit longer than I want. He'll decide when I'm healthy enough to go home, but I'm going to move in with the Browns for a few days."

The rancher also gained his feet and turned to face her. George Olson extended his hand. "We were discussing the rustled cattle before you came in. We have yours back on your range except for the hundred ninety-eight market-ready that were cut out and are in the loading corrals up the tracks as we speak. Doc made the decision to sell them for you while you were unconscious, since the market is as good as it's going to get. And you weren't in any shape to take care of them.

"While you've been laid up, everyone pitched in and we rode roundup on your range as well. Billy Rankin is taking care of your stock until you can handle it yourself. I hope that's okay with you?"

She was momentarily silent, touched by the unexpected help from her neighbors. "George. Thanks for doing this for me." She swallowed a lump. "Billy's a good hand. If it's okay with you, I'll pay you for his time when I get back to riding."

"No! It's not." He bristled with indignation. "You're not going to pay me a cent because without you, I'd have been out more than three hundred head of my own. That's a lot more than what Billy's wages would amount to."

Sue's pride was about to make her argue the point, but as she met George's eyes, she saw what she had always craved, respect. "I guess I can be a bit bullheaded at times. We'll do it your way. Thanks again."

The matter was settled to his satisfaction, so George nodded and turned to Ted. "I'll be moving on. I'm sure the two of you have matters to discuss." He tipped his hat to her and walked out the door into the falling rain.

Ted waved Sue to a chair next to the one he occupied, waiting for her. She sat down carefully, ever aware of her wound.

He drew a check from his shirt pocket and handed it to her. "This's the payment for your stock. The market is as high as it's been for some time and should meet your approval. If it does, I have some official items to go over with you."

She took the check and put it in her own pocket without looking at it. "Let's see what you have."

He spent some time going over the duties and paperwork any marshal would be responsible for. He explained, "Until somebody takes office here, you're the only sworn officer around. Unless you flatly refuse, it'll be your responsibility until someone else is sworn into office."

She nodded confidently. "I can handle it. Most of what I've read and what I've seen of law is using common sense."

"That's it in a nutshell." In a few minutes he covered the background she would find necessary for her to carry out her temporary duties. When they were done with the official business, he said. "It may not be my place to ask, but have you been through every page in every book your father left you?"

"No." She stared at him. "Why?"

"It would be playing a long shot, but maybe one of them has a name or some other clue written somewhere in the pages."

She stared at him in astonishment for a moment as he stood up. "My train is due in a few minutes. Would you walk to the station with me?"

Throat tight, she nodded. She slipped on her battered Stetson and her slicker with his help. She tried to mask her disappointment at his impending departure as he was the only man who had ever dealt with her as an equal. She walked with him toward the station, keeping to the shelter of the porches fronting the buildings on the street. The steady rain had already turned the dirt to mud. When they reached the last available shelter, she shrugged and sloshed across the street while the mud clutched at her boots.

They'd been inside for only a few minutes when they heard the wail of a whistle a short distance away.

The station agent announced, "Means they've coupled the cattle cars onto the train. They'll be here in a couple of minutes."

The train chugged into view a short distance away where the track turned sharply as it followed the shoulder of the mountain. Moments later, it screeched to a halt in a cloud of steam and smoke.

"Sue, I'm sorry I have to leave. I know you'll do a good job as the marshal." He extended his hand.

After a moment's hesitation, she held out her own. With a firm handshake, he turned, moving swiftly to board. Disappointed and dejected, her spirits plummeted even further as she watched the train begin to move but brightened when she saw his face in a window. He waved goodbye. After a few seconds of hesitation, she gave a feeble wave in return.

***

Sue rose at her usual hour the next day. The sky was clear and bright with early morning sunshine. She prepared breakfast for herself and the Browns before she walked across the yard to Doc Madison's.

She gritted her teeth as the bandage was changed and fresh ointment applied. Doc hummed tunelessly all the while. He smiled in satisfaction.

"You're healing fine. You could go home in another day or two if someone was there in case you got sick again. Since there isn't, you'd better plan to stay in town until next week." He admonished her sternly. "It's far easier to prevent infection than to cure it. I don't know what you had, and I don't know what cured it. I just want you to stay close until I know for sure you're healthy."

Sue lamented. "Doc, I'll stay in town, but I'm going to go crazy if I have to sit around all day and do nothing. If I do have to sit, can't I at least do it at the jail?" She asked soberly.

He considered her request, sighing, "You might as well. Marlin Humphrey has been serving as a temporary marshal and can take care of anything physical." He admonished her again. "But be careful!"

The jail was empty when Sue entered and her glance swept the office. An oaken gun case was against the wall to her left and a roll-top desk was against the opposite wall. A swivel chair on small casters waited on one side of the desk and a plain straight-backed chair was on the other. A coat rack screwed to the back wall completed the furnishings, while several open windows flooded the interior with light and fresh air.

She took two paces to the hallway to the back cell area and called, "Marlin. Are you back there?"

"Be right out," his muffled voice came from some distance away.

Marlin emerged from the cell area and his eyes met hers. "I know you're only holding this job temporary but I'm proud to work with you. Anybody that could outgun Snake Carson has earned it."

She flushed pink. "You probably know more about this than I do. We'll learn together."

Both of them turned as footsteps sounded on the porch.

Jack Ames, the editor of *The Wilford Messenger* walked in, clutching a newspaper in one hand. "Marshal Mason. I saw you walk in and I thought you'd like to have a copy of this week's paper." He spread it out on the desk, revealing a headline.

Sue glared at the editor, but he ignored her displeasure. "You're famous now, and soon you'll be even more so. I mailed a copy of this yesterday with pictures to *The Police Gazette.* They'd be crazy not to print it."

She was confused. "What pictures? What is *The Police Gazette?*"

"Do you remember the pictures that Harold took of you and the marshal?"

Sue nodded.

"He also took pictures of the bodies of Snake's gang in their caskets." He positively beamed. "Police Gazette is a national magazine that carries stories about crimes and criminals from all over the nation." His smile was smug. "I'm a newsman, and you are a *female* United States Marshal. You are *news* with a capital N!"

Her icy glare had absolutely no effect on the editor.

He ignored her displeasure. "You need to realize any woman wearing a badge, especially as young as you are, is rare. Literally unheard of. The fact this same young woman kills a mass murderer in a fast draw shootout has never been heard of before! I'll guarantee you there'll be a crowd of curiosity seekers in town before another week is out."

She groaned without a hint of humor as the editor beamed at her.

***

Saturday dawned in Wilford with clear skies and the cool air of high altitude. Sue was at the jail early, feeling nervous and anxious because it was likely to be an unusual day.

Marlin grinned at her. "You stood up to Snake. I don't doubt we'll have a lot of visitors. I do know you can face a bunch of curious cowboys and miners even if they do get rowdy."

She nodded but was too tense to smile. She paced the length of the room, then paced back to the doorway where she looked out. Her eyes swept the mountain peaks receding into the distance, a familiar sight which was strangely soothing.

For some reason, a memory of her father came to her, unbidden. *Duty and Honor. Duty and Honor. What a man does about them is the measure of the man.* She suppressed a fond mental raspberry. *Or of a woman. I gave my word.*

She turned to face Marlin. "You're right. We can handle it. Thanks for the vote of confidence."

Sue watched from the window or the door while the usual influx of settlers, ranchers, and cowhands became visibly swelled by many strange faces. Watching, she waited as the hitch rails in front of the saloons steadily filled with saddled horses. She glanced at Marlin, and he nodded. She shrugged and stepped out onto the boardwalk. Strangers stared, and a few met her eyes briefly before they looked away. She walked casually down the street, feeling certain everyone could tell her calm demeanor was a sham.

Her pulse was thundering in her ears when she entered the first saloon. The noisy room suddenly fell silent as she entered. Her glance swept the crowd where unfamiliar faces far outnumbered the familiar. Disbelief and consternation showed on many faces as she made eye contact with first one then another. After a nod to the crowd of drinkers, she turned and walked back out to the street. Voices erupted in disbelief behind her while she moved to the next saloon. Her legs trembled with relief.

***

They took turns inspecting the saloons, looking for any signs of impending trouble with so many strange riders and miners in town. Marlin had just returned from his latest round when they heard a rising tide of angry voices. Sue was on her feet and out the door in seconds with Marlin close behind.

He muttered, "Looks like the Red Dog, as usual. That cesspit always seems to have the most fights." His breath hissed in his teeth as he caught sight of the hitch rail through the milling throng. "There's real trouble brewing for sure. The Rafter hands are in town."

Sue had never heard of the brand. "Where're they from?"

"Just this side of Agate. Must have gotten up early to be here. They have a name for being hell-raisers."

A voice raised a shout, "Here comes the marshal!"

The crowd split, and an aisle formed while the onlookers moved back. Silence fell when she found herself facing a mountain of a man standing over an unconscious miner.

"He ain't dead," he bragged. "I just put him to sleep with my fist." The giant's face was red, and his fingers flexed near the butt of a holstered revolver. He sneered. "It was self-defense, so there's nothing you can do about it, little girl."

Sue waved Marlin back with her left hand as her mind raced. Stretching the truth, she observed calmly. "You've named me a lady. That must make you a gentleman."

His face flushed redder as a chorus of derisive laughter erupted from the crowd.

"Drunks with guns aren't welcome in this town. Since I outgunned Snake Carson and don't want to kill you, I'll make you a deal."

The giant's eyes flickered with indecision, remembering this woman was a dangerous gun slinger. He swelled, visibly ready to explode into action.

She ignored the signs and calmly continued, "We'll do a little target shooting across the creek. If I win, you'll check your guns with any barkeep in town until you leave. If you win, you keep your gun."

The giant gloated, "Deal!"

Sue shifted her glance to the crowd of expectant onlookers until she found a familiar face. "Slim, would you find us some tin cans and rocks and meet us across the creek?"

He nodded and melted into the crowd.

She pushed forward with Marlin beside her. The crowd and the drunken giant followed. They crossed the bridge into the open area below the cemetery, where the exodus from the saloons spread out.

Marlin whispered for her ears only, "Can you beat him?"

"No problem. He's drunk. I'm sober and faster. It's the only way to handle it, or we'll have to take them all on."

It was only a few minutes before they could hear Slim working his way through the crowd, offering bets on the lady marshal as he did so. Gleefully skeptical onlookers quickly took him up, delaying his arrival. As the betting frenzy spread through the crowd, the face of the giant began to look less assured.

Slim finally reached the front rank of the crowd and moved to her side, where he dropped several tin cans and a pile of small rocks. Sue held up her hand, and the crowd fell silent. Even the saloon keepers were watching in the distance from across the creek.

"The rules are simple. Slim will throw one can and one rock for each of us. Whoever gets the most hits wins. If it's a tie, he'll throw another round until the tie is broken."

She grinned at the drunk. "Since you've made claim to being a gentleman, it's lady first."

He nodded and she turned toward the open area with the crowd at her back. She flexed her fingers and raised herself slightly on her toes. "Any time you're ready."

A tin can flew high overhead, outward, and upward. Her hand flashed down and up, which was almost faster than an eye could follow. A flash of flame and smoke. The can was kicked higher and higher with each shot as flame erupted repeatedly from the muzzle until the cylinder was empty.

The echoes were still rebounding from the mountain side when Slim announced to the silent crowd. "Six for six."

Sue reloaded in seconds and slid her revolver into the holster on her hip. "Ready."

The first stone, which was about the size of Slim's thumb, followed the same path. Her Colt roared three times before the rock vanished in a spray of gravel. She turned toward the giant as she reloaded the fired chambers.

His mouth was hanging open and his face had lost its ruddiness. He dropped his hands to his gun belt and unbuckled it. "Marshal, I've never seen shooting like that! I'll leave my gun at the Red Dog."

The crowd roared in admiration as he bowed drunkenly, nearly falling. He turned on his heel and headed back across the bridge with his gun belt draped over a shoulder. Sue heaved a sigh of relief as Slim shook her hand.

"That's some shooting." He grinned. "Thanks for making me a whole lot richer."

Sue grinned in return. "Thanks for the vote of confidence. Your betting shook him up." She chuckled and turned to Marlin. "Let's head back to the jail."

They were escorted by a boisterous stream of revelers as the crowd returned to the saloons. Many a man yielded his gun belt to a favorite saloon keeper before raising a drink in tribute to the speed of the lady marshal.

CHAPTER 9

The days passed quickly for Sue while she learned her new responsibilities and established a routine. Since the wound in her side was still swathed in bandages, Marlin volunteered to do any riding which might prove necessary as well as taking responsibility for checking the saloons at night.

She found she enjoyed the daytime duties, visiting every business in town at least once a day, stopping to talk with owners, employees, and customers alike. She made a point to visit the depot whenever either of the two daily trains pulled in. As much as it was from curiosity, it was her desire to learn all she could about anything. She was fascinated by both the variety and the unexpected number of visitors arriving in Wilford, but was totally unaware of the fact her new habit had generated a rumor that spread quickly through the town—*she's lovesick and waiting for Marshal Storm to come back.*

Several more days passed. She was idly watching the afternoon arrivals stream from the train when one new arrival caught her attention as he stepped down. His back was ramrod straight and he wore a holster on his hip, radiating an aura of confidence and authority. She watched his glance flick across the other arrivals until he made eye contact and began moving toward her.

"Marshal Mason?"

She nodded.

"I've heard a great deal about you." He extended his hand with a smile. "I'm Emmet Claybourne. I imagine Mayor Wolfe told you I was coming."

Sue returned his handshake, already impressed. She was a head taller and had to look down to meet eyes that sparkled with humor. "I'm sure most of what you heard about me was highly exaggerated." She smiled in turn. "The mayor told me you'd be coming. I'll take you to meet him after you claim your bags. Welcome to Wilford, Marshal."

"They'll check my baggage into storage here. My horse was unloaded around the bend at the stock pens." A frown creased his face. "What I've heard about you is from several reliable sources. All of it good. I don't want you to think I'm trying to force you out of this job."

"Not at all." She grinned broadly. "I have a ranch waiting for me that needs my attention. Now that I have Doc's okay and you're here, I can go home to take care of it."

They found the mayor a few minutes later in front of his blacksmith shop, bent over the hoof of a horse as he critically eyed the fit of a new shoe. They watched and waited beside the horse's owner until the smith grunted in satisfaction before rapidly nailing the shoe in place.

"That should take care of this horse, Ed." He glanced at Sue and her companion. "I'll be with you as soon as I'm done here."

"Take your time," she replied. "We're in no hurry."

After the newly shod horse and its owner had departed, she introduced the two men. They sized each other up for a moment before discussing details for a few minutes.

Mayor Jake Wolfe glanced at her and then back to Emmet. "Would you excuse us for a few minutes? I'd like to talk to Sue alone."

"Sure thing. Wave at me when you want me to come back." He moved off down the street as they watched.

The mayor turned to Sue. "I think he's the right man for Wilford. What do you think?"

"I was very impressed." She kept her expression neutral with difficulty, feeling proud to have been asked for her opinion. "I think he'd do an excellent job for us."

"I do too. Unless you can think of a good reason not to, I'll tell him he's got the job."

When she nodded her agreement, he beckoned for the new marshal. They watched together as he started walking back to them.

"Thanks for filling in until Emmet got here. I'd appreciate it if you'd show him what he needs to know."

"I'll do that." She glanced at the sun. "I'll head for home as soon as we're done. I've been away too long."

The mayor extended his hand. "Thanks again."

***

Sue had scarcely reached Doc Madison's gate when he stepped onto the white-painted porch dressed in coat and tie as always. *Stately and dignified,* the thought flashed unbidden into her mind. She dismounted and climbed the steps, noticing a few wisps of gray in his beard and hair for the first time. *When did he start getting old?* He was waiting for her when she got to the last step, which placed their eyes at the same level.

"If you see the slightest sign of infection, get back here as fast as you can ride," he admonished.

"Don't worry. I will." She found it hard to speak with the lump in her throat. "Doc… thanks for everything." Impulsively, she gave him a kiss on the cheek.

"You're always welcome here even if you're not a patient."

Tears misted her eyes when she turned to go.

He continued with a smile in his voice and on his face, "When he asks you, don't turn him down."

"Who? Ask what?" Baffled, she looked at him over her shoulder.

"Ted. He'll be back."

She avoided his gaze. "I'm not sure what you're talking about, but I'll keep it in mind. Thanks again. I'll see you the next time I'm in town." She stepped to her horse and mounted swiftly. With a last salute, she was off for home.

Full darkness hadn't yet fallen when she rode into the ranch yard. Mutt dashed from the porch and raced circles around her, barking in an ecstasy of welcome. Lantern light streamed from the windows. The door opened as she dismounted, but she ignored it as the dog planted its paws on her chest and slathered her face with a welcoming lick. She hugged him in an overwhelming wave of affection.

"Sue. Is that you?"

"Yes, Billy. It's me. I'll put my horse away before I come in."

"I'll put on another can of stew to heat."

Sue dropped the laden saddlebag on the porch before heading for the corral. Her weary horse plodded behind as Mutt bounded across the yard. She stripped off the saddle, opened the gate, and watched it amble into the pasture to the welcoming whickering of other horses. She scooped up the saddle and carried it to the tack room in the nearby barn. When she placed her burden on its rack by feel, her nose wrinkled to the pleasant smell of new-mown hay drifting in the darkness.

Mutt reclaimed his rightful place by the front door when she walked into the kitchen where Billy stood next to the stove. He waved her to an empty chair at the table.

"Your stew will be ready in a minute. Make yourself comfortable." He chuckled, "Your dog is friendly, but he sure knows who his master is."

"Thanks." She grinned. "Just as long as you don't try to take him away from me. Did I really smell new hay in the barn?" She seated herself, stretching tired muscles.

He laughed, "You did. There were about a dozen of us who put up your whole cutting today. If we'd known you were coming home, we would've waited for you. We wouldn't want you to feel left out." He poured the hot stew from the pan into a bowl and set it on the table for her. "The lift on the dump rake broke just before we finished. I tore it apart and was planning to take the broken piece to the blacksmith. Since you're back, I'll head to town in the morning and leave it there on my way back to the Flying J."

While Sue ate, he reported on what he had seen and done on her range while Doc had kept her confined to town. "I 'bout cleaned you out of grub. Hope you brought some for yourself."

"My saddlebags are stuffed with canned goods."

"That's good." He got to his feet, moving to the door. "I've been bunking in the barn. I shouldn't disturb you when I leave early in the morning."

"Good night." She waited until he was almost at the door. "Billy, thanks. You've been a lifesaver for me."

He mumbled an acknowledgement, appearing embarrassed, before disappearing into the darkness.

***

Eager to check the herd she hadn't seen for far too long, Sue rode out next morning. She shivered at the gate where the violence took place but rode on. The sight of the spring crop of calves gamboling with their mothers and Mutt bounding across the open pasture dispelled that dark shadow. She rode home with a light heart and an aching side. *Don't worry about it. You haven't ridden much for several weeks.*

When she reached the ranch house, she remembered Ted's suggestion, so she plucked a book from the shelf and collapsed on the couch. She skimmed through each page, finding nothing, until she fell asleep. When she awoke, sunset was fast approaching.

***

The next few days were a blur as Sue worked from dawn to dusk, trying to keep her memories of her moments with Ted from dominating her waking hours. Often, she found herself replaying a scene in her mind and watching dreamily—walking to the train and him holding her close and looking deeply into her eyes before his lips sought hers.

Something snorted in her ear, causing her to almost jump out of her skin. She found herself halfway across the corral. When she had gathered her wits, her old pack horse was staring at her with its lips curled back in what could've been a smile. Sue glared at the offending horse before her own lips curled in a rueful smile. She shook her head and tried to concentrate on the task at hand again.

Her nighttime memories were a mix of joy and terror, alternating between her moments with Ted and the violence of the shootout. She often had trouble getting to sleep... when she did get to sleep, the nightmare of the shootout often woke her in a cold sweat. She tried reading until late, but the books from her father's library which had been so captivating, palled.

One night, she found herself outdoors, staring at the moonless night sky with tears running down her face. An avalanche of stars dipped down to the horizon in all directions, meeting the black silhouettes of mountain crests that cleaved a line as sharp as her life before and after meeting Ted. The home that had been a haven of magnificent solitude for years suddenly had become a prison of crushing loneliness. She screamed into the overwhelming silence.

"Damn you, Ted Storm! Why did you have to break my heart?"

Mocking echoes reverberated back to her. Sue stumbled back to the ranch house so numb and exhausted she fell into bed fully dressed. She slept fitfully until late in the night when she found herself in a dream, once again riding beside the marshal with his hand gently resting on hers. Strangely comforted, she fell into the first deep, restful sleep she had experienced for many nights.

She slept as if she were dead, groggily waking up to find the sun well clear of the horizon. The lassitude faded slowly as she stoked the coals in the stove to warm a pot of bitter coffee. Her mood was the lightest in many days with the tendrils of her dream wispy in her mind.

A vague feeling of urgency stirred. She checked her cupboards and was shocked to find them almost bare. *Get hold of yourself, girl. It's time to get over that man and go get some groceries.*

Sue added more wood to the fire and placed a bucket of water on the stove to heat. When it was hot, she poured it into a tin washtub, already partially filled with cold water she had carried from the spring, before bathing.

Dry, dressed in clean jeans and work shirt and her hair brushed out, she felt the best she had for many days. She hurried through the chores, saddled her horse, bridled her old pack mare, and headed for Wilford.

***

Sue turned aside as she entered town, stopping at Doc Madison's. She heard her knock echo through the house along with his footsteps.

A smile enveloped his face when he saw her. "You're looking better, girl."

"I feel better. Not totally normal, but better. I need a nap to get through the afternoon but my side doesn't hurt much anymore."

"That's good." A sly smile crinkled his face. "If it makes any difference to you, he's in town even as we speak."

Her breathing stopped. "Ted's here? In town?"

"The same. I'd suggest looking for him at the jail." His smug smile warmed her heart.

She could've burst out singing. "I will."

Within moments, she was astride her horse, feeling her heart lighter and the day brighter. She fought down the urge to whip her horse to a gallop, maintaining a sedate pace with difficulty until she drew rein at the jail a few minutes later.

Sue dismounted and left her mount and the pack horse at the hitch rail. When she turned toward the door, Ted was standing on the porch. His eyes sparkled.

"We were just talking about you. There's a man inside who'd like to meet you, since we expected you'd be in town today." He waited until she reached him before he whispered, "I'm glad to see you."

Marshal Claybourne and a stranger were standing, facing the door when she entered.

Ted introduced them. "I know you've met the marshal. This is Alex Ludens. He's a Pinkerton man."

She shook the extended hand and took the chair he offered.

When they were all seated, Alex began. "Miss Mason..."

"Please call me Sue."

"Sue, I want to congratulate you for ridding this state of its greatest scourge, Snake Carson and his gang. This world is a much better place without them." Respect was evident in his eyes as he shifted topics abruptly. "I want you to know the total of the loot recovered from the cave was two hundred and seventy thousand dollars."

Sue whistled in astonishment, "That's a lot of money!"

"You're right. Ten percent is yours as a reward. That means you get twenty-seven thousand from the State of Colorado."

Her jaw dropped.

"Pinkerton had rewards on all of Snake's gang. The reward for Snake was twenty-five thousand. The other four were five thousand each. Pinkerton regards it as all yours. Congratulations, Sue. You're a rich woman now."

"I can't take it!" She protested. "It's blood money."

"You're right," he retorted. "It was your blood that was spilled." His voice more gentle, he added, "Snake spilled a lot of blood besides yours. Why don't you think of this as a thank you from the other victims. You deserve it because a lot of people never even got the chance to fight back."

"I agree with Alex that you deserve it." Marshal Claybourne observed. "Maybe this'll help undo some of the damage Snake inflicted on this state."

Sue yielded reluctantly. "I guess I have to take it."

Alex reached into his coat pocket and withdrew two slips of paper. "Here are the checks for both rewards."

Sue took the checks with nerveless hands… unable to fathom the fortune they represented.

CHAPTER 10

Sue decided to stay the night in town, rooming with the Browns at their invitation. After supper, she walked next door to Doc's and knocked tentatively on the door.

"Come in." His warm voice echoed from within the house.

She found Doc sitting on the couch in the front room with his feet up on a footstool and a medical journal held in his lap, reading in the bright light of a kerosene lamp.

He put his feet down and beckoned her. "Come in. Sit down and make yourself comfortable."

Sue remained standing, feeling suddenly nervous as butterflies warred in her stomach. "Can I talk to you?"

"Sure." His warm smile was highlighted by the golden glow of the lamp. "Would this be father-daughter stuff?"

Her throat was suddenly dry. She shuffled her feet, staring at the floor. "…Yes."

His eyes twinkled as he patted the cushions beside him. She sat down, curled her legs under her, and turned to face him. He waited patiently while the silence lengthened.

"What do I do with my life now?" Sue finally asked.

Again, he waited patiently while another silence ensued.

"I'm now a wealthy woman, but what do I do with all that money? Who am I? What do I do now? Do I keep my ranch? Do I sell it and live a life of leisure? Do I keep this badge?" She choked back tears of frustration.

Doc waited in silence for another moment in case she had more to add before he observed. "The first thing you do is nothing."

Dumbfounded, she stared at him.

He explained, smiling, "You heard me correctly. You don't make any changes right now. You need some time to think about your options." He watched her mulling his words in her mind for some moments before he asked, "Part of your uncertainty is Ted, isn't it?"

Sue turned away, hiding her face within her shoulder-length brown hair. She choked out almost inaudibly, "Yes."

"He's the first man you've ever met who has accepted you for who you are and treated you as an equal. It's only natural for you to want it to be something more."

Her head snapped up, sending her hair flying.

He held up his hand to stop her protest as he continued gently, "It may still come to be, but you can't force someone to love you."

She ducked her face back in her long hair.

"You weren't aware of it because you were unconscious, but you owe him your life. As he owes you his. Your turn was when you killed Snake and Mel Victor. His was… I still don't understand it! You were unconscious and fading fast. Emma and I both sat with you, but nothing we did made any difference. Ted took a turn, but all he could do, all any of us could do, was to hold your hand and talk to you. I don't know what he did or what he said, but the next morning, you were much better. I will never understand it. I do know he truly saved your life that night because I believe you would've died within the day!"

Sue could see the wonder in his eyes, and the ice in her belly began to fade.

He paused as his eyes turned opaque. "I don't know what to predict about your future or whether it will be with Ted or not. What I don't see is you living a life of leisure, doing nothing. You have an exceptionally rare gift with animals, which I knew before this ever started. It was even more obvious when we found you out there when Ted told us how your dog led two horses to your aid. No one else has cattle as well cared for as yours are, and that shows as well."

She fell silent.

He shook his head. "A life as a marshal? I don't know. I don't think that is your life's calling, but you'll have to decide for yourself. You don't ask questions with easy answers," he exhaled explosively.

Sue continued to wait in silence as she mulled over his words.

"In regard to your new wealth, you've already touched every life in this community."

Startled, she stared at him. "How did you know?"

"What? Oh… I don't have anything specific in mind, so I think we're probably talking about two different things, whatever you're thinking. Let me explain." He hunched forward. "The whole country has begun to suffer from economic problems. Us included. You talked to the banker, Holtzman. This spring, he would've been within the law to have called your note due. Obviously, he didn't. First of all, he wanted to give you a chance. Secondly, he doesn't want to own another ranch he couldn't sell because no one has money to spend. Money is a strange thing. It does no one any good unless it is in use. He had none coming in, so he had none to loan out. Everybody was starting to hurt."

She watched as he grinned slyly.

"It's no secret in this town that today you deposited a huge sum of money. Even if in reality it is only an entry in someone's ledger. Now, Holtzman has money to loan for people who need to borrow. You." He pointed at her. "In all probability saved his bank and our town."

Her mind couldn't wrap around all the new information. All she could do was listen.

He smiled widely. "He did tell me you were willing to sell off your remaining herd so I wouldn't be legally responsible. I'm glad it didn't come to that."

"I never knew it was so complicated!" She was a bit dazed and exaggerated only slightly. "I just know I only had about ten dollars to my name this morning."

Doc sobered, the levity vanishing. "As to the question of who you are… You're a unique young woman in your own right. As to the family you sprang from, neither of us knows."

Doc's words and concern had lightened her mood, but Sue still had to bite back a sob. "Ted suggested I examine every page of every book in Pa's library for clues."

He nodded. "That's a good place to start," he sighed. "There is something I have to tell you. Something I once promised your father I would not."

Sue straightened in rigid apprehension.

"I know now he was wrong to ask me to do so. Very wrong! You have the right to know, and you must know. I believe his early death negated the promise I made to never tell you." Doc took her hands in his. "When your mother died, it wasn't from some disease. She died giving birth to your sister. They're buried together."

Sue stared at him, shaken and stunned by the deception, before bursting into tears. He drew her to him, nestling her head against his shoulder. He gently patted her back until the flood of tears diminished to a trickle, unmindful of his sodden shirt.

Much later, she asked in a choked voice, "Why didn't Pa tell me the truth?"

"I think he blamed himself for your mother's death. He knew there might be problems, but he didn't get her to town before she was due. Then he couldn't bring himself to tell you the real reason for her death. He did say he was always going to tell you…someday. But he was killed and then it was too late."

Her shoulders shook.

Doc tipped her tearstained face up to meet his. "Your Pa only slipped once about his past, and that was just after your mother's death. He told me they had eloped against her father's wishes and they could never go back."

***

Sue started for home the next day as a very befuddled young woman. She had planned to be up and on the way home early but ended up sleeping in as a result of her emotional turmoil. Squire and Emma were just about to leave the house when she came downstairs.

"Sue. We're going to church." Emma looked over. "Why don't you come with us?"

She was so aghast at the prospect her voice squeaked, "Dressed like this?"

112

"Of course. The Lord sees your heart, not your clothes."

Sue was torn because she hadn't been in a church for years. But she was their guest. Her hosts deserved her respect. Reluctantly, she acquiesced. "Well, I guess I could. If you really think that it would be acceptable dressed as I am."

Emma smiled in reply and offered her hand. When they reached the street, Doc was leaving his home as well. He fell in with them, offering Sue his arm. She released Emma's hand and took Doc's arm instead.

She towered over him and leaned down to whisper in his ear, "We make a rather mismatched pair."

He grinned shamelessly.

They had almost reached the schoolhouse when she halted abruptly. "Oh, my gosh! I'm wearing my gun. What do I do? I don't dare wear it to church, or tongues will really wag."

Doc gently admonished her. "Don't worry about it. Marshal Logan always wore his gun to church. You've been the law in this town as he was."

"You're sure?" Sue was trembling with uncertainty.

"Yes." Calmly and gently, his words lessened her apprehension.

She stared at him for a long moment before falling reluctantly in step. Squire and Emma had gone on ahead and were already seated. The room was nearly full, so Doc led her to two of the few empty chairs near the front. Heads turned and her ears burned as whispers swept the room. The preacher welcomed her with a nod and a smile.

Sue squirmed in her chair as the service started. After several hymns and prayers, the pastor launched into his sermon. She listened, interested in spite of her mental discomfort, gradually relaxing as the sermon neared its end. Her newfound serenity evaporated and she turned crimson when the pastor concluded.

"The Good Book tells us the strong right hand of the Lord shall smite demons and destroy evil. We welcome the strong right hand of Sister Mason into our midst today. We and the Lord celebrate your recovery from the grievous wounds suffered at the hands of the devil incarnate."

Sue turned an even brighter crimson when the entire room broke into loud applause. The preacher left his temporary pulpit at the front and stopped at her chair. Her face had begun to fade to its normal shade but returned to bright crimson when he invited her.

"We would be honored if you would join me at the door."

***

Doc helped load her pack horse while she saddled her own mount.

"I don't understand what's different," she said. "I used to be ignored by a lot of people even if they weren't openly hostile. Now, I seem to be accepted by almost everybody. And it isn't just the money because it happened even before yesterday."

"You've changed," Doc said affectionately. "Before Snake, you had a chip on your shoulder. Completely justified, I admit. You scared people because you sure don't fit the role of what most folks expect a woman should be." He snorted, "Docile and subservient, you aren't!"

Her eyes twinkled.

"You felt that the world was unfair, and it is. It's just unfair to everyone. Now you see it, it makes a difference in you. Now those people see you as a valuable, if unique, member of the community."

She digested his words in her mind for several moments before answering. "I didn't know you were such a philosopher, but thanks."

***

Sue rode out from her ranch the next morning, feeling the most at peace with herself she ever remembered. Even Mutt seemed to realize it as he raced ahead, leading the way. When she reached the gate at the canyon mouth, she dropped the bars and moved them aside. Instead of simply checking the health of her herd, she began moving them toward the open gate and greener pastures.

Cows and their calves bunched up. She forced them on until one old cow moved into the lead with the rest of the herd following. She trailed them, examining everything with new appreciation. She watched, amused at their obvious interest in new grass. Sue realized with her new insight this was where she truly belonged.

The sun was approaching its zenith when Sue rode into the ranch yard of the B-bar-F. Cathy Franklin heard the hoofbeats and was standing on the porch with three small children clustered around her, waving in welcome. Sue dismounted and climbed the porch steps.

Cathy gave her a gentle hug, minding her recent wound. "We stopped in to see you at Doc's, but you were asleep. I'm so happy you've recovered! Ben has been fixing fences in the horse pasture today. I was about to ring the bell, so he'll be here in a few minutes."

Cathy seemed to be noticing a subtle difference in her close friend that filled her with joy. Though only a few years older than Sue, unlike her, Cathy grew up under the constant care and guidance of her own mother. That experience had allowed her to help guide a young neighbor girl through the mysteries of the passage from adolescence to womanhood.

The echo of the ringing bell had hardly faded when Ben walked into the yard and joined them on the porch. Sue helped Cathy finish preparations for the meal while Ben and the rest of the family took their places. The children, Mark, Andrew and Mary listened avidly as the adults traded jibes and information in equal measure.

When everyone was seated at the laden table, Ben concluded grace, "...and we thank thee, Lord, for the company of this good friend at our table and especially for her deliverance from evil. Amen."

When they had finished eating, Sue cleared her throat with her unsteady voice betraying her nervousness. "Ben, you and Cathy were the only neighbors who helped me keep my ranch going after Pa died. Um...I know I've been sometimes nosy and stubborn, but I hope you won't be offended by me doing this for you." She reached into her shirt pocket, pulled out a folded sheet of paper, and handed it to them.

Mystified, Ben spread it flat on the table. Both adults were startled and looked up in astonishment.

Sue said with a tremor in her voice, "As you see, it's the mortgage on your ranch. Paid in full." Her voice became pleading. "Please don't be offended, because it makes me very happy to help such good friends. I know you would've paid it off in time by yourselves, but I'm now a rich woman from the rewards on Snake's gang. I can easily afford it."

Ben's mouth gaped. Cathy's face was wreathed in a huge smile as tears of gratitude streamed down her face. Her voice trembled too. "We couldn't refuse this gift from you. I love you for doing this for us." She quickly rose from her chair to give Sue a careful embrace as her tears of joy dribbled on the vest of the much taller woman.

Ben finally found his voice. "You shouldn't have done it, but we can't refuse. Thank you from the bottom of our hearts!"

CHAPTER 11

Several days later, Sue was working on haying machinery, getting everything ready for the next cutting, which was still several weeks away. She had finished repairs on the broken dump rake and was now working on the hay loader. One critical bolt was badly worn but her attempts to replace it had met with little success.

A hot, frustrating half hour after she started, she was still wedged under the machine, muttering to herself as she kept trying fruitlessly. She heard hoofbeats approaching in the distance but ignored them because Mutt made no outcry, an accurate indication it was someone familiar.

Ted Storm dismounted and dropped the reins of his horse a short distance from the machine. He chuckled to himself as Mutt lifted his head from his paws in disdainful greeting. He walked toward where Sue was wedged under the machine. His eyes swept her slender figure, and his gaze appreciated the long legs and full hips outlined against the dust. He hastily shook his head as his body stiffened.

The wrench slipped once again. Sue skinned her knuckles and cursed, using words she seldom used. When someone laughed, her heart leaped. She peered out from under her temporary prison and met Ted's amused expression as he squatted on his heels.

He chuckled, "I didn't think you knew words like that."

She grinned back. "I don't use them very often. And I'm only repeating the ones my father used, so it's all right. Could you hold that other wrench while I turn this one?"

"Sure thing." He dropped to his knees beside her.

With his help, the bolt was replaced in a few minutes. She gave a sigh of relief and squirmed her way out from under the machine. His eyes were dancing as she wiped the sweat from her face with her sleeve and settled her Stetson on her head. She picked up her gun belt lying on the ground nearby and buckled it on before turning to face him.

"Not that I mind, but I'm curious why you're here."

Amusement danced in his eyes. "It's a long story. Why don't we find some place to sit in the shade?"

"Sure. And I need something to drink anyway." She walked toward the ranch house, brushing the dust from her clothing.

When they reached the kitchen, she headed for the water pail on the counter and downed a long drink from the ladle before she offered him one.

Ted smacked his lips in appreciation. "That's mighty good water."

"It's genuine spring water from the bluff out back." Sue seated herself as he took a chair across the table.

His eyes met and held hers for a moment. "First, take a look at this." He laid a journal on the table with the title *The Police Gazette* emblazoned across the front page.

She opened it and flushed as she saw herself staring from the picture taken in front of the marshal's office. She shook her head as she read the first line. *United States Marshal Sue Mason, daughter of the late Max and June Mason, is recovering from wounds suffered during a quick draw shootout with the vilest outlaw in the West.* She read on, turning red at the editor's continuing hyperbole.

When she finished reading, her face was red. "They added a lot that was pure fiction. Jack Ames' story was at least factual. They make it sound as though I can walk on water and part the Red Sea."

He chuckled, "They do."

Sue held his gaze firmly. "Now, tell me the rest. You didn't come all the way out here just to give me this."

Ted leaned back in the chair, organizing his thoughts. "Several members of both the Colorado House and Senate have been considering establishing a statewide police force of some kind. Courtesy of Jack Ames' story and the criminal reports filed in federal court in Denver, they have a cause. They decided to form a special-session committee and invite you to testify." He grinned at her expression. "No, you wouldn't be the only witness. Just the star witness."

She asked suspiciously, "Why me?"

"You are a perfect example of a citizen who had nowhere to turn when the local law was the problem. They know you decided to appeal for help to a federal officer instead of someone on the state level." He said firmly, "They want some sort of law agency to be responsible at the local level."

"When would they want me to appear?"

"As soon as possible." He grinned sheepishly. "Actually, you're scheduled to appear Tuesday morning."

Sue glared, irritated by his making a decision for her without consulting her.

"I told them I thought you'd be willing but would wire them from Wilford if you decided you didn't want to appear." He regarded her soberly. "It really is your decision. The time element was the only reason that led me to set it up this way."

She thought for a moment as her irritation cooled. "I don't know why I couldn't testify, not that I have a clue what they want to know." She mused, thinking out loud. "I could get Billy Rankin to take care of the ranch again for a few days. That would let me catch the train tomorrow and go back with you." Ted's silence at her acceptance made her suspicious. "What other surprises do you have in store for me?"

He sighed and waved at the magazine he had brought with him. "There are rumors floating around the office that the Marshal Service in Washington wants to invite you to testify for them about funding. That would be before a Congressional Committee."

Sue stared at him in consternation. "I don't get it! What do I know about funding? Why would they want me to testify?"

"Publicity!" Ted practically spat the word. "What they want is for you to star in a dog and pony show." He pointed at the magazine on the table. "This is distributed all over America. You're the only female marshal in the Marshals Service. Also, the Eastern newspapers are fascinated by stories of fast draw gunmen. In your case, they are in a literal frenzy over the story of a fast draw *gunwoman*! No matter what you say, it won't matter to those papers. All they would care about is that this fearsome gun-slinging woman from the West is in Washington."

After a moment's consideration, Sue nodded. "I'd at least consider it if the opportunity arose. Even if the committee doesn't hear a word I say, I'll still be in the newspapers."

Ted stared at her, shocked and dismayed at her totally unexpected desire for fame.

His good opinion of her was important to her, so she hastened to explain, "I don't care if I'm in the papers or not. What I'm hoping is someone will recognize my name or that of my parents and contact me."

He relaxed, appearing to be deep in thought.

Sue waved a hand in the direction of her library. "I took your suggestion and started searching through all of those books. I've been through about a third, but I haven't found anything yet," she sighed. "I've been trying to be realistic about the chances, and I'm not counting on finding anything."

Ted met her steady gaze. "Then I'd better help you. As you said, the odds are against finding anything. Still, if we could find something, what better places would we have than Denver or Washington to follow up on any clue we might find."

Sue held his gaze for a moment with a thankful nod. She rose and disappeared into the front room. She was back a moment later with three books apiece that she placed on the table between them.

They leafed through the books quickly with painstaking accuracy. They talked only a little, fearing distraction and its consequences of possibly missing a clue.

The kitchen was beginning to grow dark when Sue asked, "Would you take care of the chores that need to be done tonight? I'll fix us something to eat."

"Sure. And I'll fix a spot in the barn for me to bunk in tonight."

She rattled off the small list of tasks that needed to be done and he was off to the barn. She stoked the stove and began preparing the meal. The stove was growing hot when the thought popped, unbidden, into her mind. *This is what being married must be like. He's outside and I'm cooking.* Remembering Doc's admonishment, she hastily quashed that train of thought.

The food was hot, and the coffee pot was steaming when Ted returned from the barn. He took a long splinter from the wood box, ignited it from the stove, and lit the lamps in both rooms before sitting at the table.

He admired her graceful moves for a moment. "I noticed one book on engineering that was well worn. Have you read it?"

She chuckled, "Some of it. Pa used it mostly when he was making sketches of dams to hold back rainfall. He used a slip scraper to build a lot of little ones to form water holes in some of the canyons. They worked, but some have eroded."

He kept his gaze toward her.

Sue shook her head. "I tried using the scraper last summer to repair one of those. The first time I hit a rock, it almost threw me over my head and under the horses' hooves. I realized right then I was about a hundred pounds too light so I quit before I got hurt. Now, I can afford to hire someone to do the hard work," she laughed.

As soon as they were done eating, she started to wash the dishes. She stared in surprise when Ted picked up the dish towel and began to dry.

He laughed at her stunned expression. "I've done dishes many times. This way, we can get started together."

They searched late into the night again, talking only a little for fear of distraction and the possibility of missing a single clue. There were only five books left on the last shelf when Ted left the table to fetch them. Before he sat down, he brought the pot from the kitchen and divided the last of the coffee between their mugs.

"This one shouldn't take too long." He grinned at the thin volume's title. "I'm not much for poetry."

"I've never looked at it either. I wouldn't know." Sue stretched stiffened muscles.

He exclaimed, "Aha!'

She dropped her own book on the table. He turned the title page so she could see the words written in faded ink, *Property of Peoria Public Library.*

She gasped in sudden excitement and was barely able to keep her voice from cracking. "A clue! Now, we have something to work with."

Ted cautioned, "Don't get your hopes too high. It might very well mean nothing at all." He waited a moment. "But then again, it might be the mother lode."

Tears of joy glistened in her eyes.

His hand covered hers on the table. "With all the bad luck you've had in your life, let's hope this is the beginning of a new life for you."

Her heart hammered at his casual touch.

He lifted his cup in salute with his other hand. "A toast to your new life."

Finally, she collected her wits enough to raise her own cup in return.

They found nothing more in the remaining volumes. After closing the last ones, both sat silently in their chairs, savoring the moment.

Ted stirred first, rising to his feet. "It's getting late. I'd better get to the barn and get some sleep."

Sue's throat was dry when she responded, "I'll have breakfast ready early, so we can ride for town."

He turned to face her at the door.

She exclaimed, "Thank you so much! Maybe nothing will come of this clue, but it's the only one I've ever found."

The lamp light reflected from her sparkling eyes as gratitude and something else shone from their depths. Impulse, not logic, guided his actions as he kissed her on the lips.

Sue gasped.

Ted, realizing what he had done, turned and fled in embarrassment.

She stood and watched him disappear into the night. Her body was frozen into immobility by ecstasy. Her knees felt weak, and her heart was pounding.

CHAPTER 12

When Ted knocked on her door the next morning, he looked as if he had had a sleepless night, probably thinking of Sue and regretting his impulsive action. When she opened the door, his well-thought-out explanation was thrown into turmoil. Instead of the frown he expected, she was smiling warmly.

"I-I want to apologize for my behavior last night..." he mumbled.

Sue's eyes were warm and smiling. "Why?"

Her demeanor threw him off. "Because I shouldn't have taken advantage of you," he explained weakly as he skated onto thin ice.

"Didn't you want to kiss me?" Now, she was frowning.

"Yes! I did!" He startled them both with his vehemence as the ice parted beneath him.

Sue held his eyes for a moment as her own glowed. Her voice was barely above a whisper. "I wanted you to kiss me..."

His thoughts caught up with his emotions. He wrapped her in his arms while his lips sought hers.

***

Much later, Ted released her from his embrace and backed away slightly. Her knees buckled as tears of happiness trickled down her cheeks.

"I'd like to come calling if I may," he whispered in her ear. He chuckled ruefully, "Right now, we have a train to catch in a few hours, and we might miss it at this rate."

"I want you to come calling." Sue sniffled. "I'll fix us something to eat."

Their intentions were noble, but it was several minutes more before she reluctantly pulled away.

***

They ate quickly, after which he headed for the barn while she finished up in the kitchen. Sue was waiting on the porch when he returned with two saddled horses. She held a single satchel, her face solemn.

"After I tie this on, there's something I have to do before we leave."

Sue tied the satchel behind her saddle and then led him around the ranch house. The overhanging limbs of a tall, solitary blue spruce sheltered two uncut stones. Her silence and the majesty of the simple scene suggested to Ted what it was she needed to do.

Her eyes were brimming with tears before they reached the graves. Unseeing and unknowing, her hand clasped his. They stood silently in front of the two faint mounds of earth for several minutes.

Her voice cracked, "Ma. Pa. I know you are with me in my heart, so I'll always have you with me. Maybe someday, I'll find your families too."

Firmly, Ted held her hand and led as she choked and turned away. Tears flooded down her cheeks. When the tears diminished, she choked again, "This is both the happiest and saddest day of my life. I'm going to truly leave my parents for the first time. Maybe to find their families," she sniffled.

He patted her back.

"We'd better go before I really break down," she whispered to the silent stones. "Goodbye."

***

They stopped at Doc Madison's house, but he was gone. Ted returned his rental horse to the livery, where Sue left hers as well. They were hungry so they stopped at the boarding house. Doc was there. He beckoned for them to join him at his table... Sue signaled the hostess to bring two meals. She was too excited to wait and began telling him of their discovery before she even sat down.

"That's wonderful news! Now, you have at least a chance to find your family."

"More family, you mean." Her love for him was obvious. "You're family to me."

"And proud to be." His pride in her was also obvious. "When you find your parents' families, I'm sure they'll be of the same high caliber you are."

Doc smiled to himself in silent satisfaction while he slyly watched the two of them during their meal. They had said nothing of their feelings for each other but their secret was too obvious to miss. Neither realized most of the other diners had also recognized the symptoms as well and approved whole-heartedly.

When they had eaten, they bade Doc goodbye and headed for the bank. They ran into George Olson on the street.

"Can I hire Billy from you for a while? And I mean hire for a few days until I get back?" Sue asked.

"Sure. I'll send him over when I get back to the ranch or from here if he's in town."

They were leaving the bank when a locomotive whistle echoed down the street. "We'd better hurry," Ted said. "That train isn't very far away."

They arrived at the station as the train pulled in. They waited while the arriving passengers disembarked before boarding.

Sue took the window seat as he slid her lone bag under the seat. "I've never been very far from home before and only on horseback." She admitted with some trepidation, "This is my first train ride, so I'm a little nervous."

Ted passed up the opportunity to tease her. "I've ridden the rails a lot. This route isn't bad at all. There are routes in other parts of the state where you'd swear the whole train's going to fall several hundred feet into a river."

She watched the scenery with a mix of apprehension and appreciation as the tracks twisted and turned uphill and down. On the rare occasions when they had a long straight stretch, the engineer would open the throttle, racing far faster than any horse she had ever ridden. About two hours after having left Wilford, the train descended into a broad valley between two mountain ranges and stopped at another station.

The conductor called out, "End of the line. Transfer here for points east, west, and south. Everyone off."

They carried their bags and moved through the station to wait next to another set of rails.

Sue stared, mystified, before asking, "What's the difference?"

Ted chuckled, "I would've been surprised if you didn't notice. We came in on narrow gauge rail, which allows for much tighter turns. The rest of our trip to Denver will be on standard gauge, which allows for bigger cars and heavier loads. The downside is the turns have to be wider."

She shook her head at another wonder. "I'll take your word for it. I just want to get there."

He laughed in response and gently squeezed her hand.

Trains were frequent on their new route, and a few minutes later, they boarded another one. Only a few miles later, their locomotive was belching a huge column of black coal smoke and white exhausted steam as it struggled up the western slope of the continental divide. Their progress was correspondingly slow until they gained the eastern slope and accelerated markedly as they roared down the mountains to the beckoning valley of the South Platte below.

They raced southeasterly for miles until the tracks made a sharp turn to the northeast for a straight run to Denver. Mile after mile fell behind, and the sun was far to the west.

Ted said, "We're less than an hour out of Denver. Do you realize how long it would've taken us to ride this far on horseback?"

"I hadn't considered it," she acknowledged thoughtfully. "It would certainly take a lot longer and require a good horse to follow a trail along the route we've taken."

"It would take most of a week and be a lot more dangerous."

***

Their train pulled into Denver's Union Station just before full darkness settled on the city. They halted on one of many parallel tracks clustered under a vast roof... adjoining pairs were separated by a shared platform.

"You can just step out level," Sue marveled.

"I've heard all the big cities in the East have this type of station," Ted replied. "That meant that Denver had to have the same. I'll grant that it makes it a lot easier to get off and keeps you out of the mud and gravel."

They followed the line of passengers into the station proper where Sue stopped abruptly.

She was amazed at the brilliant lighting. "What kind of lights are they?"

"Gas lights." She stared in wonder as he explained, "The gas is manufactured downtown and piped to the customer. It gives more light than kerosene, and it's cheaper and more convenient."

They continued through the station and outside where Ted flagged down a carriage. They were dropped off a short time later at the Drovers' House where they stopped at the reception desk. The clerk on duty glanced up and greeted Ted but dissolved in confusion when his gaze settled on Sue and the marshal's star pinned to her vest.

Ted laughed, "Sam, this is Sue Mason. She'll need a room for a few nights." He turned to her. "Sam Barker is an old friend and is always the one to welcome me home when I get back to Denver."

Sue signed the register and the clerk handed her a key. "You can have Room 210 on the second floor. It's the fourth room on the left." He barely concealed his amazement as they walked off toward the stairs.

***

They met a half hour later at the hotel dining room door. The large room was crowded.

The host explained, "There's a special show at the opera house tonight. That's why we're full, but I'll have a table for you in a few minutes."

Ted recognized many of the other diners. After they were seated, he introduced Sue to the couple at the next table. Everyone in earshot shamelessly eavesdropped. It took only moments for the introduction to spread to the entire room that Ted's attractive companion was the young woman who had ended the murderous spree of Snake Carson. Many diners took the time to stop and congratulate her as they left the dining room.

Andrew White also offered. "I have an extra pair of tickets for the show. Would you like them?"

Sue glanced at Ted, who nodded. "Thank you. We'd be glad to use them."

"Here they are." He handed them to Ted.

His wife, Polly, said, "We'll save you some seats. The house fills up rapidly when there's something special scheduled, as there is tonight."

***

There were very few empty seats left when they walked into the theater. Polly was watching for them and waved from her seat near the middle of the room. Ted waited a second for Sue to take the lead and followed her toward their seats.

Whispers coursed back and forth through the crowd as they walked down the aisle. Sue's figure was as obvious as the butt of the revolver protruding from her holster. Their seats were on the aisle, where she sat beside Polly, who welcomed her warmly.

136

After exchanging pleasantries, Sue gazed around at her surroundings. The theater looked huge to her eyes, a rectangle about three times as long as wide. The ceiling was high overhead and covered with formed metal. The walls were covered with a muted red fabric, offsetting the golden draperies of the stage curtain.

They were seated on the main floor, which sloped upward toward the back, enabling the back row to see the stage. The back third was overshadowed by a steeply rising balcony that gave those patrons a clear view of the stage as well. On either side, two individual balconies jutted out from the wall, overlooking the stage. She couldn't see how many people were seated in each, but another set of golden drapes could be drawn to give the occupants privacy. She shook her head in wonder as the gas lights along either wall were turned down and the curtain was drawn aside.

***

Sue had never seen a melodrama of any kind and was startled the first time the crowd booed and hissed the villain. Ted laughed softly at her reaction, smiling when she glared at him.

When the lights came up for the intermission, Ted could see the sparkle in Sue's eyes. They were so much more relaxed than the first time he met her. At that time, bitterness had given her face a hard edge that had since vanished. She was still too thin from a hard winter and her wound, but her health had certainly improved.

At the end of the intermission, the gas lights were turned down for the second act. The crowd buzzed in puzzlement when the hero unexpectedly appeared on stage from behind the drawn golden curtains.

He waited until the buzz faded. "Ladies and Gentlemen, I'd like a moment of your time. We all know that on stage, good always triumphs over evil. Unfortunately, in real life, that is not always the case."

The crowd waited in mystified silence.

"Tonight, I would like to present to you a real-life heroine in our midst." The silence deepened while he allowed the suspense to build. "This young woman single-handedly destroyed the Snake Carson Gang and was badly wounded herself!"

A spotlight pinned Sue in its beam, causing her to squint against the glare from a new-fangled electric arc light.

"I present to you, United States Marshal Sue Mason. Miss Mason, would you please stand up?"

Her face was flaming crimson in the bright light. Embarrassed, she turned to Ted, who gave her a smile of encouragement. Her knees felt weak as she rose, thunderous applause erupting as the crowd came to its feet.

Ted said, just loudly enough for her to hear, "Wave at them."

The applause redoubled, which came as a wave of thunder in her ears. When the adulation died away, her trembling legs eased her back into her seat. The curtain began to rise.

***

They met the next morning in the hotel dining room for a leisurely breakfast. After their meal they left and ambled through the streets of Denver on an unplanned tour. They stopped often to window-shop, sometimes talking quietly and other times just silently enjoying each other's presence. Unknowingly, they caused many cases of shock and consternation to other pedestrians because they looked like two men holding hands. Another glance would set them right… her sun-bleached brown hair tumbled to her collar, and her full hips and bosom left no doubt as to her true gender.

Sue was a bit daunted at her new surroundings. "This is quite an adventure for me because I've never been anywhere other than Wilford. I suppose this is all familiar to you."

"It is," he laughed as he enjoyed watching her wide-eyed introduction to so much that was new.

Sue was intrigued by the Wells Fargo Building where their marshal stars drew sharp scrutiny from the watchful guards. They grinned in recognition at Ted but eyed her with undisguised curiosity. They also created a similar reaction when they walked by the United States Mint Building.

Ted explained, "They don't strike any coins here, but they do buy gold nuggets and dust and cast that into bars. Millions of dollars' worth. That's why they have armed guards on duty around the clock." He gave a friendly wave to the watchful guard as they moved on.

They strolled alone some of the time… at other times only two of a mass of people, gradually gaining elevation as they moved farther away from the distant Platte. After passing a series of nondescript buildings, Sue was startled when she looked across an intersection. What looked like the bleached bones of a giant sea creature were sprawled over an area of several blocks.

She stared as her perception adjusted to the reality of a massive stone foundation, surrounded by lifting frames and scaffolding which reminded her of vultures picking at a carcass.

Ted explained, "This will be our new state capitol. They're still a few years from completion, but it will be a magnificent building when completed."

She shook her head in wonder as they walked the perimeter of the construction site.

Mid-afternoon found them sitting on a bench in a city park, thankful for the ample shade of a nearby tree. Sue snuggled against Ted's shoulder and watched in contented silence as the shadows crept up the mountains from the depths of the distant South Platte valley.

She was half-asleep when Ted called a greeting. She blinked the drowsiness from her eyes and sat up when another couple stopped at their bench.

Ted introduced her. "Sue Mason. Melvin and Elizabeth Akins. They run the finest haberdashery and millinery in the city. I think you'd be wise to stop there sometime while you're in town."

"That's definitely a good idea." She met his eyes for a moment before she turned to their visitors. "I didn't have much to select from when I left home, but I thought we'd probably be able to find someplace to shop for clothes."

Elizabeth smiled at the massive understatement. "You're taller than most women, but I have a wide selection. I'm sure I would have something you'd like."

"Thank you. We'll see you sometime tomorrow."

The Akins walked on, leaving them to lazily watch the shadows moving up the Rockies. Sue stretched and was about to suggest they leave when another visitor approached.

Ted grinned and introduced him. "Sue, meet Emil Peterson. He's a reporter for *The Denver Post*."

Emil chuckled, "You two are hard to miss but hard to catch up with. I've been tracking you all afternoon." His expression sobered as he directed his attention to her. "We reprinted the entire story about your shootout with Snake from the Wilford Messenger last month. I'd like to talk to you about it instead of just reading about it secondhand."

She gave a mental shrug before replying, "I don't know what I can add."

"Let me be the judge." He drew a notebook from his pocket and began to fire questions at her.

CHAPTER 13

The Akins greeted them warmly when they arrived the next morning at the haberdashery. Ted stayed behind while Elizabeth took Sue into the millinery next door.

After the women disappeared, Melvin observed. "Sue is a lovely young lady even dressed in men's clothes. Beth knows what will look good on her."

"I've noticed." Melvin glanced at him sharply, but Ted volunteered nothing more.

Beth urged her to expand her wardrobe greatly, but Sue limited her selections to two, a light blue traveling dress and a sweeping gown of royal purple. She explained. "I won't be in Denver very long and sure won't wear either very much in Wilford. And I'll be wearing these clothes at home."

Beth could see Sue was proud of her unconventional appearance. She smiled at the independent young woman's determination. "Just remember you look lovely enough in that gown to be mistaken for royalty."

Ted was standing in front of a mirror, examining the fit of new clothes when the women returned.

Sue admired his new outfit before asking. "Why don't you find the same for me?"

Startled, Melvin stared at her. When he saw she was entirely serious, he nodded. "I'll be right back."

Beth sputtered in indignation. "Men's clothes!" She glared at Ted, who returned an innocent smile.

When Melvin returned moments later with an armload of clothing, she firmly took Sue's arm and led her back to her shop to change.

Ted was waiting with an expectant smile on his face when the two women returned, moving to Sue's side. They were dressed identically in black Stetsons, black trousers, black vests, and white ruffled shirts. They were wearing gun belts with revolvers buckled around their waists and marshal's stars pinned to their vest.

Every clerk and customer in the store stared, probably dumbfounded at the sight.

Beth was the first to find her voice, sounding dazed. "If you wear those outfits here in Denver, you'll turn this town upside down! No one will believe what they're seeing. I can hardly believe it myself."

***

When they walked into the federal courthouse that afternoon, Sue stared in awe at the magnificence of the open rotunda arching overhead. Still in awe, she followed Ted up the marble stairs to the third floor where a secretary ushered them into the office of the Director, U. S. Marshal Service.

144

A short, burly man rose from the chair behind the desk and extended his hand as they approached. He smiled when Ted made the introductions.

"Sue Mason. This is Leonard Simpson. Leonard is the man who sent me to Wilford." He grinned at Sue. "As they say, the rest is history."

Leonard waved them to chairs in front of his desk. "Miss Mason, I'm honored to meet you. I've heard a lot about you and your exploits. All of it good, I might add." The smile left his face as he expressed his unhappiness. "I wish the Service had a medal appropriate to your courage and accomplishments that I could award you, but unfortunately, I don't. You deserve a commendation because Snake Carson was the vilest scourge to ever afflict the West."

Sue squirmed in embarrassment. She protested, "I was just defending myself."

"Yes, but you were willing to put yourself in a position of danger few men would have dared to take." He grinned. "I will not allow you to argue with me about this. The Marshal Service is proud of its only female member. There have been rumblings out of Washington that you will be 'invited' to testify before some sort of committee. I don't know at this time if anything will ever come of it. You've never been paid, so you could easily refuse." Devilish humor danced in his eyes as he handed her a check. "Now, you've been paid."

Sue laughed as she put the check in her pocket, "Ted said you could be sneaky."

"Guilty as charged. Now, tell me about yourself. I like to know all about my agents."

CHAPTER 14

The next day turned out to be unusually hot and humid for Denver. Sue and Ted met Senate Majority Leader Morgan at the downtown hotel where the Senate met in rented rooms. The committee room was already hot and stifling.

They were dressed as had been suggested, wearing their range-faded jeans and chambray shirts, gun belts well-worn and comfortable. A page took their faded Stetsons and disappeared into an adjoining cloak room.

A capacity crowd of spectators and reporters already filled the room to overflowing. When the news had broken that the committee had invited Sue to testify, the local newspapers had also reprinted the story of her experience. When it was announced a female marshal and gunwoman was to appear before a select committee, crowds of curious readers flocked to the hearing.

Sue could hear the murmurs of disbelief scurry across the room while they were led to reserved seats near the front. A low railing separated the spectator area from a raised dais occupied by a large table and five massive chairs. They were unoccupied at the moment. On either side of the aisle in front of the rail was a small desk with a single chair. The one on their right held a pitcher and two water glasses.

Senator Morgan took his seat in the middle of the row and Ted followed, with Sue sitting on the aisle. They had been seated for only a few moments when a side door to the chamber opened. A man draped in the sash of a sergeant-at-arms entered and intoned loudly, "All rise."

The crowd rose to its feet while five men filed onto the dais through an unseen door, each selecting one of the massive chairs. When the committee members were seated, the sergeant-at-arms announced to the spectators, "Please be seated."

Sue listened, butterflies warring in her middle, while the chairman called the meeting to order. A clerk who had taken the seat at the desk on the left side of the aisle read the minutes of the previous meeting. Her pulse beat faster when the clerk announced the agenda for the day's meeting of the joint committee: "The matter of testimony regarding establishment of a police force with state-wide jurisdiction. Its duties yet to be determined."

The clerk deferred to the chairman. "Will the clerk please call the first witness?"

The clerk did so. "United States Marshal Sue Mason, serving the great State of Colorado. Please step forward and be sworn in."

Sue swallowed and took a deep breath. Ted squeezed her hand reassuringly as she stood up. *You could face Snake. You can face these men.*

She was sworn in and was directed to the small desk on the right side of the aisle. She sat down, surprised at her own calm, meeting one by one the eyes of the five men facing her.

The chairman broke the silence. "Good morning, Marshal Mason. I'm Senator Taylor. On my left are Senator Smith and Senator Osgood. On my right are Representative Winfield and Representative Mason."

She started at the name of Mason. The chairman held her gaze for a moment. "I will ask the most obvious question first. What do you see as qualifying you to testify before this committee?"

Dead silence filled the room. *What are my qualifications? I'm no expert. I'm no politician.* Her thoughts raced for a moment. She surprised the committee and herself by smiling. "I'm qualified simply by being a citizen of these United States and the State of Colorado. Any action you take will certainly affect my life in one way or another."

The room buzzed while the committee members stared at her. They had been expecting the usual blandishment of special knowledge or achievements by the witness. The utter simplicity of her answer was totally unexpected.

The chairman smiled. "Sometimes we forget why we are here." He turned to the clerk. "Let the record show Marshal Mason is fully qualified to address this committee. Mister Winfield, you are next."

"Marshal Mason, what did Senator Morgan tell you to tell us to ensure we would create a state police force of some sort?"

Sue smiled. "Senator Morgan told me, and I quote, 'I'm not going to tell you a damn thing about this hearing. The committee can smell a set-up a mile away. I want them to judge your testimony on its own merits.'"

The gallery broke out in laughter while the other four men smiled. Representative Winfield's face tightened. "So anything you tell us is entirely your own opinion and observations?"

Her unwavering eyes met his. "I swore an oath to that. Yes, sir. They are."

Representative Mason's first question was totally unexpected. "Marshal Mason, I saw my name gave you quite a start. What would be the reason?"

She swallowed hard. "I've never before met anyone else with that surname. It took me by surprise."

The representative was curious and he leaned forward slightly. "Where is your family from?"

Sue paled. The room waited in dead silence until she explained in a lifeless monotone, "I have no idea."

The committee exchanged surprised glances. Senator Osgood asked, "You have no idea at all where your family is from?"

Unshed tears glistened in her eyes and her breath was short. "None. My mother died when I was a toddler. My father was killed in an accident. He never told me, but I don't know why."

Senator Smith regarded her silently. *Maybe it's some shameful family secret. Tread carefully.* "What were your parents' given names?"

"Max and June."

Senator Smith asked, curiosity evident in his voice, "Why didn't you go to your neighbors for help instead of enlisting the Marshal Service?"

Sue's attempt to keep the bitterness from her voice was not successful. "After my father died, only one of my neighbors thought I had a chance to make a go of ranching and was willing to help me. The rest either wanted to buy me out because 'No woman can succeed at ranching,' or because they wanted to marry me and get my ranch." She scowled. "Or was it they wanted to marry my ranch and get me with it?"

There was an uncomfortable silence in the room as the chairman steered the questioning away from the personal. "The state and the country both are faced with growing financial problems and cannot provide the money to do everything we're asked to do. Why should we establish a new department that is going to cost the taxpayers?"

Sue had spent hours mulling over possible questions and answers on the subject. "The first duty of all levels of government is to protect its citizens. The army and navy protect us from outside threats, while state and local governments provide protection at other levels.

"In reality, we who live outside Denver have to defend ourselves because the law is usually too far away. If it's a civil dispute, you can afford to wait, at least for a while, for the law to handle it."

Sue paused for a moment, making eye contact with the committee members. "I don't know where any of you live in the state, but for me a round trip to Wilford, my closest town, in good weather, takes most of a day by horseback, unless you're desperate. If I need to make a trip with a wagon, it's a day's journey each way. If I have business at the county courthouse, it takes an additional full day in good weather. In winter, forget travelling! I was snowbound for almost three months last winter because of snow deeper than a horse's head."

Her self-confidence grew as she met the chairman's gaze. "When I saw our local marshal meeting with outlaws, I called for outside help. When Marshal Storm responded, that was one case where the enforcement of the law needed to come from a higher level. In this case, federal"

Sue paused for dramatic effect. "Another example for the need for a response from a higher level would be President Cleveland's recent action.

I was glad to read he had forced some greedy railroads to return eighty-six million acres of land they had wrongfully claimed."

She could see frowns, wondering where she was headed. "Don't get me wrong. We need the railroads, especially for moving goods and people over such vast distances. But we must have honesty, not naked greed, in business dealings as well as in government."

Representative Winfield snapped, "I've read about your supposed heroic exploits." He scowled at her. "Don't you know it's unladylike to fight?"

Sue ignored the storm of whispers from behind her as she stared at him in stunned disbelief. "Then I'm no lady! I'd be dead if I were." Her scorn was palpable. "What do you think I should have done? Walked up to Snake Carson, shaken my finger at him, and scolded him like a schoolmarm? I was unconscious after the shootout, but the posse searched the camp and found a ledger where he had tallied killing more than thirty-eight people, both men and women. Do you really think he would have *listened* to me?"

She continued, her contempt leaking through in spite of her best efforts. "My father taught me to use a gun so I could defend myself. By your twisted reasoning, every woman that ever went west in a covered wagon was no lady—they had to fight to survive, even if it was just to find enough food for their families."

The representative's eyes were smoldering as she continued, scathingly. "Where I'm from, we have a term regarding horses to describe your attitude, but I'm too much of a lady to use it in public."

The room exploded with laughter. The chairman pounded his gavel for order, his lips twitching as he tried to suppress a smile of his own. "Representative Mason."

"So are you suggesting the state has to enforce the law directly, everywhere in the state?"

After a moment's thought, Sue replied, "Yes and no. As a private citizen I will probably never again have need for a federal marshal or some future state policeman. This time I did. Multiply me by how many thousands of people who live in this state and someone somewhere needs help from a higher authority, right now. I have faith local law usually works, but I know from my own experience that is not always the case. Justice demands we have an alternative if and when it's needed."

Increasing respect showed in four faces. Senator Osgood observed, "You seem to be well informed about these United States."

"I've read a lot from the library my father left me. I really know very little from direct experience, except for my own area of Colorado. So many things in this great country have to be seen to be believed or truly understood."

Senator Smith was next. "Do you think we should establish a police force and increase taxes to pay for it?"

"I believe we need some sort of state-wide law enforcement agency to provide a secondary source of protection for the citizens. As to how to pay for it or whether to raise taxes, I don't know. I wish I did." Eyebrows rose throughout the room. A witness before a committee had actually admitted she didn't have the solution to a problem.

Sue sighed and leaned back slightly. "You are the ones who will have to decide about something this complex. I know enough to know I don't have enough experience to offer an informed opinion. I hope you can find a fair solution."

"How would you vote on this issue?" Senator Taylor asked.

"When I'm old enough to vote, I'm sure the issues at that time will be something entirely different. At least I will be eligible to vote, since Colorado finally gave women the right to vote this past spring."

The senator was visibly startled. *A woman this poised and knowledgeable isn't even old enough to vote? She's not even twenty-one? And she's already faced down gunfighters!*

"How old are you?"

"I just turned eighteen a few weeks ago."

He was able to contain his disbelief only with difficulty. "You said earlier you were a rancher before you became a marshal, yet you say you are only eighteen?"

Sue's throat tightened. "That's right. I've run my ranch by myself since my father was killed two years ago."

Murmurs of disbelief erupted from the crowd behind her. She impaled the panel with her eyes and added firmly, "A woman could do anything a man can do, if she were allowed to."

"Even govern?" Representative Winfield interrupted with a sneer.

"Yes. We certainly couldn't do any worse. Look at all the wars men have gotten the world into over the course of history. Look at the corruption in business and government the newspapers keep reporting." She shook her head sadly and repeated, "Women certainly couldn't do any worse and could probably do better."

The crowded room buzzed. Representative Winfield seethed because Sue had unknowingly stirred his darkest secrets. Some of the spectators were aware of rumors of bribes and pay-offs involving Winfield, rumors that had been circulating in Denver for months; unknown to almost everyone, the rumors were true.

Contemptuous of women in general, a wife-beater in his own home, he took her simple statement as an attack. He exploded. "You're a damn liar!"

The buzzing room was shocked into silence. They locked eyes as an angry wave of red suffused her face. Sue's voice was hard, under tight control that amazed committee members and spectators alike. "You, sir, are the liar. It would seem to me you protesteth too much."

The chairman was as angry with the representative as Sue was. She started in her chair at the bang of the gavel. "Sergeant-at-arms! Remove the representative from this room." His angry voice carried throughout the room. "You, sir, have brought dishonor to this body by your flagrant and unprovoked attack on a witness called before us."

The room was in an uproar while the representative was escorted out, his hate-filled and terrified eyes locked with Sue's, her hand resting on the butt of her gun. She shivered at the fury she saw, reminded anew of the image of Snake Carson.

It took several minutes for the chairman to restore order, repeatedly banging his gavel until order was restored. Sue took a quick glance over her shoulder to see Ted smiling and Senator Morgan looking stunned. When he caught her eye, Ted gave her an unobtrusive thumbs-up, which made her feel much more confident.

With the hearing once again under control, Senator Taylor directed. "The clerk will enter an apology to the witness into the minutes. The personal attack by a member of this panel was unjustified." She met his eyes for a moment while he gauged her amazing self-control. "Representative Mason, it's your turn to address the witness."

Sue took a sip of water from her glass as the representative held her eyes silently for a long moment. His question was totally unexpected and hit her like a fist. "The newspapers report that you killed several men in a gunfight. No matter how justified, what is it like to kill an outlaw?"

The gallery was deathly silent, the only sound the street noise that filtered in through the open windows. Sue paled as she had not done under attack from Representative Winfield. She drew a deep breath. "It's shattering! I can only imagine it must be akin to fighting in a war, because it was kill or be killed. I was wearing a marshal's star and fired in self-defense, but I still have nightmares."

She gulped the remainder of the glass as the room waited silently. "I'll probably have nightmares for the rest of my life." Her body was rigid at the recollection and she closed her eyes momentarily. "You are about the right age to have served in the Great War. If you did, I imagine you probably faced something similar. Kill or be killed."

A shadow darkened her interrogator's eyes. His voice was flat. "I was. Memories of such horror are best left in the past where they belong. I withdraw the question."

The committee continued their questioning for most of the morning, probing topics as diverse as her understanding of the law she had studied during the winter and the prices paid for cattle.

It took great effort to stifle an audible sigh of relief when Senator Taylor closed the session. "I believe we have asked this witness enough questions to determine her views and superb qualifications. Marshal Mason, thank you for testifying before this panel." He banged his gavel. "We stand adjourned until two o'clock this afternoon."

CHAPTER 15

They ate dinner in a nearby cafe. Many of the spectators who had attended the hearing followed them and stopped at their table to talk to Sue. She was dumbfounded when several asked for her autograph, including two who asked her to sign their copies of *The Police Gazette*.

She was uncomfortable with all of the attention but tried to treat every demand on her time with tolerance. She sighed with relief when Mamma Malloy, the owner who knew Ted of old, called a halt. She good-naturedly shooed the crush away from their table so Sue could eat her meal in peace.

Mamma patted her on the shoulder and said loudly enough to be heard by the crowd, "Grab him quick, girl. He's too good a one to let get away." Sue laughed with Ted as the room cheered.

***

They were outside on the sidewalk when Ted suggested, "We're only a few blocks from the post office. I would be very surprised if they didn't have some sort of listing of every post office in the country. We could check the list, which would tell us how many Peorias there are now and give us prospects for the ones that might have had a library twenty years ago."

"I would never have thought of it. I bet you're right." She was equally excited by the possibility, and by the realization he had said *us*.

The postmaster was delighted to help. "Snake hit at least two of our mail shipments. I'm glad to give you all the help I can, knowing he's no longer a worry for me. I don't think it's adequate thanks, mind you, but it would literally take an act of Congress to do anything more." He was gone for a few minutes, returning with three heavy volumes in his arms.

"They're split up by states so it will be easy to get names. City size will be a different matter, but it will at least give you some possibilities."

Half an hour later they were once again on the street. Sue was afire with eager anticipation. They had found only one Peoria that could possibly have had a library twenty years previously—in Illinois!

"Thank you! Thank you! Thank you!" Sue was so excited that she had to stop to catch her breath before unabashedly kissing Ted on the lips. "I would never have thought of the post office." Ted grinned at her exuberance while she tried to rein in her excitement.

Sue was too keyed up to even think of sitting, so they spent much of the rest of the afternoon wandering aimlessly hand-in-hand all over the city. They talked a great deal, or rather she did.

Ted laughed when she apologized. "I'm babbling. I know I am, but I'm so excited I can't help it."

"I don't mind, and I don't blame you. You've been alone too long without knowing who you are." She made a face at him, and after a moment's reflection laughed at herself.

Sue decided later that afternoon she would return home to Wilford the next day. Their wanderings had brought them back to the vicinity of the federal courthouse, so she suggested they stop to say goodbye to Leonard.

When they entered the office, Marvin, the clerk, grabbed a yellow envelope from his desk and hurried toward them. "Marshal Mason. This telegram's for you. The agent in Wilford cabled the agency here you were in Denver. Western Union redirected it and delivered it to our office."

Sue stared at him in consternation as fear and anticipation warred in her middle. She tore the envelope open with trembling fingers and read—

MARSHAL SUE MASON STOP IT IS

POSSIBLE YOU ARE CLIENTS

GRANDDAUGHTER STOP ADVISE

FATHERS FULL NAME BIRTHDAY

IDENTIFYING MARKS STOP

REPLY SOONEST STOP

Sue's hands were shaking, and tears of joy blurred her vision as she collapsed into the nearest chair. Ted was shaken by this sign of weakness he had never before witnessed. He asked anxiously, "Are you all right?"

Wordlessly, she handed him the telegram while she tried to stem the flow of tears. His exclamation echoed as Leonard entered the room, his face showing his own anxiety at her apparent collapse.

Ted explained, "Sue might have found family today. We found a clue which narrowed her search to one city. Now someone thinks they may have found her family as well, but we have no idea which side of her family they might be."

The telegram was passed from hand to hand at her nod. Marvin offered, "If you want to dictate a reply, I'll take it to the Western Union office."

Sue nodded, snuffling as she wiped her eyes with her sleeve. After repeated tries, she managed to say, "Maximillian Howard Mason. April 27, 1851." She swallowed several times before she could continue. "Black hair, with a white forelock over his left eye."

"I'll get this right out. Unless you want otherwise, I'll give this office as the return address." She nodded agreement, unable to speak. "On second thought, I'll add the Drovers' House as an alternate, in case you were to get a response after-hours."

When they finally left the office, the sun had disappeared and night was fast approaching. Sue had regained her composure, but her voice still held a slight quiver. "I'm not hungry, but I know I need to eat something." Her voice steadied. "I know I'm not going to sleep much tonight."

Ted held her hand in silence as they walked the short distance to the Drovers' House. When they entered the dining room, he selected a table next to the wall and ordered for them both.

In spite of her misgivings, Sue managed to eat most of what was on her plate, although she took far longer than usual. When she had completed her meal, she relaxed, sipping her coffee, her eyes meeting Ted's. The lingering effects of the day's emotional storms had abated and she became aware of the intensity of his gaze.

Ted held her eyes for a moment, then reached inside his vest and took something from his shirt pocket. Their world narrowed to include only each other. Neither was aware that the buzz of conversation in the room had died, waiting in suspense. Ted took her left hand in his, eyes shining. "Sue, would you marry me?"

"YES!" Incredulous joy shone in her eyes as he slipped the simple ring he had bought days before on her finger. She blushed when applause erupted from the other diners, who were watching with anticipation.

***

They were late leaving the dining room as friends and acquaintances stopped to offer congratulations. They left the hotel and wandered aimlessly until they found another sheltered park bench. Stars sparkled brilliantly in the moonless night as Sue snuggled against Ted, her head on his shoulder, one hand in his, his arm around her as they talked and planned late into the night. The courthouse clock in the distance tolled on several occasions after the midnight hour before the night chill drove them back to the Drovers' House.

Ted kissed her good night at her door and waited until the lock clicked before he started back to his own room. They knew dawn was not far away; Sue was certain that any sleep would be difficult.

When she did awake, the sun was well above the horizon, although the day was still in its infancy. She dressed and went downstairs, where Ted was waiting for her in the lobby. He grinned and embraced her as she seemed to glow.

They ate a leisurely breakfast at a nearby eatery before returning to the federal courthouse. Some of Ted's fellow marshals were in the office and greeted them warmly. Ed Wagner was a close friend and shook hands. "Good news travels fast. Congratulations to you both."

Marvin answered her wordless query. "No telegram, but I wouldn't worry about it for a while. We have no idea what time they got your telegram and any honest lawyer would consult with their client before replying."

Leonard arrived a few minutes later and offered his own congratulations. He invited them into his office. Ted said, "I'm going to be resigning in the near future."

Sue echoed, "I will be too."

Leonard laughed. "I'm not surprised. I heard the good news at breakfast and knew it was only a matter of time." He thought for a moment before he continued. "Sue, I would appreciate it if you were to wait to resign until I know if Washington really does want you to testify. You could very well be important to the entire Service."

"That's the very least I can do. When you sent Ted to Wilford, you gave me my life and my future." Her glowing eyes on Ted said everything.

"Thank you. I appreciate that." A soft knock on the door interrupted them. "Come."

Marvin opened the door, holding a yellow envelope in his hand. "Telegram for Marshal Mason."

Sue's heart pounded as she took the envelope and ripped it open. Her smile widened. "A lawyer is coming to Wilford to see me as soon as possible. He wants to meet me in person."

Leonard opined, "I would say that makes it virtually certain you are the grandchild they are looking for. It also means your grandparents are not exactly destitute if they can afford to send a lawyer most of the way across the country to see you."

"I never thought of it that way." Her smile was blinding. "This does put some constraints on when we might be able to go to Washington. I won't go until after this lawyer has been to Wilford."

Leonard nodded.

She squirmed in excitement. "In the meantime, I have some telegrams to send." At his blank look, she explained, "We're getting married as soon as we get home. I want Doc Madison to give me away, so I want to be sure he's in town."

***

Doc was waiting when Sue stepped down from the train, his face wrapped in a smile that spoke volumes. He wrapped her in a bear hug and teased her. "You didn't say *no* when he asked?"

She laughed. "No, I didn't." She held him at arm's length for a moment as she towered over him, unshed tears glistening in her eyes. "Thanks for everything."

His own eyes glistening, Doc held hers for a moment. He abruptly turned to Ted. "Congratulations to you both! Emma has given me strict orders to take Sue to her house. She said something to the effect that she was going to get you ready to get married in style."

Sue opened her mouth to protest, but he cut her short. "No arguments. Emma informed me I would deliver you into her hands or suffer great bodily harm. I'm to take Ted home with me." Sue laughed and grabbed her small trunk while Ted followed suit.

Emma was watching and stepped outside when they appeared. She snapped imperiously, "Ted. You go with Doc. He'll get you ready. Sue. You come with me." Both submitted meekly and hastened to follow orders.

When they were inside, Emma said with a frown, "You've put the good parson in a quandary. He doesn't know if he could in good conscience marry you if you were wearing men's clothes. I assured him I'd do whatever it took to get you into a dress. Just in case, I have one on reserve at Horwick's right now."

Sue hugged her delightedly. "Thanks for caring, but I can put your mind at ease. I bought two dresses in Denver and I know which one I want to wear."

Emma's frown vanished. "I'm glad for you. Now, there's a tub of hot water waiting in your old room. You give me the dress and I'll press it while you're bathing." She waited while Sue unpacked her royal purple dress, then exclaimed in admiration.

Later, after Sue had bathed and was wrapped in a robe, Emma took a brush, comb, and scissors to her still-damp hair, shaping it and trimming the sun-bleached ragged ends from her tresses. When Sue's hair was dry, Emma helped her dress, then stood back to admire her handiwork. Sue had been transformed into a beautiful and elegant bride-to-be imagined by the society of her time. Sue herself was astonished at the image she saw in the mirror.

The royal purple material was trimmed in black around the hem, at the cuffs of the sleeves, on the seams at the shoulders and arms, and around the collar. Her new black Stetson rested atop her newly trimmed tresses, her Marshal's star gleaming on the slope of her left breast.

Emma admired the transformation while Sue turned slowly for her inspection. She laughed. "Something old, something new." Sue grinned in response as she lifted the hem of the skirt to reveal her well-worn rider's boots hidden by the flowing dress.

"Sue, you are a lovely young woman, no matter what you wear. Ted is a lucky man." Her eyes misted affectionately for her newly 'adopted' daughter's happiness. "And now it's time for us to leave. They'll be waiting for us."

Squire and Doc were waiting on the porch, and both men's eyes widened at the transformation Emma had wrought. Doc offered her his arm as he looked up at Sue towering over him. His voice was husky as he said, "You have made me very proud to stand in for your father. I know your parents are as proud of you as I am.”

She squeezed his hand fiercely for a second before they headed down the street with Emma and Squire following. They walked in silence until they turned the corner leading to the schoolhouse. Sue halted in shock and confusion; seemingly every person in Wilford lined the street, waiting expectantly.

Doc squeezed her arm gently. “You can face them. They’re proud of you and happy for you.” He grinned fiercely. “Don’t disappoint me.”

She was still stunned. “It just surprised me.” She took a deep breath and resumed walking toward the schoolhouse as the crowd fell in behind.

Ted was waiting on the steps with the parson, a smile enveloping his face. When they had arrived at Doc’s house, he had been ‘counseled’ regarding his role in the impending wedding. Consequently, he had changed into the new clothes he had bought in Denver, the black and white a perfect counterpoint to Sue’s black and royal purple.

Sue had planned to be married inside the schoolhouse/church but the crowd following behind could not possibly fit. When Ted and the parson saw the size of the gathering crowd, they decided to hold the wedding on the porch, where it would be visible to all.

Sue would always remember the simple ceremony, most of all when the pastor asked,

"Who gives this woman in marriage?" Doc's voice carried proudly to the farthest edge of the crowd, "On behalf of her parents, I do!" She hugged him fiercely and turned to Ted and the minister.

When the ceremony was over, they formed an impromptu receiving line with Doc, Squire, and Emma at their sides. The movement of the line was interrupted by a stentorian bellow from Harold Easton. He held up the line long enough to take two pictures of the new bride and groom, then ambled off like a friendly buffalo.

When the last of the well-wishers had passed through the line, the newlyweds returned to Doc's and the Browns, where they changed into their riding clothes. When they left the house, their saddled and bridled horses were waiting. After Doc helped tie their trunks behind their saddles, Sue kissed him on the cheek and Ted shook hands. They mounted, gave a last wave, and trotted out of town toward their new home.

***

Mutt was waiting when they arrived at the ranch, racing in circles around them as they dismounted. Ted took a trunk in each hand and carried them inside, then caught up with Sue as she led the horses to the corral. After the tack had been put away, they walked hand-in-hand toward the ranch house.

When they reached the porch, he stopped, holding her hand in his. He gently turned her to face him, a smile lighting his face. "Missus Storm,

I would like to carry my new bride across the threshold.”

Her smile matched his. He swept her into his arms and carried her to the door, waiting while she reached down to open the latch. Sue snuggled her face against Ted's throat as he stepped through the doorway. When he stopped to let his eyes adjust to the dimmer light, she raised her lips to his. They stayed that way for delicious moments until she said, “Down the hall. The first door on the left.”

***

Much later, Sue was nestled in Ted's arms, her bare skin pressed against his, utterly spent and incredibly happy. “Husband,” she whispered. “I love the sound of that word. I'm going to share the rest of my life with you, and I want everyone to know it.” She rolled onto her side, facing him, her breasts crushed against his chest, her lips pressed hard against his.

“I do too” was badly muffled.

CHAPTER 16

Mutt spent the night on the porch, guarding the front door. He joined them the next morning when they rode out and headed for the Franklin ranch. They took their time as Sue gave Ted a thorough guided tour of the secluded canyons where she had penned her cattle during the winter months. She then led him to an overlook part way up the sheer stone wall above the vast bowl where she had turned her herds out to summer pasture.

His horse crowded hers as he listened closely while she pointed out important features of the land and a few cattle that were visible.

"Up there." She pointed to the craggy ledge much higher and miles away. "That's where I spied on the rustlers." She shivered at the memory of the deadly chill that had permeated her bones while she crawled back from the rim.

He took her hand in his as dark memories threatened to erupt. He said softly. "I'm here now."

Her hand almost crushed his momentarily as she fought the demons of the memory. "Yes, you are. And that makes it all worth it."

Her smile was wan. She released his hand and flicked the reins against her horse's neck, moving again toward the B-bar-F. He followed suit, moving up beside her as they trotted away. Mutt followed in the rear.

***

They arrived at the Franklin Ranch in time for the noon meal. When they rode out much later, Sue's ribs were sore from the crushing embrace her ecstatic friend gave her in greeting. Ted grinned in wry amusement at her half-serious complaint and laughed aloud when Mutt's expression showed complete agreement.

They spent three more days of steady riding while Sue gave Ted a detailed tour of the ranch and its many canyon corrals and hidden forest glades. She made a special effort to show him the many trails, some hidden and others not, which connected the outlying pastures to the main ranch. Ted looked impressed with the gentle slope of some them but shook his head in dismay at others that appeared to be near suicidal to follow.

They had finished supper the third evening when Sue found her father's spyglass in the cupboard where she had left it. "This is what let me follow Snake to Lost Hope Canyon. I'll take you up to the lookout sometime so you can see what a tremendous vantage point it is." She was startled by the intensity of his gaze as he stared at the spyglass and its dull brass finish.

"This is many years old," he said. "Can I look at it?"

She handed it over, feeling her senses tingling. He took it and moved directly beneath the kerosene lamp. Slowly extending and retracting it, he turned it upside down and back, rotating it as he did so. He reached up with one hand and turned the wick of the lantern higher until it was flaring brightly, then scratched the surface with a fingernail.

"W R M. They're not your father's initials." It was a flat statement. "Are they?"

"No." Her pulse and her breathing accelerated.

"I would bet money it belonged to your grandfather or great-grandfather from the age and the first initial, W. You'd better show it to the lawyer when he gets here."

She took a shallow breath.

"What else do you have that might be added proof of your heritage?"

Sue threw her arms around his neck and kissed him. "How do you see so many clues I don't?"

He drew her close. "You've grown up with this around you all your life, so it's familiar. This is the first time I've ever seen them, so I see everything from a fresh perspective."

"Fresh indeed." She squirmed in anticipation as she pressed her body against his.

***

They rode out the next morning. Sue knew the trip to the overlook would be far shorter than her last trip. They rode steadily with no need of concealment, taking shortcuts she didn't dare use on the earlier trip for fear of exposure or bogging down in snow.

They dismounted and ground-reined their horses some distance from the edge of the cliff. They both were secure in the knowledge any horse Sue had trained would be there when they returned. Mutt trotted alongside as they advanced to the edge of the cliff. Ted whistled in admiration at the sight when he caught his first view.

Far below, the vast bowl stretched for miles, ringed on three sides by mountains whose peaks were still draped in snow even though it was past midsummer. The floor of the bowl was a jumble of canyons, brush, rock, creeks and rivers mixed together in a fantastic hodgepodge.

Sue took the treasured spyglass from an inner pocket of her vest and handed it over. "Lost Hope Canyon is over there." She pointed.

He adjusted the focus and slowly swept the area she had indicated. The canyon mouth was wide, shallow, and at the limits of the spyglass. Ted braced his elbows and searched the area until he found his target.

After surveying the sweeping panorama, he said, "I'm glad you knew what you were looking for. I'd never have found it if you hadn't shown me where to look."

"At that time, this was my territory." She affectionately punched him on the shoulder. "Now, it's our territory."

He grinned.

She continued, "And I have more to show you."

In spite of her words, they lingered a bit longer before they rode off on another trail he hadn't seen.

***

Doc heard them ride up and was waiting on the porch with another man standing beside him. Sue and Ted dismounted together and walked toward the house where Doc embraced her before turning to his guest. Sue shifted her attention and her eyes widened. The stranger was wearing what she guessed to be the latest in fashion, a tailored suit that shouted money!

Doc introduced them. "Sue Mason Storm, this is Daniel Wilson of a Philadelphia law firm of the same name."

Daniel Wilson had read and reread the story in *The Police Gazette* his friend, the Chief of Police, had brought to his attention. He read the article several times but was always in skeptical disbelief of the young woman's reported exploits. He felt the only thing meriting attention was the name of her father, Max. He brought it to the attention of his clients, voicing his skepticism, but they insisted on following one last, desperate attempt to find their missing son. That decision had led to his presence in this tiny little town in the back of beyond.

He stared in disbelief while the young woman dismounted. He had dismissed the pictures of a woman wearing a gun as a hoax inflicted on the unflappable East by Westerners. Now, he began to suspect he might have to reconsider his previous conclusions as he viewed the evidence of a gun butt protruding from the holster on her hip.

Her eyes were on a level with his before she reached the steps.

He muttered incredulously to himself, "God, she's tall…" He hardly heard the doctor's voice while they were being introduced, staring at her in slack-jawed astonishment as she stood a full head taller than him. He offered his hand in reflex action but was unable to instantly adjust his thoughts to a new reality.

Sue grinned mischievously. Her heart pounded while she waited for the lawyer to collect himself. She knew he had missed her name and introduced herself. "I'm Sue Mason Storm. This is my husband, Ted. We've been married a whole five days."

He flushed and laughed ruefully, "I must apologize. I have to admit I thought someone had tried to put a tall tale about a woman marshal over on me."

Sue laughed in return, "I've had trouble believing it myself."

He sobered. "I'm sure you're as anxious as I am to determine if you are my clients' grandchild. Shall we go inside?"

"I can leave you alone if you want." Doc offered.

She shook her head and took his arm. "You've been family to me far longer than Ted has been. I want you here."

They gathered around the kitchen table with Ted and Doc on either side, holding her hands. Mister Wilson scrutinized her face, looking for any discernible family resemblance. It was possible. She did look a little like both of them.

He asked one question after another, making notes on a legal pad, "You have no idea where your parents lived before moving to Colorado?"

Sue decided not to muddy the water at the moment by introducing Peoria into the mix. "No. I asked many times, but Pa would never tell me."

He leaned back and eyed her levelly. "Is there anything you have that might confirm your birthright?"

It took every bit of self-discipline she had to keep her voice steady. "I think so. My father left this to me." She reached into the inner pocket of her vest and handed him the spyglass.

Mister Wilson stared down at it in stunned recognition. His face was a frozen mask as he turned it over and over in what appeared as a mix of sorrow and joy. He drew a shuddering breath and looked up at her. "There is absolutely no doubt you are the granddaughter of Henry and Nancy Mason. I have seen this with my own eyes in the hands of your grandfather. It was given to him by his father, Walter Robert Mason."

Doc turned to embrace her and was nearly blinded by her smile. Tears glistened in her eyes as Ted kissed her. She blinked repeatedly before she turned back to Mister Wilson.

"Tell me everything you know about my family." Her voice was a choked whisper, "Especially why my father had nothing to do with his family."

"I've known your family for many years, but I really don't know why. I have my suspicions, but that's all they are. You'll have to ask your grandparents." He frowned at her expression. "I really wish I could answer your question, but I'm afraid I don't have all the facts."

They traded a multitude of questions and answers until they ran down much later. The room was silent for a few moments except for the distant sounds of the town.

Ted asked, "Did I miss something? I still don't understand how they wound up here in Wilford. How did an Eastern factory owner's son with no training become a successful rancher?"

Sue answered him. "I don't know."

Doc stared at Sue. "He never told you that story either?"

She shook her head.

Doc took a deep breath as everyone's attention riveted on him. "Your parents left Denver to go west for whatever reason. I don't know. When your mother went into early labor, they got off the train here. The agent sent them to me and I delivered you a few hours later. The next day, George Hawkins brought his wife to me, but it was too late. She died in childbirth but her baby girl survived. George was devastated by her death but wanted to keep his daughter rather than give up everything except the memory of his wife."

Sue trembled as she listened.

"He offered to give your father his ranch if your mother would wet-nurse his baby for a year." Tears welled in his eyes. "George and his daughter, Molly, stayed for the year, and he became close friends with your parents. George gave them the ranch, but your father paid him a substantial amount of money anyway. George is the one who taught him about ranching."

They sat in silence for several minutes until the clock on the mantle began to chime.

Mister Wilson started, then smiled. "Why don't we all go down to the boarding house and get something to eat? I'll buy."

Every diner in the place was bursting with curiosity about the stranger who walked in with them. Sue allowed the anticipation to build for a few moments. When Missus Manlick took their order, she explained how she had finally found her father's family.

Missus Manlick surprised Sue with a crushing embrace, congratulations, and a flow of tears. "I'm so happy for you! I know how you've been searching for so long."

Others heard as well. Most of Wilford heard the word in a short time as the news spread. When they were done eating, Sue and Mister Wilson returned to

Doc's while the other two men went their separate ways.

They'd been talking for a short time when Ted came in the front door with an opened letter in his hand.

His excitement showed in his eyes as he explained abruptly, "Leonard wants us to hand-carry some documents to Washington. He didn't say what they are, but they must be important." He handed her the letter and she read it quickly, noting he had appended his latest information about her testifying in Washington… still uncertain.

They shared a long moment's visual embrace before she turned to Mister Wilson. "We'll go to Washington first, then on to Philadelphia." She had to swallow against the lump in her throat. "I'll finally get to meet my family in person."

CHAPTER 17

They left for home that afternoon, having already made many preparations for their trip. Billy Rankin had promised to care for their ranch while they were gone as well as take their mounts home until they were needed. Ted disappeared on a mysterious mission while she was in the bank getting several gold double eagles for traveling money. He just laughed when she quizzed him.

"I'll tell you later. It's going to be a surprise."

She glared at him suspiciously, but he only returned a bland smile.

***

Two days later, they were again in Denver at the Federal Courthouse. They were ushered into Leonard Simpson's office and the door silently closed behind them. He rose from his chair and offered his hand with a smile creasing his face. He had never dealt with the unique aspect of married marshals before but welcomed them warmly. Obviously tense, he abruptly turned to a small safe behind his desk and drew out a slender money belt.

"The United States have suffered under a level of corruption unprecedented in our history for the past decade at all levels of government. President Cleveland did manage to begin cleaning up at the federal level during his first term, but corruption is still epidemic." His face was grim, and his voice was low. "This contains documents and other proof of corruption within the marshal's office in another state. No one is to know what you are carrying under any circumstances."

They nodded.

"You will guard this information with your lives. When you get to D.C., you will go to Senator Hill's office. Congress will be on summer recess before you get there, but he volunteered to stay in Washington D.C. for an extra week or two before he comes home. He'll put you in contact with Assistant Attorney General, Timothy Hopkins. You're to give these documents to Mister Hopkins and no one else, not even the Senator." His face was stern as he held their attention. "Do I make myself clear?"

"Perfectly," Ted acknowledged as Sue echoed her assent.

He held their eyes for several seconds more before passing the money belt to Ted, who slipped it inside his shirt and buckled it next to his skin.

Leonard's grim demeanor softened. He unfolded a newspaper on his desk and turned it for them to see. "Sue, your search for your family has given us a perfectly valid cover for the two of you to go to Washington D.C. In this case, it's a good use of disinformation."

She stared at the headline partway down the page.

She raised her eyes to meet Leonard's as Ted chuckled, "Emil's timing was perfect for putting your interview into print."

Leonard opened his desk drawer and handed an envelope to Ted. "Your tickets and some expense money are in there. I'll see you when you get back." His expression softened even more as he escorted them to the door. "Good luck."

***

They arrived at the train station by hack, carrying a single satchel apiece. When they were inside, they first checked the board for their train and then walked the long distance to their assigned platform.

An agent checked their tickets. "The train will be leaving on time in about twenty minutes." He added, "Your trunk was delivered a short time ago and has been loaded with the rest of the luggage. Welcome aboard."

True to the agent's prediction, the train departed on time and began rolling eastward. The miles and hours passed steadily as they headed across Colorado into Kansas, stopping at an occasional depot to exchange passengers or to load fuel and water for the locomotive.

Night fell long before their train rolled into Kansas City, where they booked a room in a boarding house not far from the station. They ate in the dining room.

When they left, Sue complained, "That sure didn't compare with Missus Manlick's cooking. I think I ate half a brick."

Ted's tone was as sour. "I think I had the other half."

***

Sue startled Ted next morning when she decided to wear her blue traveling dress instead of her usual shirt and jeans. She laughed at his expression, teasing him, "I just decided to be different for once. Don't you know it's a woman's prerogative to change her mind?" She sobered. "It does feel strange to be wearing a dress. I've only worn a dress a few times during the last two years, and one of those was for our wedding."

He smiled, listening and admiring.

She grinned as she picked up the handbag that held her badge, pistol, and the gun belt with its treasure in a hidden pocket. "I never thought I'd carry a handbag, but wearing my gun belt with this dress would ruin my chances to be inconspicuous."

He laughed with her as he picked up his own satchel and opened the door.

They walked the short distance to the station from the rooming house, watching heads turn.

Ted said, "I love you whatever you wear. You're a beautiful woman to me, and a lot of others think the same. Have you noticed people staring?"

He was right. Even dressed conventionally, Sue was much taller than most men and made no effort to hide it. Her boots, which were hidden by the dress, increased her height even more. Her erect posture and no-nonsense stride emphasized her vitality. Her deep tan informed watchers this young woman had spent many hours in the sun. Early risers, both women and especially men, took notice of her striking figure.

They ignored the stares while directing their own attention to the massive building they were approaching. Even from a distance, the station was an imposing structure with many spires and chimneys reaching for the sky. They had seen none of the exterior and only a little of the interior when they arrived the night before. Another pedestrian headed for the station overheard their comments and elaborated.

"It's a grand building inside. There's enough granite, marble, and carved wood to make you think you're in a castle."

Their train was on schedule. They boarded the last car and found each of the three passenger cars were about half filled. Curious, Sue scanned the car where rows of double seats lined each side. These were newer and much more ornately finished than the seats in their earlier train.

They waited for several minutes as bags and freight were loaded aboard the Wells Fargo car immediately behind the locomotive.

After the train started to move, Ted leaned over and whispered in her ear. "I don't know what they have in the baggage car, but I thought I saw someone carrying a rifle peek out the door just as we boarded. Must be something valuable on board."

"I didn't notice it, but I wasn't really looking for anything. Maybe we'll find out later."

They settled to another day of travel by visiting with their fellow passengers as the rails angled southeasterly, soon leaving the broad Missouri River valley behind.

A merchant traveling with them explained, "We'll stay south of the river all the way to Saint Louis. The river winds north and east for quite a spell before it turns almost due south. We'll rejoin the river about half way between two big bends and follow it all the way into Saint Louis."

The train plunged into a dense forest composed mostly of oak and hickory, dotted here and there by natural meadows and small clearings. Their train, an express, would occasionally stop at a small town but passed most hamlets without stopping. Sue watched in fascination when the train slowed to pass sidings filled with cars of locally mined coal or quarried rock.

Many miles fell behind as did innumerable farmsteads hacked out of the heavy timber. Most were small: only a log cabin, a barn and one or two outbuildings. The train was accelerating away from one of their rare stops when another young couple settled into the recently vacated seat behind them. Sue turned and began to converse with the new arrivals.

Naomi Henderson proudly announced she and Walter were also newlyweds, having been married just Sunday. After visiting relatives, they were now headed back home to St. Louis.

"Our house isn't very big. Just three rooms, but I love it," she exclaimed.

The train lurched as it turned sharply and began to climb a steep incline. The locomotive protested loudly at the sudden demand for increased power.

"Walter's a clerk at a bank in downtown St. Louis and has a great future." She asked, "What does Ted do?"

Uncertain whether to give a straight answer or dodge the question, Sue glanced at Ted. He gave a slight nod in return.

"He's a United States Marshal in Colorado." She hesitated for a moment in silent debate. "I am too."

Both of their seatmates stared at her in disbelief, neither ever having heard of such a thing.

Sue recognized the disbelief. "I really am. Let me show…" Her explanation was interrupted when the air brakes were suddenly applied.

She and most of the other passengers were thrown from their seats amid the shriek of tortured steel-on-steel. The train shuddered to a stop before Sue could get to her feet. She looked out the window to see a masked rider race past. Another rider pulled up at their car and bellowed from outside the door.

"Everybody stay sittin' down, or somebody gets hurt!"

Sue picked up her handbag from the floor where it had fallen and whispered to Ted, "If he comes on board, he'll never expect anything from a woman like he would from a man. I'll see if I can get the drop on him."

There was no time for Ted to protest. The second rider swung aboard, and seconds later, he appeared in the doorway.

"Ever'body sit tight!" he roared. "When I come through, put your money and your valuables in my hat. Don't nobody try to hide anything 'cause I'll be mighty unfriendly if you do."

They were sitting in the third row from the front. Sue drew a quick breath and slowly stood up, moving into the aisle with her heavy bag in her hand. She could see the bandit smile under his mask as his revolver pointed carelessly at the ceiling. She heard the smirk in his voice.

"That's right, girlie. Now, just let me see what's in your bag."

Her free hand was hidden in the bag as the bandit stepped toward her. He froze in shock when the Colt 45 suddenly appeared with the barrel aimed directly between his eyes.

Her voice was cold. "Hold it right there. Keep your hands up and don't move."

Ted slid out of their seat and took the gun from the outlaw's unresisting hand. Sue knew there was no time to waste and swung her revolver hard against the masked head. He collapsed limply.

Ted turned with the gun and asked the well-dressed man in the next seat. "Do you know how to use this?"

The man nodded.

"Good. Use it if you have to, but keep him quiet."

Gun shots broke out from the front of the train near the baggage car. "We're running out of time." Ted turned and called softly to the car. "Everybody get down on the floor. There's likely to be more shooting." He smiled faintly as everyone quickly complied as best they were able to.

Sue took her gun belt and the marshal's star from the handbag while Ted was issuing orders. She buckled the belt around her waist and pinned on the star while Ted pinned his own to the front of his vest.

They started forward as she turned to whisper. "I think I can draw the outlaw in the next car back here. We can get him out of the way and get closer to the baggage car without being seen."

He stared into her eyes for a second. "Be careful!" He followed when she stepped into the gap between the cars.

Ted was filled with both pride and fear: pride in her courage and initiative and fear for her safety. He had been in shootouts before with other marshals by his side, but the fact Sue was his wife as well as his partner changed everything. He knew each had to depend on the other and any effort to protect her was far more dangerous to both of them than to trust her judgment. He swallowed his fear and followed her through the doorway.

Sue stopped at the door into the next car and carefully cracked it open. As she expected, there was another masked man in the aisle with his hat held out. Under the threat of his gun, passengers reluctantly dropped their money and other valuables into it. Hiding behind the door and showing only a portion of her face, she called out in a shaky, teary voice.

"Mister Outlaw. Your friend in the next car threatened to kill me unless I came and told you he needed you."

"Why's he need me?"

Sue added more tremble to her voice until it nearly broke. "I didn't ask, and he didn't tell me."

The outlaw snickered as he accepted her explanation. He called out to the other passengers as he strode toward her. "Don't nobody move 'cause

I'll be back, and I don't like people that don't do as they're told."

Sue stepped back from the door to give it room to swing open. As she raised her revolver to eye level, Ted did the same. The masked man opened the door and froze in shock as a muzzle appeared in front of each eye only inches away.

"Not a sound," Ted murmured as Sue took the revolver from him. "Now, back up real slow."

Sue held the door fully opened while the outlaw complied. When they were safely inside the car, Ted swung his revolver as Sue had done. The second outlaw lay unconscious on the floor. He handed the revolver to a man on the aisle and repeated his instructions. Moments later, the passengers were also making the most of the meager protection offered by being on the floor.

The shooting outside had stopped. They bent low to stay out of sight below the windows as they scurried down the aisle. Safely at the front of the car, Ted peeked out a window to see three masked riders, who were pointing guns at the door of the Wells Fargo car.

One of the trio yelled, "You have one minute to open up, or we'll blow you apart!"

Ted took one side of the stairs while Sue took the other one step above him, giving herself room to safely fire over his head. When they were both ready, he leaned out slightly.

Ted bellowed, "You're under arrest! Drop the guns!"

The stunned outlaws twisted in their saddles to face the new threat and started shooting, sending their bullets flying wildly. The element of surprise gave the marshals the advantage, so their return fire was far more accurate. One outlaw doubled over at the waist and fell from his mount and another twisted to the side as the embattled occupants of the baggage car rejoined the fight. Faced with the unexpected odds from behind them, the remaining robbers fled. Seconds later, they were joined in flight by the masked man from the front car.

An eerie silence descended over the train.

Ted called out, "You there, in the baggage car. I'm U. S. Marshal Storm, and I'm going to step out. Don't get nervous and start shooting."

"We'll hold our fire," a muffled voice called back.

Ted and Sue both stepped down from the train and walked together toward the locked and barred door. A few minutes of suspense passed before the door slowly slid aside and two guards holding ready rifles appeared in the opening. Amazement flashed across their faces when they realized one of the figures facing them was a woman in a dress, wearing a marshal's star and a gun belt. The equally amazed fireman and engineer stared from the cab of the locomotive.

"I'm Marshal Sue Storm, and this is my husband, Marshal Ted Storm." She added with a chuckle, "This isn't exactly the best way for people to get acquainted."

Behind them, with the threat of the masked riders gone, passengers erupted from the cars to find out what was going to happen next. Ted explained to the guards that they had two captives on board and suggested they be transferred to the baggage car.

The conductor and fireman enlisted a force of volunteers from among the male passengers. Everyone pitched in, and within a few minutes, the roadblock of trees and stone was removed from the track. They were free to move once again. The volunteers re-boarded... the engineer applied steam to the drivers before coaxing a raucous song of triumph from his whistle.

When they got back to their seats, they were greeted by an incredulous Walter and Naomi, who gasped. "I didn't believe you before, but I do now! You really are a marshal!"

CHAPTER 18

Their next stop was almost a half hour ahead, where the local law was informed of the attempted train robbery and began forming a posse. One of the Wells Fargo agents hurried to the station and a few minutes later the telegraph lines winged a message to St. Louis.

TWO CAPTURED TRAIN ROBBERS

TWO MARSHALS STORM

ARRIVING TRAIN NO 732 STOP

MEET UNION STA STOP

***

When the train rolled into St. Louis, it was only twenty minutes late despite the attempted train robbery. The first indication of the city they saw was the increasing number of buildings and roads along the tracks.

Walter and Naomi were eager to point out prominent features of the city and its environs as the train rolled onward. "We're a big city now," he proclaimed proudly. "The last census counted almost ninety thousand people and our population's been growing by leaps and bounds ever since."

Their train slowed as it wound its way through the city proper. Naomi pointed to a tall spire in the distance, partially obscured by the rooftops along the track. "We'll be at the station in a few minutes," she explained. "That's the clock tower at Union Station. When we make the next turn, you'll be able to see the roof of the whole station. It's the biggest building in Saint Louis."

The train crept forward slowly until it moved into the station and was engulfed in shadow. Sue looked around, curious as always. Platforms extended in both directions, separated by pairs of rails. Many people were crowding the nearer platforms, staring at their train.

"I wonder why there are so many people..." Walter was mystified. "I've never seen such a crowd before."

Naomi laughed, "Don't you think word of our adventure was telegraphed ahead? I bet they've heard about the train robbery."

The train coasted to a gentle stop, followed by a blast of steam as the safety valve on the locomotive relieved excess pressure.

The conductor had ridden the last few miles in their car and his call echoed through the car. "Saint Louis. End of the line. All passengers must disembark."

Walter and Naomi wished them well as they picked up their bags and joined the line of passengers headed for the exit.

Ted led the way and was abcut to step onto the platform when a uniformed police lieutenant asked, "Marshal Storm?"

"Yes."

"Would you please come with me? The sheriff would like to talk to you about the train robbery."

Ted stepped aside when he reached the platform to allow Sue to join him. The lieutenant stared, his mouth agape, when he spied Sue, a marshal who was a woman in a dress and wearing a gun. He'd been informed by his superiors of the entire telegram, but only now had the enigmatic *Marshals Storm* dawned on him.

He managed to mumble, "Marshal and Missus Storm?"

Sue corrected him. "Marshal Ted Storm and Marshal Sue Storm."

The lieutenant gaped for a few seconds before regaining his composure. "Would the two of you please come with me? The rest of the people involved in the investigation would like to meet you at the baggage car. The Sheriff would especially like statements from you before he files charges against the three in custody. Assuming the wounded robber survives to stand trial."

Ted agreed, "We'd be glad to help. Lead the way."

The lieutenant turned and headed up the platform that'd been kept clear except for the passengers leaving the station. The watching crowd began to buzz with excitement when they realized that the young woman in the trio was wearing a holstered gun.

One astonished voice carried above the rest. "She's wearing a marshal's star!"

The lieutenant had recovered his composure before they reached the baggage car and announced calmly, "Sheriff Olsen, I'd like you to meet Marshal Ted Storm and Marshal Sue Storm."

The two Wells Fargo guards had already informed the small crowd about the female marshal: the sheriff, several deputies, more city police, and two other men dressed in civilian clothing. They were better prepared than the lieutenant but were still unable to completely conceal their amazement at their first glimpse of Sue.

She smiled at the crowd. "It's nice to meet you, Sheriff. Do you approve of the three captives we delivered for you?"

He acknowledged dryly, "I certainly do." He eyed her momentarily before he indicated the two civilians. "Marshals Storm. I'd like you to meet Miles Howard, the local Wells Fargo Agency Superintendent. The other gentleman is Wilson Hickory, Section Supervisor for the Saint Louis division of the Missouri Pacific Railroad."

The two men acknowledged their introductions with a nod. The sheriff continued, "We're taking the two down to the jail and the wounded one to the hospital. Would you mind coming with us? We'd like to get statements from the both of you before we file charges."

"We'd be glad to."

Wilson Hickory interrupted, "Would you like us to take care of your baggage and deliver it to the Holly Oak Hotel for you? We'd be glad to take care of all your needs for you while you're in town."

"Sure." Sue added, "We'd appreciate that since we're not familiar with the city."

The buzz of voices from the watching crowd intensified as the group left the baggage car. Three groups of deputies escorted the surly captives.

Ted whispered in her ear, "See the group over behind the constables? They look like a bunch of reporters to me."

It was a bunch of reporters, and they were seething at having been kept at bay. Unable to reach the marshals and bombard them with questions, they scurried after the other passengers instead. When they learned Walter and Naomi had ridden with the mysterious pair, they descended on the young couple. Basking in the limelight, they answered the questions fired at them as best they could.

One reporter asked, "Did you know they were both marshals when you first met them?"

Naomi answered, "No. Sue told us Ted was a marshal in Colorado before telling us she was one too. I didn't believe her at first, but that was just when the robbers attacked." She shook her head, remembering what happened. "I didn't believe it myself until it was all over and she came back wearing her star."

An astounded voice suddenly interrupted, "A woman marshal from Colorado! There can't be two such! She has to be the one that killed that outlaw, Snake Carson, and his gang!"

Only then did Naomi realize it had to be Sue she had read about in the newspaper a few weeks before. She protested, "She's too nice a person! She couldn't have killed anyone."

Her protest was lost in the rising hubbub.

When they were alone later, she repeated that denial to Walter and he replied. "I read the story too, but it had to have been her. If you remember, she fought in self-defense after being shot and wounded.

"Don't judge her too harshly. Nobody knows how they would react if they had to defend themselves or someone that they love. Besides, you know the newspapers always exaggerate."

***

Several hours later, Miles Howard and Wilson Hickory escorted Sue and Ted the short distance to the Holly Oak Hotel. When they entered the lobby, she stopped in amazement and stared in awe at the vaulted ceiling. The walls and floor were finished in polished woods, brasses, and marble. The whole place shone with reflected light from gas lights and massive chandeliers, the focal point being the elaborately carved reception area.

"This is the finest hotel in Saint Louis," Miles declared with pride. "It's an honor for us to show you our appreciation for what you did today so we're taking care of your expenses. This certificate is good for passage anywhere on any railroad associated with Wells Fargo."

Sue and Ted exchanged a look of surprise.

Having observed their ethical standards firsthand in dealing with the Sheriff, he added, "This is just a small, inadequate token of our gratitude."

Ted tried to refuse, waving his hand. "We were just doing our duty."

"You did your duty and did it well. Take this anyway because the two of you probably saved lives and many people a lot of grief and money."

A uniformed bellman approached them, waiting respectfully until they turned their attention to him. "Mister Hickory, the suite you requested is ready. Would you like me to escort your guests to their room?"

Mister Hickory nodded and turned back to them. "If I don't see you before you leave in the morning, thank you again."

Both men shook hands and quickly departed while the bellman led Sue and Ted to the elevator.

Sue was mesmerized by the splendor of the lobby and the magnificence of their suite. Every solid surface in four rooms and a bath was highly polished and gleamed brightly. Velvet drapes graced the windows, brilliantly flowered paper covered the walls. The bed was made with fluffy down pillows, satin sheets and a silken spread. The bath was finished in white porcelain and shiny brass. Brightly lit gas lights reflected from every solid surface.

The bellman waited until his dazed guests turned their attention to him. "Your luggage is in the closet over there." He indicated a satin cord and a small box with a cover beside the doorway. "If you need something, just pull the bell cord and talk into the speaking tube when someone responds."

Sue and Ted turned to look.

He flipped open the cover of the box and pointed to a funnel-shaped object before adding. "Don't try to blow out the lights. Turn them off with the valves at each light. The unburned gas is poisonous and could kill you."

Overwhelmed, both stared at him. He closed the door, leaving them alone to explore. They were simply amazed and amused at the excesses of their accommodations. Although the day had been hot and sultry, their rooms weren't uncomfortable because of the opened, screened windows and a gentle cross breeze. The windows opened high above the ground, overlooking every building around and high enough to mute the sounds of the traffic on the streets below.

"It's going to be cooler tonight," Ted said flatly.

Sue looked at him, wondering how he knew.

He grinned. "See that line of clouds at the horizon? They're thunderheads. Once storms like that pass through, you have cooler weather, even if only for a few hours." He chuckled in anticipation. "You haven't see weather until you've been through a real thunderstorm."

Darkness arrived early, hastened by the towering wall of black clouds to the west. They were still eating the multicourse meals that had been delivered to their room before the first distant rumble of thunder entered the opened windows.

"It's going to be a powerful storm," Ted predicted. "The slower they move, the stronger they are."

As the thunder continued to increase in frequency and volume, they had just finished their meal when a sudden blast of wind gusted through the windows. They hurried to close them as raindrops began to splatter against the screens.

Ted turned all of the gas lights very low before rejoining Sue in the sitting room. They stood by a window, watching bolts of lightning flash between the clouds and the ground. The boom of thunder was almost continuous as the sky lit up from horizon to horizon, banishing the night with unending flashes of lightning.

Sue watched the storm pass slowly and was amazed by the unimagined fury. They stood together until the pounding rain slackened and moved on with the storm. The thunder was muted before she spoke. "I thought I'd seen severe storms in the mountains.

Now, I know. I've never seen anything to compare with this!" She turned from the window with her eyes sparkling in the faint glow of the lowered lamps.

He grinned.

"It was magnificent! I'm glad I got to see it," she laughed. "Now, tell me why it's so much more violent than any in the mountains."

Ted laughed in return, struck once again by her desire to know about anything and everything. "I don't know. I don't think anyone knows for sure." He sobered. "My best guess, and it's only a guess, is it has something to do with the higher temperatures in this part of the country."

CHAPTER 19

They departed from St. Louis shortly after sunrise the next morning, still marveling at the grandeur of their hotel room. "I'll never see such a fairytale castle like this again," Sue exclaimed. "Who'd believe such extravagance? The four rooms are bigger than our ranch house. I never want to get accustomed to something that fancy."

Ted was less vehement but agreed completely, "It was quite a spread for two youngsters from the mountains. This trip has been quite an adventure for us."

Their car was a Pullman sleeper. As they watched out the windows, it began to rumble slowly onto the Eads Bridge spanning the Mighty Mississippi. Sue paled and her stomach flipped as they entered the lacy network of steel supporting their passage high above the river.

The man sitting across the aisle noticed her pale face and teased with a chuckle, "If it makes you feel better, it hasn't fallen yet."

"I sure hope it doesn't now," she laughed shakily. "I'll feel a lot better when there's solid ground under the track."

Their route wandered easterly and southeasterly until they met the Ohio River on its endless flow toward the Mississippi and the Gulf. Their train paused for a short time to let the passengers board and depart the cars. Meanwhile, the train exchanged the locomotive for one already fueled and watered. With a wail from the whistle, they rolled eastward once more.

***

The echo of the conductor's call died away in the rattling car. "Next stop. Washington Union Station."

Other passengers began to gather their belongings as Sue whispered in Ted's ear, "I've never been so glad to hear something in my life."

His grin was lopsided. "Me too. It's been a long ride."

The train slowed to a near stop as buildings began to multiply along the tracks. During one slowdown, Ted spotted a pointed stone spire showing above the trees in the distance.

He commented to no one in particular, "I wonder what that is…"

A man sitting behind them volunteered. "That's the Washington Monument. The tip is over five hundred fifty feet high. You can climb to the top and look out over the entire city. It's on the Mall between the White House and the Capitol. It's impossible to miss."

Their train arrived exactly on time as the airbrakes locked the wheels. The conductor's final call echoed through the car as the noise died away. "End of the line. All passengers will disembark."

They joined the departing line of passengers with their luggage in hand and followed the stragglers into the station.

A young man who was scanning the arrivals moved to greet them. "Marshal Storm? Marshal Mason?"

Ted replied, "Marshals Sue and Ted Storm."

The young man beamed. "It's good to finally meet you. Mister Simpson has written a great deal about you." He grinned slyly as he turned to Sue. "He never wrote a word about your name change though. I gather that's a recent development?"

She laughed, "Very."

"Senator Hill sent me to meet you. I'm Alex Wilson, his secretary. I'm to take you to your hotel and get you settled in before I take you to his office."

They carried their luggage across the street to the Harmon House, a modest building only a few blocks from the Capitol. The clerk's back was turned to them as they entered and stepped to the counter.

Alex asked loudly, "Do you have reservations for Storm and Mason? We'll only need one of them."

"Yeah. I'll have your key in a minute." The clerk completed his task and turned to his guests. When his glance found Sue, he gasped in astonishment and collided with the corner of the counter.

They stifled grins while he recovered and offered the registration book to Ted. After signing the registration and receiving their key, they looked to Alex for guidance.

"Why don't you get settled in your room? I can come back in an hour or even later if you want more time."

"No. That'll be fine."

***

Alex was waiting when Sue and Ted returned to the lobby. "The first thing I'm supposed to do is take you to the Capitol to meet the senator. Nothing was said about taking the most direct route, though. I'll show you some of the sights along the way." He grinned.

He led them on what turned out to be a roundabout route, pointing out important landmarks as they passed. When they walked past the Library of Congress and the Supreme Court buildings, both were taken aback by the history that radiated from both buildings.

Alex led them along the east and south faces of the Capitol, then to the west steps. At the top of the steps, he turned to look to the west and explained, "The open space you're looking at is the Mall. During the Great War, they grazed herds of cattle there for the feeding of the city dwellers. Midway on your right, north of the Washington Monument, is the White House. The public can go through on tours, but if you're ever invited, your social status in this town is assured."

Sue chuckled, "Not much danger of that happening to us."

They followed Alex into the imposing building and down one corridor after another until he turned into a large office. "Please wait here. I'll see if the senator is free."

They gazed around the room filled with heavy carved furniture, massive doors, and wood trim.

"Senator Hill will see you now. Please follow me."

They entered a smaller office to meet a man of medium height and spare build with graying hair beginning to thin on top. "Marshal Storm. Marshal Mason. Welcome to D.C. I'm glad to meet you both."

Alex interrupted. "Senator, I just learned that they're both Marshal Storm. I just realized they haven't been informed they are to have supper with Mister and Missus Hopkins tonight. We need to allow them time to get ready."

"Yes, of course. And congratulations on your marriage." The senator explained, "We've arranged for you to dine with the Assistant Attorney General and his wife tonight. We've taken care of the details... they'll pick you up at your hotel at seven."

His eyes met Ted's, whose bland look and an unobtrusive hand movement indicated the hidden belt with its documents. The senator nodded in satisfaction.

***

Assistant Attorney General and Missus Hopkins greeted them in the lobby of their hotel shortly before seven. She had been forewarned by her husband but was still startled by her first glimpse of the marshals from Colorado. They were very young, tall, slim, and dressed in identical black Stetsons, vests, and trousers. White ruffled shirts, new rider's boots, well-worn gun belts, and bright marshal's stars completed their matching outfits.

She knew the young man's appearance was striking enough to turn heads in staid Washington D.C. and that every eye would be drawn to the young woman whose man's clothing emphasized the curve of hips and breasts. She had dealt with people of many nationalities at diplomatic functions, but none of those occasions had compared to this meeting. She stifled her unease as her husband introduced her and was immediately put at ease by the much younger woman.

"I'm Sue Storm, the strange woman from the West I'm sure your husband warned you about," she laughed softly at her own description.

Timothy Hopkins flushed at the gentle barb, laughing as well before introducing Marsha in turn. "I have a carriage waiting outside for us. Shall we be on our way?"

Their reserved table at the Washington Ambassador's Club was waiting when the four of them arrived. They were escorted to the dining room foyer where hats and shawl were collected and taken to the cloak room.

They were shown to their table and quickly seated. Sue stared at her surroundings with wonder, once again feeling like a hick as she marveled at the ceiling above their heads. Huge chandeliers hung at regular intervals, brightening the walls covered with paper in ornate floral patterns. They were accentuated by intricately carved wainscoting and numerous pieces of artwork. Her gaze kept returning to the chandeliers, unable to determine the source of their brilliance.

Missus Hopkins smiled when Sue asked, "I've seen kerosene lamps and gas lights, but I've never seen anything like these. What are they?"

Tim answered from her left, "They are electric lights, the newest invention to hit Washington. All of the major buildings in the city either have them or soon will. As you can see, they provide much more light than gas or kerosene."

Their waiter arrived at that moment and gave each a menu and left them to discuss their choices. Sue knew she was in far over her head socially and gladly accepted when Missus Hopkins asked if they would like some advice on ordering.

"I sure would. I can't even read the menu." Sue smiled in bewilderment. "What language is it?"

"It's French. There seems to be an unwritten rule in this city which says if the menu is in a foreign language, they can charge more for the same meal." She winked.

Their waiter returned a few minutes later and they placed their orders. After he left, Missus Hopkins smiled. "Missus Storm, this is the traditional moment when we women go to the powder room and leave the men to themselves. Would you like to go with me?"

Sue gratefully accepted and followed closely until they were beyond the dining room door. She asked hesitantly, "Missus Hopkins…"

"Please call me Marsha."

"Thank you. I'm Sue." Relief colored her tone. "I don't know much about society functions like this. Could you give me some pointers on what to do or what not to do?"

Marsha appeared sympathetic. "I'd be glad to. You have no reason to know, but you're just a bit younger than my daughter. Why don't I treat you as a new daughter to make it easier for both of us?"

The foyer to the dining room was beginning to fill when they returned. Several diners were standing just inside the dining room doors, talking to the maître d'.

Marsha suggested, "Let's wait here for a minute. They'll be moving soon, and we won't have to push through the crowd."

***

Theodore Leonard Preston, Junior, was in a foul mood when he and two companions entered the Ambassadors Club. He was young, handsome, and a member of the idle rich, but his marriage proposal had been spurned by a young woman from one of the finest families in D.C. Humiliated, he stomped out in a furor and turned to his favorite form of solace, a bottle. Several hours had passed and he was now thoroughly drunk. A mean drunk.

When he and his companions entered the foyer, they found their path blocked by two women. His recent rejection and subsequent drinking had so clouded his mind the only things he noticed about the younger woman were her gender and that she was dressed in black.

In an exaggerated tone of joviality, he encircled the young woman's waist with his right arm and squeezed. "Hello, my lovely. Why don't you ditch your friend and share my table?"

The young woman staggered at the pressure of his arm. Theodore sneered and thought, *Weak-kneed bitch. They're all helpless.*

The young woman wheeled to face him, her face showing fury. He smiled and turned his cheek to offer a better target for the usual dainty slap. Instead, an unexpectedly powerful left hook buried itself in his soft and unprotected belly. He doubled up in agony as his descending chin met a right uppercut that lifted him off his feet and sent him crashing into his two companions.

CHAPTER 20

Sue's knees nearly buckled when the crushing pressure on her barely-healed bullet gouge set it aflame with pain. She turned in a rage which exploded when she saw the smile on the face of her assailant. Both of her fists swept outward and upward even though the impact hurt her knuckles. Ignoring the minor pain, she exploded at the two men holding the unconscious body upright.

"You get that worthless son of a bitch out of here! When he wakes up, tell him I'll shoot him if I ever see him again!"

Sue's angry voice carried clearly throughout the club... Ted was instantly on his feet and moving toward the foyer. He was close enough to hear when one of the companions tried to protest.

"You can't tell me..." The protest died with a strangled gasp as the muzzle of a Colt 45 ground into the underside of his jaw. He rose on tiptoes to escape the pressure.

George Elston, also a member of the idle rich, was well on his own way to being drunk when they entered the club. He sobered up suddenly with a gun muzzle under his chin and cold eyes boring into his. A voice that brooked no argument penetrated the fog of drunkenness.

"I told you to get him out of here. Do it, or I'll bend this gun barrel over your stupid head."

He found himself in no position to argue. "Let me go," he croaked. "I'll do it."

Ted halted beside Sue, watching warily as the young man grunted his surrender and was released. He gently placed his hand on her shoulder, scanning the horrified crowd standing in the foyer while the two men dragged their unconscious companion out the door.

Sue didn't realize that she was still holding her revolver in her hand until the three men disappeared. She re-holstered her Colt and turned toward Ted but met Marsha's eyes that were wide and staring at her in shock.

She explained with no apology, "He darn near crushed my waist."

Marsha continued to stare in shock at the polite young woman, who had so suddenly transformed into a menacing tigress. When the significance of the simple statement dawned, she gasped. "Tim told me you'd been shot in the side in a gunfight. There's no way you could be fully healed in so few weeks. He must've hurt you terribly!"

Onlookers gasped at the astounding statement.

Sue apologized, "It hurt bad enough to just about put me on my knees. I'm sorry I lost my head and embarrassed you."

"No apology is necessary," Marsha snapped, indignant and adamant. "If he'd done it to me, I'd have only slapped him. I'm sure you made a much greater impression on him than I would have."

Sue ignored the stares and whispers as Ted and Marsha escorted her back to their table.

When they were seated, Marsha explained to Tim, "Sue was assaulted by a drunken fool, the young Theodore Preston."

Her husband grimaced in distaste. "That ass! I hope that he got what he deserved."

Marsha smiled. "He certainly picked the wrong young lady to get fresh with this time. Sue laid him out cold with two punches."

Fully aware of the nearby tables unabashedly eavesdropping, she explained in a whisper to Sue, "This man has a reputation that is not the best around here. Some of the young women he has been associated with have been seen with bruises and black eyes at one time or another."

"No one has ever reported witnessing him beating his companions," Tim added in a whisper, "And none has ever pressed charges against him. That might be because his father is one of the richest and most powerful men on the East Coast."

Sue scowled as she considered the character of the man she knocked out cold. "I meant it when I told his friends I'd shoot him if I ever saw him on the street. It sounds as though I would be doing the world a favor if I did."

Marsha managed to stifle a gasp at the brash young woman's statement, glad she had done so when Sue explained. "I've never drawn a gun on a man unless it was self-defense. You don't have to worry about me starting anything here."

"You said the father is rich and powerful." Ted observed. "It sounds as though he spoiled the son."

Tim chose his words with care, knowing many people were listening. "That may be the case. The father has been involved in many rough-and-tumble business deals over the years and has a reputation as a hard man. Some of that could easily have rubbed off on his son."

Their meals arrived, diverting everyone's attention. As their conversation ebbed, attention from the surrounding tables waned.

Tim added, "Your decision to come here was timely. When you were featured in the *Police Gazette*, Congress was about to adjourn for the summer break. However, several East Coast members of Congress eagerly volunteered to be called back to talk to you when you arrived," he laughed. "My take of the situation is they can't believe there really is such a person as a female marshal and gunfighter. They have to see you for themselves."

Sue flushed.

"I don't want to embarrass you, but the Marshal Service needs your help. When Mister Simpson notified us you were coming, we decided to have you testify before the special committee. We distributed copies of your story to the local newspapers... they're going to print the story tomorrow."

Marsha saw the grimace on Sue's face. She laid a sympathetic hand on her arm but gently admonished. "Like it or not, you're a celebrity now. You're the only female marshal in the United States, so anything that you do will be news."

***

George Elston was terrified simply by being in the same room as the elder Theodore Preston. Even more terrified of the consequences if he were to flee, he shrank back.

The older man roared, "Tell me again what happened, and make it quick!"

George stumbled over his words in his haste to comply, "We were standing in the Ambassadors Club when Theo patted some woman on the back. She spun around and hit him on the chin. Theo was unconscious, so I dragged him out of there, flagged down a hack, and brought him back here."

He was too terrified to admit the whole truth, much less tell of their erstwhile companion. That brave soul had deserted them after he had helped load the unconscious Theodore into the carriage.

George had heard rumors regarding the shady reputation of the father of his friend but had always dismissed them. He shivered in fear, having witnessed the man's display of temper, which put some truth to the rumors. He now realized others believed them because when he snarled the address at the driver, he tried to dump them back on the street. George now understood why the terrified driver had sped away after unloading his passengers at the mansion's front door, not even waiting for his fare.

Theodore had since regained consciousness but was still groggy as he tried to mumble something through his broken jaw.

His father whirled to face him in demonic fury. "Don't you even try to speak to me! You've failed at everything you've ever tried, and now you've let a goddamned woman knock you out! In public!"

He whirled back to George and screamed at the hapless young man. "You're another worthless whelp! Get the hell out of here and don't ever let me see your face again!"

George fled from the room and nearly ran from the house. He was terrified by the face of the beast he saw exposed. He slowed only when he was safely off the grounds, stumbling in fear along the street.

Theodore Preston the senior was in a towering rage that knew no limits. He had hated women all his life since being abandoned by an alcoholic and abusive mother, and now his sniveling son had been knocked unconscious by a woman. His rage fed on itself, intensifying to a white heat as it had once before when the mother of his son rebelled at his abuse and cleaned out the family safe before she fled. *That* was one body that would never be found.

He made his decision and turned to the drape behind him. He pulled twice on a hidden bell cord and turned back to his son who was slumped on the chair in front of his desk. He glared without a word until the eyes facing him dropped.

"You rang, sir?" The quiet voice of the butler interrupted his glare.

"Yes, Alfred." His voice sounded like velvet, which was the more threatening for its mildness. "I have a job for you."

Alfred O'Hare had served the household for many years as the butler, valet, secretary, and secret emissary. He had been summoned by his master many times before but never had he seen him radiating such cold fury. Wisely, he kept silent while waiting for his new assignment.

The senior Preston snarled through his gritted teeth. "Alfred, I want you to go to the Ambassadors Club. You are to find out the names of two people who ate there tonight. They would seem to be visitors to the city who don't know their proper place in our society." He savored his words before he continued, "When you have their names and determined where they live, I want you to contact our friend, Mister Raven. He is to exercise his specialty with one qualification at the earliest opportunity."

Alfred listened to the instructions with utmost care.

The rage simmered close to the surface as he instructed. "That qualification is that he does not kill the woman. The man doesn't matter. I want her so crippled she never walks again and so disfigured no man would ever want to look at her." His smile was as cold as death. "If Mister Raven and his fellows want to share her among themselves, they have my blessing."

"Yes, sir."

He picked up an envelope and handed it to his secretary. "Mister Raven's usual fee applies with a bonus of one thousand dollars for satisfactory completion. I expect him to personally lead his men. When they leave her after completing their mission, he is to tell her Theodore Preston sends his greetings. I want her to know that no one crosses me or my son."

***

The foyer was empty, and the dining room nearly so when Alfred arrived at the maître' d's unoccupied station. He was a patient man and waited quietly with his back to the dining room, until the man returned.

"May I help you, sir?"

"Yes, Ramon."

Ramon's face turned a pasty shade of gray when he recognized the voice, not that it mattered that he couldn't see the face of his visitor. He struggled with his own voice until he was able to emit a strangled reply, "How can I help?"

"What was the name of the woman who struck young Mister Preston this evening?"

Ramon swallowed hard, knowing he was condemning the young woman to death and that he would be committing suicide if he did not. Bile burned his throat and he nearly strangled on the bitter words.

226

He blurted, "Sue Storm. Mister and Missus Ted Storm. They're staying…I think they're staying…at the Harmon House." Too terrified to think, he neglected to add *they're both United States Marshals.*

Alfred purred with his voice pure silk, "Very good of you, Ramon. I'll check out the address personally." Without turning to face his latest informant, he walked calmly out the door, leaving a terrified Ramon staring at the retreating figure.

***

Sue and Ted met another pair of marshals at noon, one of whom brought copies of the local newspapers.

Wilbur Anderson grinned. "I've never seen so much interest in someone who wasn't a politician or a war hero before. You have to understand it was only because of professional curiosity that I bought these. I watched a lot of people who bought papers and then stood there reading the story for themselves," he laughed.

Sue and Ted smiled.

He held the paper to show the bold headline midway down the front page. *Lady Marshal To Address Congress.* He chuckled as Sue groaned, "They don't have the facts right as usual. You're only to testify before a joint committee."

Wilbur and his partner, Abe Swanson, shepherded them for the rest of the afternoon while they visited several offices in the Justice Department

Building. Sue ignored as best she could the stares and looks of disbelief many passersby sent her way.

The afternoon was fading when she protested, "I don't know about the rest of you, but I think that's enough business for today. We'd still like to visit the Washington Monument, and if we wait much longer, it'll be too dark to see anything."

CHAPTER 21

Their escorts agreed to call it a day and they separated, Sue and Ted heading for the Monument. Soaring skyward in solitary splendor, it rose from a small rise overlooking the nearby Potomac and its marshes. They approached slowly, awed by the magnificent spire marking the Mall in front of the Capitol and the White House.

The guard at the entrance recognized his famous visitors, who were featured on the front page of the morning papers. "Welcome to the Monument. I'm glad you didn't arrive any later, or you might have had to wait for another day. It takes so long to walk to the top we won't be taking very many more admissions for this afternoon. I'm glad you came on my shift. My wife and children will be thrilled to hear I've met someone famous." He grinned brightly.

They moved out of the guard's hearing range toward the stairs. "More like infamous," she whispered.

Ted chuckled as they began the long climb to the top. They stopped at each of the landings as they went, reading the inscribed carvings on the many stones from around the world that had been set into the walls.

They were both in excellent physical condition but were tired before they reached the top of the Monument. "I've never climbed this far before at one time," he admitted. "Let's make it worth our time while we're here."

They took their turn and moved from one small observation window to another, looking in turn at the city laid out far below them. The elevator operator, who was patiently waiting for the crowd of tourists, pointed out some of the features visible from their vantage point.

"You're looking east, and it's easy to recognize the Capitol. The building in the foreground is the Smithsonian, our national museum." He moved to another window. "That's north, and that's the White House there in the middle. Just to its right are both the Treasury Building and home of Commodore Stephen Decatur."

They followed the remaining crowd as he moved to the west window.

"You can see the Potomac winding through the marshes in the middle distance. Just across the river on the rise is the former home of General Robert E. Lee. The Union confiscated it after the Great War, and its grounds are now Arlington National Cemetery."

Their last view was to the south, showing much of the city with vehicle and railroad bridges that were being rapidly lost in the shadow as the sun dipped below the horizon. Streetlights far below began to wink on one by one when lamplighters began their rounds.

Ted and Sue joined the remainder of the visitors on the steam-powered elevator for the trip to the ground level. Both shivered as they began their first elevator ride, knowing their ornate cage was suspended above the earth only by steel cables.

Their guide explained, "You're privileged to be able to visit this monument because it hasn't really been open to the public for very long. It took forty years to construct from the laying of the cornerstone to the opening."

Their elevator ride took a long twelve minutes. Everyone stepped out at the ground level, and the guard locked the gate behind them. Sue and Ted stood in silence while the other tourists and the guards departed in their various directions. Full darkness had fallen when they once again stirred, walking slowly across the Mall.

They were only a few blocks from their hotel when Ted, as habitually alert as ever, whispered, "I think we're being followed. I wasn't sure what I saw wasn't just a shadow when we left the Monument, but now I'm positive. I just saw someone duck back into the shadows when we turned that last corner. It was too furtive to have any good intentions for us."

"Better to be safe than sorry," Sue whispered agreement.

They left the circle of light falling from a nearby street light. Each unobtrusively inserted another cartridge in the empty chamber under the hammer of their Colts. The street was bereft of other pedestrians and lined with deep shadows that offered concealment. Sue listened with keen ears for footsteps from behind while Ted's eyes swept the sidewalk ahead.

They'd almost reached the next intersection when four men with clubs suddenly stepped out of the shadows and blocked their way. When they halted abruptly, Sue spun on her heel to cover their backs. Unsurprised, she calmly announced, "Four more behind us. They don't look very friendly either."

The silence of the empty street was shattered by a shrill whistle as the eight men charged as one. Ted and Sue responded instantly with right hands flashing down and guns spitting fire as they came level. Sue aimed low, knocking the legs out from under two assailants with three rounds, but the other two still came on. Her gun rose a fraction and spat fire as she squeezed off a round that missed. Her last two shots hit one man in the chest at short range, while the fourth swung his club savagely.

Sue ducked and spun away as his momentum carried him past her, left hand punching cartridges from her belt loops. Seconds later, she had three rounds chambered and no more time. She fired at point-blank range as the last assailant swung viciously again. The impact of the bullet in his body deflected the thug's aim and he went down.

She was knocked to the ground when the club bounced off her shoulder instead of crashing into her head. She was stunned and shook her head to clear it. A wave of fire stabbed through her abused side. Sue looked up to see a thug rushing at Ted from his blind side. She fired a desperation snapshot that slammed into him. He stumbled and fell at Ted's feet as his club flew along the sidewalk until it crashed into her.

She was dazed but still able to move. As she rose to her feet, she automatically punched fresh rounds into empty chambers. Ted was still on his feet as she called anxiously. "Are you hurt?"

"I think I broke a wrist when I stopped a club, but otherwise, I'm okay. What about you?"

Instead of answering immediately, she roared at one of the shadowy figures trying to get to his feet. "You're under arrest for attempted murder! Stay down, or I'll put a bullet through your head!"

Sue watched the shadow settle back. "I just have a bruised shoulder. I think." She listened to frantic whistles in the distance that were fast approaching. "What's all the commotion?"

Ted almost laughed aloud, "Those are police whistles. They obviously heard the shooting."

The police had heard, along with everyone else for blocks around. Lights were turned down, but windows were forced fully open all along the street as the curious peered cautiously from their second-floor residences. As the first officer pounded into sight, Ted yelled a warning.

"Federal Marshals here! Hold your fire!"

The officer slowed his pace. When he was in easy earshot, he asked, "What the hell's been going on here?"

Ted explained briefly while more officers arrived at a run.

The first arrival bellowed at one of his fellows. "Amos. Call the station and tell them we need a paddy wagon and the Captain as soon as possible."

Amos walked to a box on a nearby lamp post, opened a door, and held something to his ear.

Mystified, Sue asked, "What's that thing?"

The officer gave a startled gasp. In the excitement and poor lighting, he hadn't realized her gender until she spoke. When he recovered, he said, "A telephone. It's like a telegraph, except you can actually hear whom you're talking to."

Sue and Ted both stared in amazement.

Amos spoke briefly before calling loudly, "They're on the way."

Standing at a respectful distance, a crowd of curious onlookers soon surrounded the officers and the wounded thugs. Sue and Ted stood with Constable Blackstone until the paddy wagon arrived and forced its way through the throng. They watched as a shadowy figure stepped down from the paddy wagon into the circle of light from the officer's bull's-eye lanterns.

The shadow gained substance as it approached, and Constable Blackstone saluted. "Captain Miller. I'd like you to meet United States Marshals Ted and Sue Storm."

***

Much later that evening, they were seated together in Captain Miller's office, having returned from the local hospital. Ted's wrist was not broken but badly bruised. It had turned a mottled black and blue. Sue's shoulder was also badly bruised. Under her shirt, she was a matching mass of black and blue. She was very uncomfortable and found it hard to sit still because the pain of her injured shoulder merged with the residual pain from the bullet gouge in her side.

The captain eyed the unusual young couple momentarily before he spoke, "Only one of the thugs got away, and from the bloodstains, we know he was wounded." He smiled in smug satisfaction. "We arrested the five you captured. They're all in the hospital under guard."

Sue winced a little in pain.

He hesitated for a second before continuing with no trace of regret. "The doctors have indicated to us some of them probably won't survive and will join the two we already hauled off to the morgue."

Ted nodded.

His expression changed to one of pure satisfaction. "Not bad results for one night's work, because they're all members of the most vicious gang in the city. Their leader, known as Raven, admitted to the officers they could see you were wearing guns. They were so arrogant they were sure they could get to you before you could possibly get your guns out. My guess is they were used to the speed of my officers here in D.C., which is nonexistent. Your speed certainly saved both your lives tonight."

***

Later, they were finishing up signing the statements, dictating to a stenographer when another officer entered the room. He held a sheaf of papers in his hand and swept the waiting trio with his eyes.

"Captain, I think you'll find these statements from the Raven Gang and the summary very interesting." He laid the reports on the captain's desk and quickly exited, leaving them alone again.

Captain Miller skimmed the statements before reading the summary much more carefully. He raised his eyes to meet theirs. He spoke flatly, "Interesting is an understatement. The two of you weren't picked just by accident. These statements confirm Theodore Preston senior hired those thugs to kill you, Ted, and maim Sue for life."

Ted's face flushed with barely suppressed rage. His voice was frigid as he asked through clenched teeth, "Who the hell is Preston?"

Sue's tone matched his. "Marsha said the name of the man I knocked out last night was Theodore Preston junior."

The captain's eyebrows rose. "Tell me all about it."

They did while the captain took notes. When they finished, Ted was still furious, snarling,

"You'd better tell me where he lives because I'm going after him!"

Aches and pain forgotten for the moment, Sue's voice and face echoed his. "I'm going too!"

Captain Miller understood their anger, but his exasperation showed as he snapped, "No! You're not. Neither of you is going. Number one, neither of you are in any condition for another gun battle tonight. Number two, neither of you knows anything about the city."

Ted glared at him.

His voice softened, "I'll get search and arrest warrants for everyone in the house. You're federal officers, so I'll take some of my officers, enlist some of your fellow marshals, and go pay him a visit. Tonight."

They were frustrated but had to bow to reality. Neither was in any condition to pursue their quarry in unknown territory by themselves. When the captain sent them on their way, they resentfully returned to their hotel for an uneasy, painful night's sleep.

After breakfast in the dining room, they checked at the desk and found a message from Captain Miller asking them to come to his office late that afternoon. Unaccustomed to inactivity and with most of the city as yet unexplored, they spent most of the day as tourists.

They were in Captain Miller's office late that afternoon and were joined a few minutes later by Wilbur Anderson. They could see bloodshot eyes that indicated both men had been up for many hours. Their observation was confirmed when the captain began.

"Your work last night has solved a lot of criminal cases for us."

"How so?" Sue asked.

Captain Miller stifled a yawn. "We went to the Preston mansion last night with eight men. Wilbur had the warrants and knocked on the door. When the butler answered, the rest of us forced our way in with drawn guns. The butler, Alfred O'Hare, drew a gun and wounded one of my men before he was shot down."

Wilbur interjected, "We arrested everyone in the house including both Prestons and two other men. Four of our officers took them to the jail while the rest of us searched the mansion from top to bottom and found a lot of evidence of criminal activity." He took a long drink from his cup of coffee. "We also found the door to one storeroom not only padlocked but nailed shut. We broke in and found it empty, which made us very curious. We searched it very thoroughly and found someone had dug up and re-laid stones in the floor."

Ted and Sue listened with curiosity.

His face turned stony as the gruesome scene replayed itself in his memory. "We found a skeleton under the floor. A woman's skeleton. We found a locket with it, but there was nothing to positively identify the body. When we finished our search, we went to the jail and leaned on all four of the suspects we'd arrested."

Sue urged, "And?"

His grim demeanor softened. "The three older men stayed as quiet as clams. The younger Preston recognized the locket as his mother's and went wild. When we finally got him calmed down, he told us his father told him his mother ran off years ago and abandoned him. When we found the body, he knew his father had murdered his mother."

Captain Miller continued after a few moments, "The father has always belittled his son, and he in turn, hated him for it. He dearly loved his mother, and when he found out she had been murdered, he started telling us everything he knew or even suspected about his father's crooked dealings."

Ted let out a sigh of shock and relief.

"With the documents and other evidence we found in the house, even without the son's testimony, we have enough to hang the father and a half-dozen of his 'business associates'. We can easily prove they're guilty of every crime imaginable from murder to embezzlement and bribery to forgery, just to mention a few." He shook his head in frustrated disgust. "The bastards were sure organized."

Both men gazed at Sue and Ted for several moments with profound respect.

"The best thing that's happened in D.C. for many months was that the two of you came to visit."

Wilbur addressed her with admiration, "We've solved more major cases in three days than in the previous three years. All because you had the guts to slug a man who abused you."

Captain Miller asked, only half-joking, "Can you stay for a couple of years? You'd clean up my entire case load."

Both men yawned as one.

Wilbur said, "I have to go home and get some sleep. Tim asked me to tell you that you're scheduled to testify before the committee tomorrow morning. He said someone will be at your hotel in the morning to pick you up. He was sorry he couldn't give you more warning, but he only learned of it a short time ago."

CHAPTER 22

The next day promised to be as hot and humid as only a summer day in the South could possibly be. Assistant Attorney General, Timothy Hopkins, accompanied Sue and Ted to the Capitol the next morning, where he led them to a small reception room near the much larger room assigned for the joint committee meeting.

They had dressed as Senator Hill had suggested, again wearing their work clothes, which were range-faded jeans, chambray shirts, and well-worn and comfortable gun belts. A page took their faded Stetsons and disappeared into an adjoining cloakroom. He returned and directed Sue to wait while he led Ted and Mister Hopkins to seats in the meeting room.

When Sue was led in a short time later, the committee members had already been seated, and the room was overflowing with a crowd of spectators and reporters. Mister Hopkins had confirmed on the ride to the Capitol that the local newspapers had reprinted the entire story that had first appeared weeks earlier in the Wilford Messenger. Curious readers had devoured the earlier story, while this morning's reports of another shootout involving the Marshals Storm were once again headline news. The subsequent arrest of one of the most powerful men in the city had raised interest in the female marshal to a fever pitch.

Sue could hear the murmurs and see the looks of disbelief as she was led toward the front of the room. Ted and Mister Hopkins were seated in the first row of spectators and both gave her smiles of encouragement.

A low railing separated the spectator area from a raised dais occupied by a horseshoe-shaped table and eleven chairs. On the center, just outside the curve of the table, was a single desk with a chair. The only items on the desk were the usual provision for something to drink for the witness.

Her escort pulled back the chair and gestured her to sit. When she did, the chairman called the meeting to order. A clerk who was seated off to one side announced that there were no minutes of a previous meeting. Her heart was hammering as the clerk announced the agenda for the day's business of the Joint Select Committee.

"The matter of testimony regarding financing for Justice Department operations, specifically the Marshal Service."

The clerk deferred to the chairman, who intoned, "Will the clerk introduce the first witness?"

The clerk managed, only with difficulty, not to stumble over the absurdity of a female on the witness stand. "United States Marshal Sue Storm, presently serving in the great state of Colorado."

Sue was amazed at her own calm but reminded herself again. *If I could face Snake, I can face these men.* Her eyes traveled from one end of the table to the other, meeting the eyes of the men facing her one by one.

The chairman introduced himself and the other committee members: five senators and six representatives, all from states near the Atlantic Seaboard. "Marshal Storm. I doubt you can appreciate the interest you have sparked in both in the government and the public, of your exploits."

The room waited silently, watching as his face turned grave.

"We have heard much about you. The Marshal Service has submitted your name as qualified to address this committee. In your own words, what are your qualifications for testifying before this committee?"

"Sir. I will repeat what I told a joint committee of the Colorado State Legislature. I am simply a citizen of these United States." She watched the faces that were examining her closely as she let the tension build for a moment. "Whatever action you take here will undoubtedly have an influence on my life at some point, whether directly or indirectly."

The committee members stared at her in surprise as murmurs raced through the watching crowd. After a moment's consideration, the chairman nodded. "That will be satisfactory." He turned to his right. "Senator Orion."

The senator was unsmiling when he met her eyes. "Why did the Marshal Service want you to testify before us?"

"I can only surmise their reasons. Perhaps you should ask someone from here in D.C."

He glared at her. "Let me rephrase my question. Why are you here to testify?"

Sue met his unfriendly gaze levelly. "It's a long story."

"We have lots of time." His mouth twisted as though he had bitten into something sour. "Go on."

"My mother died when I was a toddler. My father was killed two years ago in an accident. He had always refused to tell me about their families. Why, I don't know." The room waited in silence as she took a sip of water to ease her throat. "When the story about my experience as a marshal was printed in *The Police Gazette*, which, by the way, was highly exaggerated, someone in Philadelphia noted the name of my father. From that chance occurrence, I found my father's family. When we decided to come east to meet my grandparents, the Marshal Service asked if I would testify on its behalf while we were so close."

The room fell silent.

Sue took a deep breath before she continued as her even soprano carried clearly. "I could not refuse because I owe the Marshal Service my life." She turned slightly with her eyes meeting Ted's for a moment. "And my love. I owe the Service my life and my love. I could not refuse their request."

The senator nodded curtly.

The chairman spoke, "Representative White."

The man's eyes were not unfriendly but wary. "Would you recap the circumstances of your little adventure for us?"

Sue's face hardened, and her eyes turned cold at the intimation her travails could be casually dismissed as a *little adventure*. The representative flinched at the transformation into such a menacing figure, but in a moment, she had regained her composure.

"Certainly, Sir." Her tone was cool as she recalled her memories of those terrible days, explaining step by step what had transpired. No one interrupted, but many in the crowd stirred in shock or dismay.

When she told of the ambush from behind that almost killed Ted and forced her into the open, she halted abruptly and took a long swallow of water from the glass by her side. The room remained deathly silent, waiting in fascinated anticipation.

"Snake Carson shot out of hand the outlaw that ambushed us. He was smiling, not only enjoying the killing but looking delighted." Her voice caught, "I knew I had but two choices. One was to fight back and possibly live or at least die quickly. My other choice was to meekly surrender and die slowly at the gang's hands."

Her words hung in the deafening silence.

"I survived, but I was wounded. It nearly killed me, but I've managed to recover in the weeks since." She leaned back in the straight-backed chair while the room erupted.

***

The next morning, a headlined editorial in The Washington Post summarized the chaotic committee meeting.

This reporter has never seen such universal interest in the appearance of any witness before any government committee. United States Marshal Sue Storm, the only female marshal in the Marshal Service, astounded and confounded committee members and observers alike. Marshal Storm, at only eighteen years of age, is a survivor of violence and travails that would have killed men many years her senior. Though she dresses in man's clothes as a practical necessity, she is a lovely young woman. Lithe and willowy, on the witness stand she was the personification of a tigress, sleek and potentially deadly.

Her most astounding feature noted by this writer was that this remarkable young woman never raised her voice in anger. While she answered every question civilly to the best of her ability, on several occasions, a single icy glare would instantly silence a critic. This young woman is obviously well-read and knowledgeable about many subjects. She presented several well-thought-out arguments to the committee. The most important was that the first duty of government at all levels is the protection of the citizenry. She emphasized self-defense is the responsibility of the individual, but there needs to be higher levels of protection against abuse of power by any level of government.

Sue Storm is an amazing example of young womanhood. We wish her the best of luck in her search for her family.

CHAPTER 23

When the chairman at last excused her, Sue rose, feeling her knees weakening with relief. The clerk escorted her to a seat next to Ted's while she ignored the dozens of staring eyes. When she was seated, Tim Hopkins leaned over,

He whispered, "Well done."

The chairman addressed the rest of the committee, "Let the record show Marshal Sue Storm has given us some unique and fresh views on the problems we and the Marshal Service must deal with. I would recommend we consider her observations and suggestions very carefully during our deliberations."

***

They met that afternoon in Tim's office.

He grinned smugly. "The committee was well aware of Senator Hill's position before you testified. Most of what you told them supported his views, but you did contradict him on several points. That's good politics because they know you weren't just parroting him. They want input from all sides before they make a recommendation to their respective chambers. Sue, as the chairman stated, you made some points they need to examine further. That's another one of the good results that can come from a committee meeting."

They were interrupted by a knock on the door. A clerk entered, obviously bursting with curiosity but who still managed to present a dignified demeanor. "Mister Clark from the White House would like to meet Mister and Missus Storm for a moment."

They all stared at each other before Tim answered, "Please send him in."

Mister Clark entered, apologizing. "Mister Hopkins, I hope this is not an inconvenience for you."

"Of course not. What can I do for you?"

"I was informed I could find the Marshals Storm here in your office. President Cleveland asked me to deliver this letter to them and wait for their reply." He drew an envelope from his coat pocket and handed it to Ted.

Mystified, Ted opened the unsealed envelope and unfolded the handwritten note. He turned it so Sue could read it as well.

Marshals Ted and Sue Storm,

I would appreciate the pleasure of your company in my office in the White House tomorrow morning at 10:00 A.M.

President Grover Cleveland

They stared at each other in consternation while Tim watched, bursting with curiosity.

Sue found her voice first. "Mister Clark, we'd be honored. Please tell the President we would be delighted to accept his invitation."

Tim's eyes widened.

Mister Clark smiled warmly. "The President requested that you come to your appointment dressed as you were for the hearing. He's read a great deal about you while you've been visiting Washington and would like to meet the two of you in person."

****

They were so excited they slept poorly that night. Consequently, they were ready early and were waiting when Mister Hopkins arrived in a hired coach to escort them personally. When they stepped down from the coach, they gazed at the majestic three-story mansion waiting for them. They faced the main entrance, whose soaring pillars rose to support the portico arching high over their heads.

Tim brought them back to reality with a discrete cough. "I know this building has been here going on four generations and has a great deal of history," he said with a laugh. "But you do have an appointment with the President."

Ted inhaled deeply, "You're right. But it's a bit much for two youngsters from the mountains."

Sue nodded agreement, feeling overwhelmed by the majesty of the surroundings.

"I obviously wasn't included in your invitation, so I'll wait for you at my office." He added with a smile,

"The staff here will take good care of you. Good luck." He shook hands and stepped into the waiting coach.

Sue and Ted climbed the steps to the main entrance where they were greeted by a uniformed doorman. They were ushered inside where they were met by a butler, who led them down one hallway after another to the entrance to a spacious office.

They were greeted by a secretary. "Please come in and take a seat. We'll let you know when the President is ready for you."

A row of chairs was arrayed along the wall to the left of the secretary's desk. Sue sat down first. As soon as Ted was seated, her hand sought his. He held it gently with one finger brushing her wrist. Her racing pulse was only slightly more rapid than his.

Ted scanned his surroundings, meeting the wary eyes of the secretary. They showed great tension... his thoughts suddenly clicked. He stood and unbuckled his gun belt while a startled Sue lifted her own eyes to meet his.

He explained softly, "We don't want to appear threatening to the President. Let's leave our guns here."

The secretary visibly wilted with relief. No law prevented them from entering the office carrying arms, but several years and another presidential assassination would pass before the Secret Service was given responsibility for the protection of the President. Ted wrapped both of the belts around their holsters and laid them on the desk.

The secretary breathed a sigh of relief and exclaimed, "Thank you!"

Time dragged. They waited silently, trying not to be obvious as they stole repeated glances at the clock on the wall. Sue would've sworn the hands were frozen in place, but they at last showed ten o'clock. Her pulse accelerated even more. Still, more eons ticked by before the secretary's voice broke her thoughts.

"Marshals Storm, the President will see you now."

***

President Grover Cleveland was sitting at his desk, reviewing the notes that had piqued his interest in the two marshals who were next on his calendar. Both had been described as young in years but old in experience. Both had been wounded in gun battles in Colorado but had survived. Both also survived an ambush in the Capitol city only because of their extraordinary speed with guns. He shook his head in disbelief.

He raised his eyes, thinking for a moment that two young men were facing his desk with both wearing marshal's stars. He realized he was mistaken because one was a lovely young woman.

The secretary announced, "Mister President. Marshal Sue Storm and Marshal Ted Storm."

The President stood, leaning slightly across his desk to shake the hands of the young couple in turn. "Thank you, Andrew."

The secretary turned away, silently closing the door behind him. The President indicated two chairs waiting in front of his desk. "Please be seated."

Sue was nervous as she sat down in the surprisingly comfortable, overstuffed chair and met the eyes of the President. She saw a very heavy man of middle age with his dark hair combed back on his head and wearing a warm smile. She began to relax as he studied them in turn.

President Cleveland had fought corruption and dishonesty on all levels of government during his service in public life. He had fought for enactment of the nation's first civil service laws during his first term, suffering the wrath of his own party when he refused to endorse the old system of distribution of political spoils with every change of administration.

His overriding personal tenants during his entire life had been honor and duty. As a sheriff, he had personally sprung the trap under two condemned killers. Regarding it as his elected duty, he had refused to shunt the gruesome task onto some unfortunate deputy.

"Missus Storm, from the reports I've read about you and your husband, we hold several precepts in common." He smiled broadly. "One of those is to be an implacable foe of corruption."

Sue blushed, assuming that the President meant her fight against Snake.

"Another is that we both place great value on family. My sources tell me you know little of your family history. Is there something I could do to help you in your search?"

Stunned, Sue stared, stumbling over her words, "T-thank you f-for the offer. We've been able to find my father's family, and we've pieced together a little information…which makes us believe we know where to search for my mother's family. I hope our leads pan out."

"I wish you the best of luck." He turned his attention to Ted. "Mister Storm, what can you tell me about the state of the economy in Colorado?"

The national financial panic that had struck that spring was making its effects felt all across the country. No one, not even the President, had any idea it would deepen into a depression which would hamstring the nation for the next four years.

"Well, the cattle market has certainly been hurt." His glance shifted momentarily to Sue at his side, knowing she had sold hers just in time. "The bottom fell out of prices just during the past month. A lot of ranchers are going to get hurt. Miners are complaining about the low price for silver although gold is steady."

"I'm afraid a lot of people are going to be hurt, but if we follow the wrong path, they will get hurt far worse." The President sighed, "I'm afraid we must stay the course."

They watched him turning slightly and looking out the window, gazing at the green lawn surrounding the White House.

"I've never seen the Rockies, but I hear they are magnificent. Please tell me all about them."

President Cleveland was enjoying himself immensely as he asked the young couple questions that led to other questions in return. He found them to be a refreshing change from the stream of professional politicians and bureaucrats who constantly placed demands on his time. These young people weren't jockeying for money or power. They were visibly relaxing as they enjoyed themselves too. He regarded them as the true strength of this country, the common citizens who make things work. The country was in good hands.

CHAPTER 24

The President's secretary was anxiously looking at the clock. The two marshals, who were allotted fifteen minutes of the President's busy time, had been in his office for almost an hour. The Secretary of State had just returned for the third time, obviously upset at having been kept waiting.

The door to the President's office suddenly swung open and the two marshals emerged, stopping at the secretary's desk. They picked up their wrapped gun belts and buckled them on as the Secretary of State stared in utter disbelief at the sight of a woman with a gun.

The President followed them to the hallway door and bid them goodbye. "Please be sure to come tonight dressed as you were at the Ambassador's Club and don't forget your guns. Nowhere else in the world would anyone not part of the King's Court be allowed to be armed in his presence."

The two waiting men stared when the outrageously dressed young woman assured the President they would do so. Both men watched, stunned, until the young couple disappeared down the hallway.

"Add the names of both Marshals to the guest list for tonight's State banquet," the President ordered as he turned away from his departing guests with a smile. "I want to show our guests true democracy in action tonight. Those two young people are prime examples of the opportunities our country offers to those who are willing to work hard and take chances."

***

Sue and Ted returned directly to Tim's office after they left the White House. When they told him of their invitation to the State banquet, his eyebrows met his hairline. He chuckled, "This is a job for Marsha. She knows just how to handle something like this." He dashed off a note and called for his secretary. "Get this to my wife as fast as possible. She'll need all the time possible to help the Storms prepare for the reception tonight."

***

Marsha was waiting when they returned to their hotel after a quick meal. She immediately took charge. "Ted. There is a barber shop three doors down. They're waiting for you as we speak. Sue, you come with me. My hairdresser is waiting."

Her expertise was invaluable. Both Sue and Ted were back at the hotel with time to spare. Marsha was waiting nervously in the lobby when they came downstairs. She inspected both as closely as any army officer had ever reviewed his troops while other astounded roomers watched.

They waited patiently until Marsha nodded her satisfaction. "Ted, you're a handsome gentleman in that outfit. Sue, the fact you're already married will break many hearts tonight." She gently placed her hands on Sue's shoulders, looking up at the young

258

woman towering over her. "I couldn't be prouder if you really were my own daughter."

Sue's eyes misted at the unaccustomed mothering as she promised, "I won't let you down."

****

A closed carriage dispatched from the White House picked them up at their hotel door, and a short time later, it was waiting in line at the mansion. They were swiftly escorted to the front door. As they entered, a massive grandfather clock struck the hour of seven.

Another butler met them and asked politely, "Marshals Storm?"

They both nodded.

"Please follow me."

There were many people congregating in the entry hall. Sue ignored the raised eyebrows of other guests who were staring at their holstered guns. The butler halted momentarily at a cloak room where they left their Stetsons before continuing down the corridor toward the State Dining Room. They rounded a corner and found themselves at the end of a line of dignitaries.

Their escort whispered, "Just follow along. This is the reception line for the President and First Lady. Someone else from our staff will greet you after you've gone through the line and answer any questions you might have."

She whispered the information to Ted as the couple in line ahead of them turned.

In a heavy accent, the matronly lady greeted them. "Good evening, sirs."

"Good evening to you, ma'am." Sue struggled to stifle a giggle at the shock on the other woman's face and of her husband at the sound of her soprano. "We are United States Marshals Sue and Ted Storm. Am I correct you are visitors to our country? If so, please accept our personal welcome."

Whispers raced down the line and heads turned.

The gentleman acknowledged in his own heavy accent, "I am Hans Schmidt, an ambassador from Germany. This is my wife, Helga. Thank you for your welcome."

Other arrivals followed, and those curious newcomers engaged them in conversation. The line was moving slowly but steadily, and in a few minutes, they entered the dining room. Two visiting ambassadors, the Secretary of State, and their wives were in the official receiving line with the presidential couple.

President Cleveland greeted them with a smile. "I've overheard others in the line and knew you were here. I'll visit with you later in the evening, so enjoy yourselves in the meantime."

The First Lady greeted them warmly. Her husband had talked to her about his meeting with this young couple, and she was anticipating meeting them. When they shook hands, Sue eyed a woman not many years older than herself. The First Lady was several inches shorter than her husband, which was almost a foot shorter than Sue. She radiated an air of confidence and compassion that greatly impressed Sue. They chatted for a few moments until they were forced to move on by the steady pressure of the line.

Sue and Ted sat across from each other, not far from the head table. Their own table was impeccably set with a white linen tablecloth, red napkins, white china, shining silver, and clear crystal goblets. Sue shivered at the thought of dropping any of the delicate items gracing the table. "I sure hope I don't break any of these."

Her fellow table guests, seated on either side, were the ambassadors from Canada and Australia. Across from her were their wives who sat on either side of Ted. Both women smiled.

The Australian said, "I don't believe that is apt to happen. I read in the newspapers you've been in far more dangerous situations than this and handled them beautifully."

When Sue had been seated, both women immediately took her under their wings since it was obvious she was both young and inexperienced. They took turns explaining what was happening, offering suggestions for the proper responses surrounding the intricate details of diplomatic functions. Her unabashed innocence and eager acceptance of their advice endeared Sue to both women. The appropriate diplomatic formalities were observed when the meal was over, as toasts were drunk and speeches given.

At the conclusion, President Cleveland announced, "Ladies and Gentlemen, this ends our official evening's activities. Please join my wife and myself in the ballroom where we hope you enjoy yourselves."

Neither Sue nor Ted had ever heard an orchestra. Their only exposure to music was limited to the occasional fiddle or banjo at a dance held in a home or the schoolhouse. When the orchestra struck up the music for the first dance, a waltz, they listened in awe-struck amazement. They watched while the President and First Lady took the floor, feeling overwhelmed by the music and the fairytale atmosphere as the couple glided across the dance floor.

Ted whispered, "I know I'm not much of a dancer, but we'll regret if for the rest of our lives if we don't get out on that floor at least once."

Sue sat entranced by the music and dancing. Her eyes were aglow. "I agree," she whispered in turn. "Let's wait for something slow and take our turn."

They watched through two more dances before moving onto the floor when the third started with a much slower tempo. She melted into his arms, swept up in the magic of the moment as the music flowed around them.

When the music rippled away and the mystic moment ended, the enchantment faded. Sue moved to the sidelines, savoring the moment.

"May I have this dance?"

She turned her head to find the President and First Lady standing there.

She gulped, managing not to stammer, "Of course."

The President explained with a smile, "It's customary for both couples to exchange partners in this situation."

Sue swallowed before replying, "We would be doubly honored to share this dance with you."

The orchestra struck up another number at the President's wave, and they took the floor. He was a magnificent dancer in spite of his weight, leading her smoothly through the movements. He raised his voice enough for her to hear over the music. "Have you been enjoying yourself?"

She was entranced. "Yes! This is a night I'll remember all my life. I keep expecting the clock to strike midnight, the carriage to turn into a pumpkin, and find this is all a dream."

"You're not dreaming," he laughed. "This is reality, not a Cinderella story." He led her into another turn, gracefully dodging her holstered revolver as he did so.

Her glance swept over his shoulder and caught Ted's eye as he danced past with the First Lady. The moment of magic ended with the music, and they returned to their seats on the sideline. Sue collapsed against Ted, marveling at the experience and enjoying his presence as their dance partners disappeared together again onto the crowded dance floor.

The dance was in its first stages when she whispered in his ear, "Have we done something wrong? Everyone is staring at us, but we've been here long enough for them to have gotten accustomed to us wearing guns."

He was equally mystified. "I don't know what it would be." The matter remained a mystery to them until the next morning when a totally unexpected source gave them the reason.

***

Marsha Hopkins was ecstatic when she met them.

She was bubbling with excitement when she hugged Sue fiercely. "I knew you would set official D.C. on its ear. I checked with my usual sources, and they all agree the two of you were the stars of the evening. Sue, you weren't dressed in a gown, but you impressed every man that talked to you. They're all so used to diplomatic doubletalk your direct answers left them confused. The women all wanted to protect you because you were so honestly innocent."

Sue turned crimson.

She laughed, "Ted, you didn't do too badly yourself being the handsome gentleman, but handsome men are a dime a dozen in this town." She chuckled, "The White House has never seen such an unusual package of youth and poise dressed as you two were."

Ted grinned.

She paused for breath, continuing more calmly, "The two of you had no way to know how truly special you made last night for the President and First Lady."

Their faces showed their bewilderment.

"They don't normally exchange dance partners with anyone because there are so many diplomatic and political sensibilities to consider. You were the only guests who attended who were not associated with any government or bureaucracy. That meant they could share part of their evening with you without having to worry about any political repercussions."

They stared at her for several moments.

"I never suspected that," Sue stammered. "I thought they were just being nice to us because we were the only young people attending."

"That wasn't the only reason." Marsha was bubbling again. "The two of you gave them a night to remember as special to them as the night they gave you. Treasure the memory always. My sources confirmed the foreign diplomats were dumbfounded you wore your guns. I'm glad you explained to me why the President asked you to wear them. He certainly made his point that royal privilege has no place in our system of government."

CHAPTER 25

Tim Hopkins sat at his desk, facing the Storms and reviewing the whirlwind of activity they'd created for multiple law enforcement agencies in the city. His staff would have many weeks of work resulting from the documents Ted had passed to him on their ride to the Ambassador's Club that first evening. Other departments would also have many weeks of work as the result of one event—the arrest of the senior Theodore Preston.

His reverie was interrupted by a knock on his door. His secretary entered a moment later.

"Mister Hopkins. I hate to interrupt, but Mister Shoemaker needs to see the Storms on official business."

"Send him in."

The man who entered the office a moment later was in uniform, wearing a District of Columbia Police badge. "Marshal Sue Storm. Marshal Ted Storm. I have subpoenas for your presence in court two days hence." He handed an envelope to Ted and one to Sue. "I'm sorry I have to do this."

Mystified, they read the summonses.

Disbelief was evident in Ted's voice as he explained, "There's a preliminary hearing for Raven and the other surviving gang members. Their lawyer is trying to get the case thrown out and is demanding to question us." He shook his head in bafflement. "This doesn't say on what grounds he's seeking dismissal."

Tim scanned the subpoena Sue handed him and snorted in derision, "Dirty Dan Taylor. He's been a lawyer for dubious characters for many years. Rumored to have done a lot of legal work for Preston. Crooked as a rail fence but too slick to ever have anything stick. He has something up his sleeve. That's for sure."

***

Sue squirmed uncomfortably in the straight-backed, woven-cane chair. Ted was seated across the small waiting room, looking as uncomfortable as she felt. She turned her head slightly, gazing at the other three inhabitants of the room. Two of them were women who also had been called as witnesses for this morning's hearing. The third was a uniformed bailiff who was monitoring his charges.

They had been warned as a group to say nothing to any of the other witnesses before the hearing. She found that less difficult than she imagined and credited it to her years of solitude living in the mountains. She twisted in her chair and stretched her long legs again, trying in vain to find a more comfortable position. She sat up when the door creaked open.

Another uniformed bailiff by the doorway beckoned, "Marshal Sue Storm. Please come with me."

She stood, feeling grateful to be free of the chair. She was apprehensive, not knowing what to expect during her first-ever appearance in a courtroom. The prosecutor had warned her about the favorite tactics of Dirty Dan Taylor.

"He loves to attack and confuse people so badly they begin to question their own recollections. Then he gets them to change their own testimony, one way or another."

The unspoken words, bribery and extortion, hung in the air. Sue followed the bailiff down the hall. They were almost at the doorway to the courtroom when she asked, "Am I allowed to wear my gun on the stand?"

"Yes, you are. Some of the judges don't allow it, but Judge Haverson is one of those who does."

A few minutes later, she was sworn in and took her seat on the witness stand. Her glance swept the courtroom, surprised to see it packed with spectators, even though it was only a hearing. There were hostile glares from the four defendants, and the hate and cold viciousness reminded her once again of Snake Carson. *Raven is aptly named.* She thought.

Black, glossy hair, as long as her own, flowed to brush his shoulders. A triangular, sharply pointed nose gave him a hawk-like countenance. The other three men in the dock were grubby, loutish-looking men, who could be counted on to be unthinking hatchet-men.

Guards hovered behind the four men, who were dressed in striped prison clothing, wearing handcuffs and leg manacles. Every time they moved, the chains would clink and rattle. Raven's left arm hung limp and his hand started to curl as the result of a bullet that had damaged muscle and nerve. The other three showed various bulges under their clothing from bandages and splints.

Sue's eyes met those of their lawyer and knew instantly he was aptly named. Standing in front of his clients, he appeared cold and contemptuous. His eyes held hers for a fleeting moment. His face was clean-shaven but marked with old scars. His nose was flattened and askew, obviously having been broken at some time in his life and poorly set. He looked like a pugilist. *This man is dangerous.*

"Marshal Storm!" The lawyer addressed her with a sneer. "That is certainly descriptive. Your gilded reputation precedes you. You've been stirring up a storm of trouble for quite some time now, haven't you?"

She kept a tight rein on her temper and her voice civil. "No, sir. All I've ever done was to defend myself."

"The old claim of self-defense!" He leaped to the attack. "How convenient. My innocent clients were a half block away when you opened fire on them for no reason. They were merely trying to defend themselves by running at you."

Unable to believe the audacity of his charge, Sue stared at him. "Defend themselves by running at us? They were only about ten yards distant in front of and behind us, carrying clubs. We were outnumbered four to one, so when they charged, we used our guns."

"You keep saying *we*." His smile was oily, his voice velvet over steel. "Obviously, you've been discussing this case with someone else, which is a breach of both law and justice."

"Only with the other victim of this brutal attack, my husband."

His grin was that of a shark. "Let the record show this witness has admitted discussing this case with another witness outside the courtroom."

Sue managed to stifle her retort only with difficulty, afraid of digging herself in deeper.

His smile was patently false when he approached the stand. "You claim my innocent clients were less than ten yards away when you opened fire. That proves that not only you attacked them without cause, but you are a liar." He waved a sheet of paper at her. "This fraudulent statement that you signed claims you didn't draw your gun until they ran at you. By your own admission, that wouldn't have given you time to get your gun out of your holster. If they were that close."

She smiled and turned to the judge. "Your Honor, if I may approach, I can prove who's lying in this court."

Lawyer Taylor suddenly objected.

"Overruled," Judge Haverson admonished. "You're the one who opened the charge of lying. The witness may approach."

Sue stepped down from the witness stand and approached the judge. "Your Honor, I would like to draw my revolver so I can eject the cartridges in the chambers. Then I will demonstrate the actions I took that night when I was attacked. I will not fire the last three rounds because I have no blanks."

The judge considered her intentions, glancing at both lawyers. "So be it."

Sue carefully drew her Colt, breaking the action as soon as it had cleared her holster to avoid any hint of intimidation. She ejected the shells from the chambers and laid them on the bar before showing the empty cylinder to the judge for his inspection. He nodded for her to continue.

Sue snapped the action shut and smoothly returned the gun to her holster. She moved away from the bench, turning to face the empty space at her right. The crowded courtroom buzzed with anticipation, falling silent as they waited.

The room was deathly silent, every eye riveted on her. She rose slightly on her toes. Her hand flashed down and back up with the Colt. Six clicks of the hammer on empty chambers were still echoing in the room when her left hand began to punch rounds from her belt loops. The action snapped open, three rounds went home, and it snapped shut.

She counted the pretend shots aloud, "One! Two! Three!"

Bedlam reigned as the crowd erupted in amazement. The judge pounded his gavel angrily until the tumult subsided. "Let the record show Marshal Sue Storm has demonstrated to the satisfaction of this court she is indeed capable of firing and reloading as rapidly as she has attested in her previously filed statement."

"Thank you, Your Honor." She approached the bar where she retrieved her ejected cartridges. In one fluid motion, she reloaded two of them, spun the cylinder, and lowered the hammer over the empty chamber. Her left hand returned the unused cartridges to her belt loops before she slipped the Colt back into its holster. Sue returned to the witness stand, glancing at lawyer Taylor.

His jaw was tight, and anger smoldered in his eyes. "Marshal Storm. Your statement alleges one of my clients struck you with a club." His voice was deceptively mild but as taut as a loaded trap. "How is that possible when you claim to be so fast on the draw? Surely, you are lying now."

She thought warily. *You've made him a liar once already. Don't mess up now.* "I didn't down all four men during the first attack and had to dodge to reload. One of them came at me again and swung his club just as I fired. If I hadn't shot him, his club would have hit my head instead of my shoulder, and I'd be dead."

"So you claim!' he almost shouted, spitting his words like bullets. "Isn't it true your so-called bruise was the result of one of your earlier escapades?"

The prosecutor objected vehemently while the courtroom buzzed. Sue clamped her jaws tightly until order was restored.

The judge addressed her, "The witness will answer."

"No. The bruise is not from an earlier time." She turned her head and addressed the judge, "Your Honor. I'm willing to show the bruise on my shoulder to the court, in private. I believe any fair-minded person will agree from the appearance that it is only a few days old. As I've sworn, the bruise resulted from the defendants' attack on me."

The courtroom was silent while the judge pondered her offer. He ordered both sides to approach the bench where Lawyer Taylor's face reddened as a low-voiced argument ensued. The judge banged his gavel and announced. "We will take a ten-minute recess while the witness and lead lawyers adjourn to my chambers."

A few minutes later in the judge's chambers, he said, "Marshal Storm, you offered to prove your bruise is only a few days old. If you would be so kind…" The judge's voice tapered off into embarrassed silence.

"Certainly, sir." She turned her back to the three men and pulled the shirt-tail out of her jeans. She partially unbuttoned her shirt and slipped it off her right shoulder far enough to reveal her shoulder blade and upper arm.

"Gentlemen." The judge addressed the silent lawyers, "I will enter into the record that the witness has voluntarily shown us her injured shoulder and arm. They're both discolored by a large bruising of black, blue, and yellow with the intensity supporting her statement regarding the aforesaid infliction of the injury. The evidence is consistent with the timing of the alleged attack."

Lawyer Taylor opened his mouth to protest but was silenced by Judge Haverson. "Don't say another word. What I have to say to you will be in open court." He directed his next words to Sue's back, who had already slipped her shirt back over her shoulder. "Marshal Storm. We'll wait in the hall while you get dressed."

CHAPTER 26

Chief Prosecutor Rufus Murdock was amazed at the poise of his star witness. He had had deep reservations regarding her ability when he first met her, not knowing what to expect from someone so young and female. Now, he found himself admiring her maturity on the stand where she had not only deflected the attacks by Dirty Dan but had turned them back on him. He watched her calmly listening while the judge upbraided the lawyer for making demonstrably false accusations regarding her testimony.

Lawyer Taylor was tightlipped with anger when the judge finished his tongue-lashing. "I have no further questions for this witness." His voice filled with anger. "Your Honor. May I have a short recess to confer with my clients before the Prosecution questions this witness?"

"Certainly. Court is recessed for ten minutes."

Prosecutor Murdock was watching with heightened interest when the defendants returned with their faces glum. Lawyer Taylor bypassed his own seat at the table and laid a sheet of paper on the table. "Do we have a deal?"

The prosecutor read the note carefully before nodding. "They plead guilty now, and they get ten years. If they insist on going to trial, I'll go for twenty years. You know I'll get it."

***

Raven and his gang were among the most hated men in the city—especially by rival gangs whose members had suffered horrendous injury when cornered by the sadistic group. It would be no surprise Raven would die in less than a month as his body was found in a pool of blood in the prison yard. The knife that cut his throat was entwined in his long hair. Two of the others would take their own lives within two years, despondent over the constant beatings they received in retaliation. The fourth would die of natural causes in less than five years. None would be mourned, neither inside nor outside the prison.

***

Sue watched from the witness box while the two lawyers talked in low voices. When the judge reentered the courtroom, she stood with the rest of the spectators, growing tense with anticipation. She was mystified when both lawyers approached the bench after the hearing was gaveled to order. The whispered conversation lasted only a few minutes before the lawyers returned to their seats.

Judge Haverson declared, "Let the record show the witness is excused." He turned to address her directly. "Marshal Storm. You may step down."

Her stomach fluttered with relief while she followed a bailiff out through a side door. He led her to a small room that was empty except for two chairs. "Wait here. Someone else will be back for you in a short time." When she looked at him questioningly, he grinned. "I think they're going to cut a deal and plead guilty. You put them on the road to prison in more ways than one.”

Sue was startled. Before she could frame a question, he turned away. Her 'thank you' followed his retreat.

***

Later that day, they met at Tim Hopkins’ office where Marsha welcomed Sue with a hug and a smile that warmed the room. Her pride in her 'daughter for the moment’ was obvious. Tim confirmed the reason for the sudden adjournment of the hearing… the defendants opted to plea bargain for a shorter sentence.

“Your testimony by itself, with the physical evidence, would have convicted them. The testimony of the other witnesses would’ve been unnecessary. They get a lesser sentence, but they’ll still be behind bars for a long time.” He beamed as he shook their hands vigorously. “Thanks for taking a bad bunch off our streets.”

Marsha was also beaming as she broke the momentary silence. “I know you want to leave to see your family in Philadelphia as soon as possible, but I would like to host a going-away party for the two of you tonight.” She added with a wistful tone, “You could still leave on an early train tomorrow.”

Despite the short time they’d known one another, Sue had grown very close to Marsha and her mothering. She smiled in return. “I’d like that very much.”

Marsha glowed. "Then let's get started because there's not much time to plan." She turned to the two men and issued orders, "Ted. You will be at our house at six. I'm taking Sue with me right now, and we'll be ready at seven. Be there!" she laughed.

Sue accompanied her obediently and soon found herself in what Marsha declared to be the finest millenary shop in the city. "I've been scouting for a dress for you for several days, and I finally found the perfect one." She waved at the proprietor, who disappeared into a back room but returned a moment later with a dress folded over her arm.

"Claudia. This is the young woman I told you about. I'm putting her in your hands." She smiled as Sue was led away to the fitting room. "I'm getting you this gown as my present. You will be the most beautiful woman in the city tonight."

***

The two men were waiting 'more or less' patiently in the front room of the Hopkins' home at the appointed hour. Ted was dressed as he was at their first meeting in white shirt, black trousers, and vest, sporting his gun and marshal's star.

"Gentlemen. Allow me to introduce the new Missus Storm," Marsha announced from the doorway with her eyes glowing with undisguised pride in her new charge.

Ted turned at the sound of her voice and his eyes widened.

Sue stood just inside the door, her face pink. The new dress was a shimmering royal purple silk that belled out to sweep the floor, emphasizing the curves of her waist, hips, and breasts. The shoulders were padded with the neckline puffed high on the back and cut low in front. Marsha's skillful application of makeup had lessened the contrast of the deep tan of her face and neck against the white of her exposed skin while a glimpse of cleavage was emphasized by the low neckline. Sue's reservations melted at the undisguised adoration in Ted's eyes.

He took her hands and held them for a moment. "You are the most beautiful woman I've ever seen. I'm proud to have you as my wife."

Marsha's eyes glowed as Tim chuckled, "Our carriage is waiting. We don't want to be late for our own party."

They joined in the laughter. Ted offered his arm, proudly escorting Sue to the waiting carriage for their ride to the Ambassador's Club.

***

The sinister faces were half hidden in shadow, emphasizing the menace in the atmosphere. "We're agreed then. Slick will wait for them in Saint Louis." The leader smirked evilly. "The law there will blame the escaped train robbers when we kill her."

CHAPTER 27

Sue's middle was populated by a huge flock of butterflies when the train pulled slowly into the station in Philadelphia. Fear and anticipation warred within her as the conductor announced the stop. Ted squeezed her hand gently as they stood and joined the line moving toward the door. He stepped aside to let her be the first one off. Her eyes anxiously swept the waiting crowd but failed to recognize anyone. Her foot had just touched the platform when a voice called from her left.

"Sue! Over here."

She turned to see Daniel Wilson a few feet away, standing beside a white-haired man and woman. An instant later, she was enveloped in the arms of the woman who exclaimed brokenly through tears of joy, "My granddaughter! My granddaughter!"

Sue was nearly crushed by the strength of the embrace as her own eyes streamed tears. After a moment of time savored but not measured, she raised her eyes from those of her grandmother to face her grandfather. Her face turned white and her knees turned to jelly. She sagged, dragging the other woman down with her.

Her grandfather asked anxiously, "Is something wrong?"

Sue's voice cracked and was barely audible. "If your hair weren't white, I would swear on a stack of Bibles you were my father's ghost!"

Henry Mason's heart leaped with joy. "Your father always did look like me." He choked, tears streaming down his face, "How I wish I could see my son again."

Lawyer Wilson walked with Ted as they led the way through the station. Sue and her grandparents walked arm in arm, exchanging questions and trying to fit a lifetime of discovery into a few moments. Grandmother Nancy was on her left, holding her closely as though she would never let go. Grandfather Henry kept pace on her right.

When they were seated in the waiting carriage, Sue asked in a breaking voice. "I have to know! Why did my father have nothing to do with either you or my mother's family?"

A silence stretched for some time before Henry explained, "I'll answer the easy part first. I have no idea why he had nothing to do with your mother's family." His voice caught, "We never knew he was married, much less that he had a daughter. You."

Another extended silence followed before he continued with obvious reluctance. "Your father and I argued for years about his future. I insisted he follow me into business, but he wanted to be a professor. One spring day Maximillian just disappeared, leaving a note telling us not to bother trying to trace him." Bitterness, hurt and anger were reflected in his eyes. "We, of course, ignored his instruction and immediately started a search for our only child. We never did discover how he left the city or where he went. All those years, we never had a single clue to his whereabouts or his fate until your appearance answered our prayers."

***

The closed carriage brought them to the front door of a huge mansion set back from the street. When the rig stopped on the curved drive, a uniformed footman stepped down and opened the door, greeting them one by one.

Sue stepped away from the carriage and stood silently beside her grandmother, staring in awe at the house. White pillars rose to support the roof overhead, reminding her of the White House in spite of the red brick of the rest of the structure. Trees and flower beds stretched in all directions, disappearing behind the house.

She whistled silently before asking, "All of this is really yours?"

"Yes." Grandmother's smile was restrained as she admitted, "It is a bit much for just two of us." She sighed and an edge of bitterness crept into her voice when she continued, "It takes a staff of four to maintain it, which makes it feel more like a hotel than a home."

Sue glanced sharply at her grandmother, who ignored her questioning gaze. A butler held the front door open.

"Let's go inside. Dinner will be ready soon. Then we can talk."

The dining room reflected the magnificence of the exterior of the mansion with ornate furnishings and draperies everywhere. The meal was one exquisite course after another. When they could eat no more, her grandparents led them to the library where they talked into the evening.

When Sue came downstairs by herself the next morning, she found her grandmother sitting at a small table on the veranda. Nancy welcomed her with a loving hug.

Her face glowed as she continued wistfully, "Good morning, dear Granddaughter. I never thought I'd be able to say that." She gazed lovingly into Sue's eyes for a long moment. "Ted has gone for a walk in the gardens. He asked me to signal when you came down for breakfast."

"All right."

Her smile dimmed. "Henry has already gone back to work at the factory. Why don't you let me show the two of you some of the city's historical sights today?"

"We'd love to do that."

"What would we love to do?" Ted asked as he rounded the corner of the mansion and stepped onto the veranda.

"See the city with Grandmother as our guide."

"We sure would."

Nancy's smile returned with their enthusiastic agreement.

They left shortly after breakfast. Strolling slowly, they enjoyed the beauty of the immediate grounds. They soon left the estate, following wide brick sidewalks toward downtown Philadelphia. Nancy stopped often, explaining the significance of everything of interest they passed. They stopped often as Grandmother exchanged familiar greetings with many of the pedestrians, glorying in the attention they showered on her newfound granddaughter.

An hour's stroll found them standing in front of a red brick building trimmed in white. The clock tower soared, drawing their eyes heavenward. Nancy smiled at their reaction to Independence Hall.

"This building took eighteen years to build starting in 1730. It was first the home of the Colonial Government for Pennsylvania before it became the home of our state government. The Declaration of Independence was debated and signed here. When we go inside, you can almost feel the presence of giants like Washington, Jefferson, and the other men who signed that historic document."

Sue shivered in anticipation as they entered the bell tower and saw the massive Liberty Bell for the first time.

"It was hung in the tower in 1753. After the Declaration of Independence was signed here in 1776, it was rung every Fourth of July until it cracked in 1846. The only exception was for the two years it was hidden from the invading British during the Revolution."

They saw many other visitors in the old Pennsylvania State House as they explored the historic building. Sue could see they shared the same reverence she felt as the silence in the chamber was broken only by street noise that filtered in from the outside.

***

The next few days flew by in a flurry of activity as they toured a city steeped in history. Each evening was filled with activity as they were introduced to relatives and friends during the galas her grandparents held in their grand ballroom.

Sue was as surprised as Ted was when her grandmother announced at breakfast one morning he'd have to fend for himself for a while. "We ladies are going walking." She smiled affectionately at Ted as she patted Sue's hand.

Grandmother led but was uncharacteristically silent and solemn while they followed a gently curving path through the wooded landscape. She selected a spreading oak on a grassy knoll and sat down with her back to the trunk. She beckoned Sue to sit beside her.

Instead of sitting, Sue took her grandmother's extended hand and squatted on her heels in rider fashion, facing her. She met an intense look from the older woman's eyes and was bewildered by their fixity.

Grandmother swallowed before she spoke, "I hate to have to say it, but you must leave us. It must be soon."

Sue jerked in shock, being so abruptly shut out of the family she had just discovered.

Her grandmother saw the hurt and hastened to explain, "I mean you must leave, not that I want you to leave. Your grandfather is a rigid and vindictive man. How I've put up with him all these years since he drove your father away, I will never know!"

Grandmother's face was pale, and her body shook with suppressed sobbing. "He plans for you to stay in Philadelphia and for Ted to take over the factory. He has no thought for any plans you may have for your own lives. I'm afraid if you don't leave now, he will never let you go," she choked.

Sue was shaken, her thoughts in turmoil, but she answered with surprising calm. "I'll never allow any man to dictate how I must live my life. What you just said isn't a total surprise because I've seen and felt things since I've been here. I can see Grandfather trying to run my life." Her voice was burnished steel. "I'll never let him do so."

Grandmother dabbed her eyes.

Sue was breathing hard. When she had regained control, she continued softly, "I've been uncomfortable around him mostly for what was unsaid rather than what was said." Her eyes held those of her grandmother's. "I love you very much in spite of only knowing you for such a short time, but I've felt at arm's length from Grandfather from the beginning."

Her grandmother pulled Sue close with her arms tightly enveloping her. "I love you too, Granddaughter Sue. You've made me very proud of you and proud of your father for producing such a strong and independent young woman. It hurts so much to have found you after so many years, and it hurts even more to lose you so soon."

***

Dessert had been served following the evening meal when Sue caught her grandmother's eye. She said without preamble. "It's time for us to be going home. We'll be leaving tomorrow."

Her grandfather blanched, and his face turned white then red before he erupted, "You're our only grandchild! You can't leave! You have to stay because Ted must take over my factory!" He stormed on while Ted held her hand.

When Henry finally stopped for breath, Sue responded in a voice edged with steel. "Yes, I am your granddaughter. That much is true, but this is not my home nor is it my life. This is *not* where Ted and I plan to make our own life together." She met her grandfather's unforgiving glare. "I don't want to leave here in anger after finally finding my family, so don't drive me away as you did my father."

Henry's face flushed red while her grandmother's face paled.

Sue's voice was pleading when she continued, "I'd think someone in the family here in Philadelphia would be willing to take over the factory for you, but we are not!" She was pale, meeting her grandparent's eyes in turn. "Our world is mountains and open spaces, hard work and hard winters. It is sometimes violent, but it is *our* world." Her voice softened, "Philadelphia is not like that, so we are going back to our world tomorrow."

Grandfather turned away from her pleading eyes with his jaw clenched. Sue waited in the chilled silence as the clock in the background ticked away the seconds. After an extended period of silent hostility, she turned away and stood up. She gently stroked her grandmother's tear-stained cheeks with one hand before walking out of the dining room with Ted silently following behind.

They retreated to their room in silence. Ted sat down in the huge rocking chair and held out his arms, inviting Sue into his embrace. He held her tightly while she curled up on his lap, crying silently against his shoulder. He waited in silence, comforting her simply by being there.

She whispered brokenly, "Does having family always hurt this much?"

"No. It doesn't." He continued to hold her as tears trickled down her face. "I can certainly understand why your father left Philadelphia."

Both Sue and Ted were surprised when both her grandparents saw them off the next day, riding with them to Union Station. Henry watched in rigid silence when Grandmother Nancy hugged them both at the train and kissed Sue goodbye. She held Sue at arm's length for an extended period, looking into her eyes.

Her voice quivered. "We'd like to visit you next summer…if you'd have us."

Sue's voice was also unsteady. "We'd be happy to have you visit us anytime. Just let us know when you are arriving, and we'll meet you at the station in Wilford."

Grandmother and Granddaughter waved to each other until the train carried them out of sight. Sue turned to Ted with tears on her cheeks.

He whispered, "Don't feel guilty about leaving. We have our own lives to live."

CHAPTER 20

Their tickets were for a Pullman sleeper car that was supposed to be an overnight express to Chicago via Cleveland and the shore of Lake Erie. A more direct route to Peoria was possible, but the schedule would've added two more days of travel on a series of local stops with numerous layovers. Sue watched the miles click by, becoming more and more depressed. She was afraid of finding nothing but a dead end in the search for her mother's family.

They arrived at Chicago's LaSalle Street Station in the middle of a hot and sultry summer afternoon. They were a day late because of a balky locomotive and a major derailment that had blocked the tracks ahead for hours.

Sue was weary and exasperated while they waited for their luggage. "This is more than enough travel for today! Let's find someplace to stay for tonight. Tomorrow is soon enough to face that damn heat again."

Ted agreed heartily. They checked their heavy trunks at the station and kept only one overnight bag. They found their way to the street where Ted flagged down a hack. The driver pulled to the curb, giving them a startled double take when he spotted Sue's marshal's star.

"Where to, folks?"

"Someplace reasonable for one night is all we need," Ted responded. "Where would you suggest?"

The driver grinned. "I'd suggest from your outfits you'd probably be most comfortable at the Drovers' House. Most cattlemen stay there."

"Sound's good to us," Sue said, aware of the same name as their hotel in Denver. "The Drovers' House it is."

The driver dropped them at the front door of the hotel a short time later.

When Ted paid the fare, the driver winked and said conspiratorially. "You've got a real keeper there, Mister." He chuckled and pulled away into traffic, leaving Ted laughing in his wake.

Sue demanded to know what was so funny. He repeated it... she reddened until she saw the humor and laughed as well. They registered but stayed only a few minutes in their stifling room. They were soon outside on the street, walking the few blocks to Michigan Avenue and window shopping as they went. They were in no hurry, stopping often when one or the other pointed out some unique or especially beautiful item.

They crossed Michigan Avenue, dodging heavy traffic of every kind. Strolling along the shore of Lake Michigan, they enjoyed the cool breezes blowing from offshore. Sue marveled at the unending expanse of water extending beyond the horizon to the east.

"I'll probably never see an ocean, so this is the next best thing."

"You're probably right," Ted agreed.

A large steamer sailed past, heading toward the mouth of the Chicago River and its inland port. They watched until it disappeared into the river channel before ambling back toward the hustle and bustle of the city.

They resumed strolling and window shopping amid the crush of pedestrians. They hurried across busy intersections, dodging heavy wagons and light carriages alike. Shouts and curses from the many teamsters added to the raucous air of the city.

Ted suddenly stopped, causing Sue to bump into him. She followed his gaze and inhaled sharply. Her eyes were drawn to a wondrous selection of jewelry winking at them from a store window.

Ted was eyeing an exquisite locket which drew her eyes as well. "It's time for me to get you something to celebrate our wedding."

Sue started to protest, but it was as if he could read her mind.

"You didn't exactly marry a poor man." He grinned slyly. "I did manage to save some money before I met you."

She met his eyes for a moment before following him into the store. The owner was eager to please and quickly brought the display tray to the counter for their inspection. Sue tried several lockets before deciding on the one that had first caught Ted's eye. As he held it up, it sparkled brightly in the late afternoon sunlight. She took the locket in her hand, admiring its beauty.

Ted indicated their selection to the clerk. "We'll take this one if you'll take a check from a Denver bank."

The owner's smile faded. "I'm sorry, but I don't take checks, not even from a marshal. There's a bank just around the corner that does a lot of business with Westerners like you. I'd imagine they'd take your check and you could pay me in cash."

Ten minutes later, they were seated in the office of the chief teller for the Montgomery Bank. Ted filled out the faded check blank he had produced from his wallet.

The teller inspected it closely for a moment. "This will only take a few minutes. Please wait here while I get it cashed."

The door had scarcely closed behind the teller when a woman's scream pierced the air. A coarse voice carried clearly through the thin walls.

"This is a holdup. Everybody face down on the floor. Don't look up, or you'll get yourself shot." The voice turned even more menacing. "Put all your money in the bag!"

Ted was on his feet a second before Sue. "Cover me," he whispered as he tiptoed to the door.

She followed, her own revolver at the ready. Ted pulled gently on the door and cautiously peered through the crack. His limited field of view showed two masked men with guns facing the barred teller's cage on his right. A third was holding a gun on the dozen customers lying helplessly on the floor. His vision to the left was blocked by a short wall. Taking a calculated risk, he slipped through the door.

"Freeze! You're under arrest!" His crisp order froze the trio in their tracks. He waited a few seconds and took another step forward and to the right. Sue was about to follow when a cold voice to her left sneered.

"Freeze yourself, cowboy."

Sue peered around the edge of the open door and saw another masked man barely two feet from her, his gun aimed at the small of Ted's back. Her gun came up silently, closely level with the back of the head.

She ordered coldly, "Drop your gun, or I'll put a bullet through your head!"

"That's the oldest trick in the book, bitch," the thug laughed without turning his head. "You can't fool me."

The click of a hammer going to full cock and the pressure of her gun muzzle against the back of his head froze the thug. Ted turned, his free hand taking the gun from a shaking hand. Sue swung hard with her Colt and the thug dropped senselessly to the floor.

One of the masked men attempted to take advantage of the momentary distraction and spun, his gun spouting flame. The other robber between them pitched forward, downed by his companion's gunfire. The marshals' guns roared in return.

The gunfight was over in seconds. Four robbers lay sprawled on the floor while Sue and Ted kept watch, guns smoking. The echoes died away and silence descended.

She called, "I'll reload. You cover them."

A few seconds later Ted acknowledged, "I'm ready."

He turned his attention to the prone customers. "You're safe now. When I tap you, get up and move over by the door. Wait there until the police get here because they'll want to talk to you." He tapped the nearest prone figure and instructed, "Go outside and find a policeman. I'm sure at least one heard the shooting and is on the way."

The pale and shaken accountant had barely stumbled through the door when the first constable pounded through the gathering crowd.

He bellowed, "What's going on in there?"

The erstwhile victim gathered his shaken wits enough to respond, "The bank was being robbed when two marshals broke it up. I think they killed all four robbers."

Additional reinforcements arrived rapidly. Some kept the curious crowd back from the door while others rushed into the bank. Constable Peter O'Hara was the first inside where two tall men wearing marshals' stars were holding guns on four prostrate figures.

"D' you want to tell me all about this?" he asked quietly.

O'Hara was known to be unshakeable under fire as he had proven on several occasions during his police career. Despite that experience, he was dumbfounded when one marshal turned out to be a woman.

She answered matter-of-factly, "We tried to arrest them but they decided to shoot it out. Obviously, they lost."

***

When the investigation had been completed, Sue and Ted left the bank with two policemen as escorts. Ted had a roll of cash in his pocket pressed on him by a grateful bank president, who tore up the check he had written a short time earlier.

Constable O'Hara and another officer led them through the remainder of the curious crowd to the jewelry store. Ted paid for the locket and fastened it around Sue's neck.

He whispered, "I'd like to kiss my bride."

Constable O'Hara again took the lead. A short time later, they found themselves at the local precinct. He led them to Captain Mallory and excused himself, promising to return as soon as he completed his written report.

Captain Mallory eyed the two marshals, who were examining him in return. He waited several moments before he said dryly, "You two don't have a clue how much trouble you've stirred up around here, do you?"

He noted with approval as they suddenly turned wary and shifted in their chairs.

He explained, "The four men you shot it out with belong to an underworld gang that controls the court with jurisdiction in this precinct. They've bought off the judge, which we can't prove and you never heard me say. That means the three who've survived so far will probably go free."

His face was bland while his two visitors stared at him in consternation. Sue's disbelief was palatable. "I hope you're joking."

"I wish I were."

A thoughtful expression flitted across Ted's face. Sue was prepared to say more when she saw it and held back, waiting.

He mused. "The bank robbery would be a crime under state law. What if we filed charges in federal court? Say attempted murder of U.S. Marshals? Maybe even go for murder since one of them did kill his accomplice. Take the legal proceedings away from this precinct and the crooked judge."

The captain's face erupted in a huge smile. "That's brilliant! I love it." He leaned back in his chair and did a cat-like stretch. "I like it so much that's what we'll do. If you're willing to help, we'll transfer them to the Federal Court House right now."

"We'd be glad to," Ted agreed heartily.

"There's something you said earlier I wanted to ask you about first." Sue said, making her mystification obvious.

"What was that?"

"I've been wondering what Greek mythology has to do with criminals?"

The captain stared at her in confusion, trying to recall his own words. "When did I ever say anything about Greeks?"

"You said the bank robbers were part of an underworld gang. The Greeks are the only people I ever read about who believed in an underworld."

The captain exploded in laughter, tears of mirth running down his cheeks. He was still chuckling when he explained, "The land along the edge of the lake used to be much lower and would flood badly. That area was filled in to raise the flood plain, and a lot of basements of old buildings were just covered over, leaving a rats-nest of places where the criminals moved in to live and hide. They live underground, so we call them the underworld."

Sue grinned sheepishly while Ted chuckled. "That makes more sense than Greek mythology."

The captain led the way to the cells, and a short time later, they found themselves perched on the seat of a paddy wagon headed for the Federal Building. It wasn't far, and very shortly, three bitterly protesting prisoners were locked in cells or the small infirmary.

Captain Mallory and Marshal Lawson were old friends, so both were aware of the criminal influence within the city court. "I certainly appreciate the assistance your men gave my fellow marshals," the marshal offered blandly.

"Since my fellow marshals aren't familiar with the city, I'm glad you brought them here with no delay. We'll file the charges tonight, so the judge can arraign them in the morning."

The captain handed over the file with the written statements of his officers and the witnesses. "We were glad to be of help." He winked as he turned and departed.

***

Sue and Ted were involved in several court proceedings over the next two days, which were avidly reported by a mob of reporters to a public demanding more information about the unusual Marshals Storm. Two badly wounded bank robbers continued to be held in the infirmary under armed guard. Another, recovering from a severe headache, was in jail... the fourth had been hurriedly buried.

The second night of their unplanned stay, Sue was cuddled in Ted's arms in the privacy of their hotel room. "I hope we don't run into another holdup on the way home," she lamented. "If we do, we'll be old and gray before we get there."

***

The clerk in the Washington Post office looked up when a voice asked, "Any general delivery for Ed Smith?"

He turned to his rack and checked before handing over a plain white envelope postmarked in St. Louis. The recipient's appearance was unassuming, but the eyes were so cold the clerk's skin crawled. He hastily averted his own gaze.

The man tore open the envelope and read the short message, breaking into a string of curses. The unsigned message was cryptic.

Chickens flew coop some other direction. No see one week I go roost.

CHAPTER 29

Sue's heart was racing even before the conductor walked through the car, announcing loudly. "Peoria, next stop. All passengers for Peoria, next stop."

Ted felt her racing pulse as he held her hand. He whispered an encouragement, "Don't forget all of the research we've done. This is the only Peoria that was big enough to have a library twenty years ago. This is the right town." He kept his own doubts to himself. He hoped there was still someone living here who would remember Max or June Mason.

Sue flashed him a smile, but his words did nothing to slow her heartbeat as the train pulled to a stop. She practically leaped to her feet, but he kept his grip. She was forced to slow for him.

As soon as they were on the platform next to the station, Ted headed for the baggage car to claim their trunks. Sue hurried inside to the ticket window where she waited until the clerk looked up. "Could you tell me where to find the town library?"

The clerk was obviously startled by her appearance but directed, "Out the front door. Left three blocks, then turn right for another six blocks."

"Thanks. Where would I find a hack for hire?"

"There's a livery just across the street next to the hotel."

They left their luggage in the checkroom at the station before crossing the street to the livery, where they engaged a hack. A few minutes later, they pulled up in front of a substantial brick building. Their driver assured them it was the finest library in the state outside of Chicago.

"Wait for us." Sue's voice showed her tension. "We may be only a few minutes, or it might be hours. We'll need you when we're done here."

She almost ran up the steps to the door while Ted followed. "Take it easy," he cautioned. "A few seconds won't make any difference after all these years. We don't want you to trip and break your neck."

"I know that!" She snapped. "I can't help it."

She pulled the heavy door open, and they found themselves in a large foyer with a desk centered in the middle. Shelves of books stretched away in all directions with numerous patrons seated at small tables placed at regular intervals. A young woman not much older than Sue herself was seated at the desk and looked up, obviously startled by their sudden appearance.

"May I help you?"

Sue tried to stifle her disappointment at not finding someone old enough to have ended her quest. "I hope so. Would you know who the librarian was here about twenty years ago?" Time stood still as she felt her hopes suddenly evaporate.

The librarian broke into a smile and Sue began to breathe again. "Yes, I do. My Aunt May was the librarian then. You can find her at the office of The Peoria Reporter. You've made me very curious. Would you mind my asking why you want to know?"

"Thank you!" They'd already turned and were headed for the door. Sue called back over her shoulder, "She may be my only link to my mother's family."

The librarian's *good luck* was cut off by the closing door.

The waiting driver knew the city well and dropped them off a few minutes later at the door of a rambling brick building. Sue clasped Ted's hand tightly as they walked through the doorway, her heart beating so loudly she was sure it could be heard across the room. A low counter separated them from three desks arranged along the back wall, two of which were occupied by young women. The third was occupied by a woman who looked old enough to be their mother and who was intently writing in a ledger. The clatter of machinery drifted through an open doorway in one corner.

"I'll be with you in a moment," one of the young women offered.

Sue moved to the counter and braced her shaking body against it. One hand gripped her Stetson while the other crushed Ted's hand as she waited in an agony of suspense.

"How can I help you?" The young woman asked.

Sue's voice was shaking and her words were abrupt. "I'm looking for someone named May. I understand she was the librarian here twenty—"

The older woman instantly looked up at the sound of Sue's question. Her face turned ashen. She gasped, "June! Is it really you?" Her face fell as she said, bitterly disappointed. "No. It can't be. You're much too young."

"My mother's name was June." Sue offered in confusion.

May's voice abruptly rose in pitch and volume. "What is your father's name? Tell me, please!"

Sue's voice and body were quaking as she gulped. Her voice squeaked, "Max Mason."

The two seated young women stared in astonishment as May leapt from her chair. She raced from behind the counter and threw her arms around Sue in a fierce hug. She wailed. "You look exactly like your mother, niece of mine! Tell me about your mother! Tell me your name! Tell me! Tell me!"

"I'm Sue." Tears of mingled joy and sorrow streamed down her face. "Mother died when I was four. My father was killed in an accident two years ago."

May crushed her cheek against her much taller niece as broken sobs shook her body. "I knew my sister had to be dead." She blubbered, "If she were alive, she would've written to let me know."

The two young women had left their desks and were standing a few feet away, staring in shock at the sobbing pair who were oblivious to their surroundings.

Ted said dryly, "It would seem Sue has found her family at last." He introduced himself and asked. "You would be…?"

"I'm Lucy." The older of the two nodded in the direction of the other. "She's my sister, Anna. This is quite a shock for all of us. We never knew we had another cousin."

"Sue didn't know until about a month ago that she had any family at all," Ted explained. "This is as overwhelming for her as it is for May. Is she your mother?"

"Yes." Lucy turned to her sister. "I'll go start telling the rest of the family that Aunt June's daughter has found us. They should meet us at Mother's house as soon as possible."

She started for the door, and Ted called after her, "Take our hack. We won't need it for a while. Tell the driver I'll settle up with him later."

Ted and Anna waited until May finally released Sue from her crushing embrace. She drew back to arm's length with her eyes fixed on her niece's face. Tears continued to trickle down her face. "I've known for years my sister must be dead because she never, ever, wrote. It hurts to know she's gone, but the uncertainty was far worse." Her Adam's apple bobbed several times. "How and when did she die?"

Sue's tears matched her aunt's. "She died in childbirth when I was four."

May wiped her eyes with the back of her hand. "Your grandmother is living with me. Let's go break the news to her." Only then did she turn her head and realize one of her daughters had disappeared.

Anna explained. "Lucy went to tell the rest of the family that June's daughter is here and they should meet at your house."

May's laugh was a bit shaky. "Then we'd better get there before everyone else starts to arrive. Anna, tell Maurice he'll have to watch the office for a while."

May released her grip on Sue and stepped back, seeing for the first time the marshal's star pinned to the faded blue shirt. Her eyes widened more when she realized there was a gun belt buckled around the slim waist as well. "You're a marshal!" Her voice squeaked in amazement.

"Yes." Sue grinned.

"And this gentleman is your husband?"

"Yes. I'm now Missus Ted Storm."

"Tell me about yourself, please." She paused for a second... before Sue could respond, she added, "If you want to wait until everyone is at the house, that's fine. That way you won't have to repeat everything."

Sue followed her aunt outside where May and Anna fell in on either side. Ted followed.

“As I said, I’m now Missus Ted Storm. We’re both United States Marshals but will be ranchers when we get back to Colorado.”

CHAPTER 30

May's home was only a few blocks away. They moved briskly along the red brick sidewalk shielded from the hot summer sun by a succession of leafy maple, oak and elm. Several people who knew May tried to engage them in conversation as they passed, but May politely declined, telling each. "It's a long story and Mother needs to know first. I promise to tell you about it as soon as possible."

They covered the short distance in just a few minutes. They were taking a short cut through an alley to the back of her house when May stopped abruptly. "Your appearance has been such a shock I didn't realize until now you probably don't even know your mother's maiden name, which was Ashworth. Your grandmother's name is Ruth. Your grandfather died eight years ago."

Sue was silent, feeling overwhelmed by the rush of events.

They followed May into the kitchen where they left their Stetsons on the table. "Mother is usually in the parlor at this hour. I'm sure we'll find her there." She smiled sadly at her daughter. "Anna, why don't you wait here?"

She raised her voice. "Mother. You have visitors."

Sue gulped, and almost crushed Ted's hand as she followed her aunt into the parlor. An elderly woman with white hair was seated on a couch, knitting. She turned to them, her smile vanishing instantly when she saw Sue's face for the first time.

May's voice was gentle. "Mother, this young woman is your granddaughter, June's only child. Her name is Sue Mason Storm. The gentleman is her husband, Ted. I'll let her tell you the rest."

Ruth's face had paled at May's explanation. Tears began to stream down her face as she held Sue's eyes. "I can see from your faces my June is dead," she choked. "May. Would you leave me alone with my new granddaughter? I want to have her to myself for a while."

Ted assumed he was included in the gentle dismissal and followed May out. Her grandmother beckoned Sue to the couch beside her, both beginning to cry before the door had closed.

***

Sue asked uncertainly through her tears, "Do I call you…Ruth?"

"All of my grandchildren call me Granma. You're just my newest one."

Sue's voice was unsteady when she continued, "I've learned a little about my father's family but know nothing about my mother's…yours." She asked haltingly. "I have to know. Why did they have no contact with you?"

Her grandmother wrapped an arm around her. "Your grandfather, Albert, could be a proud and unreasonable man. When your mother told us she wanted to marry your father, he was furious. He did not trust an academic... your father was a young professor at the local college and a man of the wrong religion. When he forbade your mother from even seeing your father, much less getting married, they eloped. He made such a scene I'm sure they felt they would never be welcomed by anyone in the family."

Sue's eyes glistened with tears.

"Only once did I tell your grandfather he was a stubborn and unforgiving man... the night we found them gone. I know he regretted what he did until his dying day. I pray that June could forgive him when they met again."

There was a comfortable silence for some time before Sue felt she could control her voice and began to relate her life following the death of her mother and the following death of her father. She continued through the years of living alone and hesitated. "I hate to admit it, but I do owe Snake Carson a thank you for bringing Ted and me together."

"Snake Carson? That name sounds ominous. Tell me about him."

Sue's heart was in her throat, expecting condemnation as she told her grandma a condensed version of her encounter with Snake and his gang, resulting in the gun battle that caused so many deaths.

She wilted in relief when Granma said, "I came to this state as a young girl in a covered wagon. We had to fight off outlaws and bandits, all of them white men, both on the trail and after we settled here." She smiled wanly at Sue. "Sometimes good people have to meet violence with violence just to survive. You have done nothing to be ashamed of and I'm proud of you."

***

May whispered fiercely to Ted before the door had fully closed behind them. "Tell us everything you can about my niece and her parents, please."

Ted obeyed, following May and Anna through the kitchen and onto a wide porch cuddled against three sides of the rambling house. Several people were already waiting and they clustered around Ted and the two women.

More visitors of all ages trickled in as Ted answered their questions, which were passed on to new arrivals. The mass of people was beginning to crowd the porch.

He asked, "There's getting to be quite a crowd. How many brothers and sisters do you have?"

May laughed through her tears of joy. "Our father had a sense of humor in some things. There were four girls. He named us April, May, June, and Summer. He named our brothers Albert Junior, Julius, and August." She caught her breath. "June was the next to youngest. April is the oldest, but she lives quite some distance from Peoria, so it'll be a while before she arrives."

There was a momentary interruption when Sue and her grandmother stepped onto the porch holding hands. In her hurry to spread the word to the rest of the family, Lucy had neglected to include any specific details. Astonished gasps and widened eyes resulted.

Ruth announced in a trembling voice, "I want you to meet your newest relative, Sue Mason Storm. I want you to know I'm very proud of this young woman! I know you will be too when you get acquainted. May, would you introduce Sue to everyone?" Her voice strengthened.

***

The hour was late when they clustered around the table in May's kitchen. Physically and emotionally exhausted, Sue braced her elbows on the table to support her head in her hands. Her euphoria had evaporated but she gathered enough energy to say. "May. You know almost everything there is to know about me. Tell me about yourself because I know there aren't many women who are newspaper publishers."

May's smile was pensive. "I met Henry Lawson when I worked at the library and he worked at the paper. He bought the business the year we were married. We had five good years and two daughters before he died." Her glance swept the table and smiled fondly. "You and I are very much alike, Sue. I wasn't about to let anyone tell me I couldn't make a go of it just because I was a woman. It has been hard work, but it's been worth it."

Sue smiled agreeably.

There was steely pride in her voice. "Lucy and Anna have both worked in the office since they were toddlers. They're the ones who pushed me to get a Linotype machine to set the type even though I didn't think we could afford it."

"Really?"

Her face brightened. "We've proved the naysayers wrong and developed a successful business. Best of all, my daughters have husbands who love and respect them. Nothing else really matters."

***

May organized a huge picnic dinner for them on the day before their planned departure. She invited all of Sue's newfound relatives as well as many family friends.

The dishes were washed and put away. Sue was taken from one group to another, being welcomed by the adults and viewed with awe by the youngsters, especially the girls. She was seated next to her grandmother and surrounded by a cluster of all ages when her uncle Julius approached her for the first time.

He snapped, "I suppose you came back, so you could claim your mother's inheritance?"

Shocked and furious at such callousness, Sue still managed to keep her voice civil. "I have never, ever, considered such a thing! You've had family around you all of your life and can never appreciate how empty life is if you don't have any!" she snapped. "I have no need of any money my mother might have been entitled to. I'm a wealthy woman in my own right."

He was skeptical, and his tone just short of a sneer. "I suppose you inherited a fortune from your professor father?"

She responded in like tone. "I inherited a small ranch from my father when he was killed. The rest of what I have was earned with my own sweat and blood."

Her cousin, Ellie, the librarian, tried to divert her uncle and soften the mood. "Did you really run a ranch all by yourself?"

Sue responded matter-of-factly, "Yes, I did. That's what led to the rustling that brought Ted into my life." She recounted those days with a brief review of the events that led Ted to Wilford, elaborating only to the extent she had met him in town.

Eleven-year-old Audrey, who had been listening avidly, piped up, "That's so romantic."

Julius snapped. "Hush!" He turned angrily to Sue. "I suppose you're going to tell me you found a gold mine or something else just as unlikely."

Sue was more civil in her reply, but her anger was obvious. "We were both wounded in an ambush. I had a shootout with the gang and its leader, who kept a tally of the thirty-eight people he murdered. There were large rewards on their heads."

Shocked silence ensued but was broken by Grandmother Ruth. "I told everyone I was proud of my newest granddaughter! She has made her world and ours a safer place by eliminating such evil."

Julius flushed and stomped off, never looking back.

"He's always been a tightwad, even as a child," Ruth told Sue softly. "Sometimes, I'm not proud of my own son. Don't you worry about him."

***

Sue's head nodded against Ted's shoulder, keeping time with the clickity-clack of the wheels on the rails. They'd risen very early to catch the train headed north toward the Mississippi River towns of Rock Island and Davenport. The warmth of the early morning sun combined with minimal sleep for several nights had her drifting in and out of a doze.

Sue started fully awake when the conductor walked through the car, calling. "Galesburg. Next stop."

She blinked, meeting Ted's smiling eyes, blushing when he whispered, "Lo, my sleeping beauty wakes as through the yonder window morning breaks." He chuckled at her expression.

"That's a bad imitation of Shakespeare, but you are a lovely woman."

She returned his discrete hug. "If we're at Galesburg, we should be crossing the Mississippi sometime around noon if my memory serves me correctly. Which means we'll be at your folks' sometime tomorrow."

Her memory was correct. Their train rolled onto one of the bridges spanning the mighty river just as the bell of an unidentified clock tolled the hour. They stopped for a few minutes at the Army's Rock Island Arsenal station while several uniformed officers disembarked before continuing on to the Iowa side into Davenport.

Midafternoon again found them on their way. Their route was tight against the bank of the wide river. They watched in fascination as each mile displayed one or more river craft from the smallest of rowboats to large stern and side-wheelers.

Rail traffic was also heavy, their train occasionally taking its turn on a siding, waiting for opposing trains to clear. The miles rolled by as they stopped at one river town after another: Camanche, Clinton, Sabula, Green Island, Bellevue and Dubuque.

They had a half-hour break and time for a quick meal while the locomotive took on fuel and water before rolling into the gathering dusk. Full darkness had fallen before they rolled into the small river town of Guttenberg.

"They planned to name it after the first printer, Gutenberg," Ted explained, "but whoever filed the papers misspelled the name."

Their train halted for only moments as mail sacks were loaded and unloaded before they were on their way once more. They were both exhausted when the train screeched to a halt a short time later.

"Marquette," the conductor announced. "All passengers must disembark. Trains for all points depart in the morning."

CHAPTER 31

Sue woke shortly after dawn, feeling much refreshed despite having slept for only a few hours. Quietly, she lay beside Ted, who was still asleep, stretching her stiffened muscles as languidly as a big cat. The first trace of dawn light allowed her to lovingly watch him sleep for a few minutes before she silently slipped out of her nightdress and began to run her fingers gently over his body.

Her gentle touch had the effect of holding a lighted match to a fuse. He awoke, returning her touch eagerly. He nipped her hardened nipples with his lips. Her body was transfixed as tremors shook her. His body hardened as he followed the curves of her body with his hands.

Much later, delightfully sated by their passionate lovemaking, she whispered in his ear, "This is why I would rather have stayed in a boarding house than at Aunt May's."

They ate a filling breakfast in the boarding house dining room before venturing into the early morning sunshine. A heavy curtain of fog obscured all sight of the river, limiting her view to a few yards horizontally. In marked contrast, the sky was clear overhead with the sun warm and bright. The fog was a thick blanket of white, accented by wisps and streamers and undisturbed by any breath of wind.

"It's like looking through a window of diamonds," she breathed. "I've seen fog and mist over mountain streams but never anything even remotely like this."

They viewed the shifting fog for a few minutes before Ted broke the silence. "If you look downriver to the first bluff showing above the fog, that's Pike's Peak. It was discovered by and named for the same Zebulon Pike who discovered Pike's Peak in Colorado."

He turned away from the river. "Almost all of this stretch of river, for miles up and down stream, has only a very narrow strip of flat land along the shore. Sometimes, it's only a few yards wide, just enough for a rail bed, before the bluffs start rising steeply. In some places, five hundred feet or more."

Sue followed his lead, listening.

He indicated the town crowded around them. "The railroad built their junction here because that small valley coming down from the west gave them a straight east-west route across the river. It's the only spot where they could do so for many miles up or down river."

Ted held her by the waist and turned Sue to face the rising mist over the river. "You can't quite see it yet, but the mouth of the Wisconsin River is right across from us. That's where the first Europeans ever to see the Mississippi, Frenchmen named Marquette and Joliet, entered the river."

They walked to the depot, arriving with time to spare, claiming their luggage from the check room and prepared to board.

Sue stared at the waiting train for a moment, mystified. "Why in the world do we have two locomotives? We've never had them before."

Ted started to reply but was overwhelmed when a safety valve on one of the locomotives suddenly popped to relieve the excess steam pressure. He raised his voice to be heard above the noise. "It's hard to believe, but the grade from here to the top of the bluff is steeper than any other we've traveled before. Even in the mountains. The valley we're going to follow is too narrow to build switchbacks, so they add more power to get up the bluff using brute force."

The safety valve closed and quiet returned once more.

His voice returned to normal. "They'll drop off the engine at the first stop because the land levels out. They don't need it for the route farther west. They'll add it to the next train on the return trip to give them added braking power."

***

The sun was midmorning high while they watched the extra locomotive being coupled to an east-bound headed for the river. After it departed, they snuggled against each other on the iron bench, waiting for their connecting train. The morning sun bathed them with its warmth while they enjoyed the closeness.

"This is about as close to heaven as I'm likely to get," Sue whispered.

A short time later, the distant wail of a whistle announced the impending end of their solitude. A few minutes later, a short train of mixed passenger and freight cars pulled up at the tiny station. Twenty minutes later, they were under way once again on its return trip southbound.

"Ours will be the second stop, so it won't be long before we get there," Ted said. "The curves aren't as sharp, and the grade isn't as steep as in your beloved Colorado, but you'll see some similarities."

Sue could see the parallels as the track twisted and turned, following a flowing stream fed by springs instead of snowmelt. A heavy forest of hardwoods, instead of softwoods, crowded the right-of-way, occasionally forming clearings for a homestead or small meadow. Their route descended steadily for miles until they reached the floor of a river valley and turned sharply east. Shortly after, they pulled into a small town where they halted for the few minutes necessary to load and offload passengers and mail.

They rolled to a stop again less than ten minutes later. Ted laughingly imitated the conductor's chant, "All passengers for Canada will disembark. Canada!"

They were the only passengers to get off. They waited for the baggage and freight to be unloaded onto the station's freight wagon. The train departed with a blast from the whistle as the station agent bent to check the tags on the trunks before he turned to them.

"Hello, Silas," Ted greeted him.

The agent's face twisted first in bafflement then in recognition. "By all that's holy! Is it really you, Ted Storm?"

"It sure is." Ted's hand was enveloped in a hearty embrace as Silas boomed an enthusiastic welcome.

Ted grinned. "Silas. I'd like you to meet my wife, Sue." He turned slightly to Sue. "This is an old friend of mine, Silas Wilson."

The agent turned to face Sue and gasped when he realized the young man with Ted was really a young woman. He managed a weak greeting. "Pleased to meet you."

"Glad to meet you." She smiled and offered her hand.

Ted chuckled at his friend's discomfiture. Silas grinned sheepishly before offering them a ride to the livery. A few minutes later, they were squeezed into the seat of the delivery wagon headed for the stable a half mile away. Shortly after, they were on their way with their luggage lashed onto the back of a buggy pulled by two spirited bays.

They clattered across a nearly new iron bridge on the way out of town and were quickly lost in shadow. The road cut a narrow path overshadowed by a forest of oaks, maples, and myriad of other hardwoods. Ted let the team set its own pace, a rapid trot that slowed only slightly when the trail began to climb steeply.

He pulled the team in at the top of the mile-long hill and held them to a walk, allowing them to cool slowly. He waved with his left hand at a clearing that sheltered a farmstead as they passed. "Almost all of the land around here was originally solid timber with only a few open meadows. Every field and farmstead you see has been carved out of the forest one tree and one stump at a time."

Sue was impressed. "That's even harder work than ranching."

"It sure is." Ted's grin was lopsided. "One of the reasons I left Iowa."

The sun was high when they turned into the farmyard. The house faced south, a rambling structure... one end built of logs and the other of sawed lumber. A tall barn with a hip roof faced the yard, slightly down hill and downwind from the house. A cluster of draft horses were tied at the water trough in the shade of a huge elm.

"Looks like everyone is here for dinner," Ted observed as he drove the team up to the same trough. "Our timing is perfect."

Ted's back was to the house when he stepped down from the buggy and turned to help Sue down. When he turned to face the house, a wild yell erupted from an open window.

"It's Ted!"

A mass of people streamed from the opened door of the house, calling joyful greetings as they spread out to engulf Ted. The flow divided once again to allow a tall woman to reach him and envelope him in her arms with tears of joy streaming down her face. A moment later, a rotund man joined her to pound him joyously on the shoulder.

Ted savored the tumult for a few moments before he gently lifted his mother's tear-streaked face up from his chest. He raised his voice so the throng could hear. "Ma. Pa. Everybody." When the hubbub had subsided, he announced. "I brought someone with me I'd like you to meet."

With their attention riveted on him, Ted stepped to Sue's side and wrapped his arm around her. "I'd like you to meet my wife, Sue."

There were a few seconds of stunned silence before Beth Storm took two steps and wrapped Sue in a welcoming embrace. She raised her own eyes to meet brown eyes set in a pale face. "Welcome to the family. I'm delighted to meet my newest daughter."

***

Sue's legs were unsteady as she stood with her back to the buggy. She was clearly overwhelmed by the flood of family surrounding Ted. The lack of any family in her own life did not prepare her for such a rush and she was suddenly afraid—afraid of not being accepted by her new family.

When the tumult quieted for Ted's announcement, she froze while everyone turned to her. Tears of relieved joy wet her cheeks as her color returned at the warm welcome. Beth's own face was damp as she held Sue in a welcoming embrace while the rest of the family added their greetings.

Beth released her grip so she could get the full measure of the young woman who towered over her. She stared at the marshal's star pinned to the man's shirt before her eyes dropped to the gun belt and revolver. She gasped, "You're a marshal too!"

"Yes." Sue's waning confidence returned. "That's how I met Ted, but it's a very long story."

"You can tell us over dinner." Beth turned slightly, one finger rapidly selecting four youngsters. "You kids take care of the horses and their bags."

The four teenagers broke from the crowd to take care of their new duties while the rest of the family flowed back to the house. Two plates were added to the table while Beth complained good-naturedly about the bread that burned while she was outside to greet the newlyweds.

When everyone was seated, Ted introduced his three sisters, his brother, and their spouses. He begged off introducing the numerous nieces and nephews. He grinned. "Some of this mob was born after I left home. Most of the rest were babies or toddlers. They've grown so much I can't keep them straight now."

After an extended period of conversation and eating, Ted joined the other men when they returned to the field to bring in the day's cutting of hay. Sue remained behind with the women and girls as they began to clear the table and wash the dishes.

Beth smiled and steered Sue to a tall stool near the window. "Sue. This is one time you get to take it easy. Tell us all about yourself. We'll listen while we do the dishes."

Sue wanted to protest not helping, but a gentle shake of Beth's head changed her mind. She left out nothing, wanting her new relatives to know who she really was. Little girls and grown women listened in fascination. Their emotions ran from shock to admiration and envy. She was interrupted frequently by questions but the dishes were washed, dried, and put away long before she finished.

"...and then we pulled into the yard. I was shaking but I couldn't run," she laughed nervously.

Beth swept Sue into her arms. "I called you daughter already. You're still my newest daughter. We're proud to have you in the family. I'm sure you'll be the only one of us to ever dance with the President." She smiled broadly.

***

Ted's brother, Fred, and sister-in-law Wanda, shared the operation of the home farm with his parents. During the next few days, Sue came to regard Wanda as the sister she had never had, and Beth as the mother figure she had lost so many years before.

They spent many hours together while preparing for and cleaning up after meals, or just sitting and talking. Sue was taking her turn at the dishpan. "Beth, I'm so happy I met Ted. Before I met him, I was always angry. Angry at the ranchers who were trying to marry me off. Angry at Ma and Pa for dying. Angrier at the rustlers. Angry at the world in general."

She fell silent and Beth patted her shoulder comfortingly. "Being in love makes the whole world better, doesn't it?"

"It sure does." Her throat constricted when she uttered a word she hadn't used for many years, "Thanks, Mom."

Beth's eyes were moist with unshed tears. "If you ever need me, just write and I'll be on my way."

"When I know I need you, I'll write immediately and include a train ticket."

Beth smiled knowingly. She patted Sue gently on the back before turning to her bread dough.

***

The small community of Canada had been buzzing all week long with the news that Ted Storm was back to visit. Fact and rumors regarding his new bride had also spread widely—a bride who was wearing a gun and a marshal's star. Rumors of gunfights and train robberies abounded, embellished with each retelling.

Ted's parents and his brother's family filled the farm wagon to almost overflowing for their usual Saturday trip to town. Ted shook his head with a laugh when they were invited to squeeze in, electing to harness the team of his rented rig.

A heavy rain shower the night before had turned their dirt road muddy, so the pace of the small convoy was slow at first. Clear skies, warm sun, and a stiff breeze had nearly dried the road's surface before they rolled into town.

The street and boardwalks were crowded as the Storms drove into town and halted at a hitch rail. Old friends and curious onlookers descended on the newlyweds when Ted helped Sue down from their rig. He turned to face the crowd who were clustered around them, bursting with poorly concealed pride. He greeted many friends, introducing each of them to a poised and confident Sue.

Ted and Sue were surrounded and bombarded with questions all morning long by neighbors, friends and family as they moved slowly up and down the street. The rest of their immediate family was also pigeon-holed by their own peers, especially the youngsters who were the envy of their own circles of friends. More than one story about aunt and uncle was embellished to some degree by the youngsters as they basked in the admiration of their peers.

Beth spent much of the day with her own circle of friends, emphasizing her pride in Sue's steely independence. She also shared Sue's triumph over being orphaned and alone. Those friends listened raptly as Beth related Sue's days in Washington D.C. and looked most envious when they learned Sue and Ted had danced with the President and First Lady.

CHAPTER 32

Sunday promised to be an even bigger day for the entire Storm family. Friends, neighbors, and extended family gathered at the small neighborhood country church following morning services. The guests of honor were dressed in their finest with Ted in his black marshal's outfit. Sue wore the purple silk gown she had worn in D.C., eliciting envy and a multitude of compliments from the women in attendance.

They were in constant demand as they moved from one group to another. Beth watched with amusement from a distance while an admiring gaggle of girls of all ages trailed Sue. They hung onto her every word with an almost visible cloud of hero-worship surrounding them.

The sun was dipping low in the west before the reception broke up. The majority of those in attendance were farm families who then hurried homeward to take care of the ever waiting chores.

****

Ted and Sue stood together away from the lights of the house and from obstructing trees, admiring the slowly fading colors in the sky as darkness descended.

Sue said softly, "The sunsets here sure last a lot longer than they do back home."

"They sure do. Without the mountains, it takes quite a while to get totally dark."

She snuggled against him as he wrapped her in his arms. He continued with a twinge of sadness in his voice. "Enjoy it tonight. Tomorrow, we'll be headed back to our own home and its sudden sunsets."

His lips lifted in a smile as he sought her sparkling eyes. He said softly in return, "I'd say finding family has agreed with you."

Her smile matched his as her eyes danced. "Yes. I did find there are a couple of stinkers in the family, but now I know who I am and where I'm from." She kissed him. "And I know who I'm sharing my future with."

***

They watched the Iowa countryside change as the miles rolled past. Rough and rolling forest gradually changed to the gentle rise and fall of open prairie. Sue was fascinated by the contrast with her native Colorado mountains but decidedly not impressed by the heat and humidity of a scorching late summer Iowa afternoon.

She leaned toward the opened window, searching for what little comfort was available from the flow of coal-smoke laden air. Perspiration streamed down her face and soaked her shirt collar as she panted against the heat. Ted was equally uncomfortable, restlessly trying to relax by stretching his legs under the seat in front of them.

"Leonard will be lucky if I don't give him a pounding when we get back to Denver," Sue growled, only half joking as she gasped at the blast of hot air.

"The only reason I won't is because he had the good sense to send you to Wilford so I could marry you."

"I'll be sure to tell him how lucky he is," Ted laughed. "In the meantime, you'll be glad to know we'll be crossing the Missouri River into Omaha before long. When we change to a night train it'll be a lot cooler than this oven."

The sun was dipping low to the horizon when they rolled into Omaha. Lengthening shadows covered the bridge and the water below while butterflies multiplied in her middle as they rolled high above the water, dissipating only when they rolled onto the solid ground of Nebraska.

The conductor's song rang through the car, "End of the line. All passengers must disembark."

Ted sighed, "Only one more end of the line before we'll be home in Denver."

Sue smiled. "It's been quite an experience, but it will be nice to be home again."

Their next train was an express that rolled westward, following the sun into the dusk and the darkness of full night. When the tracks met the Platte, they turned northwestward.

The conductor found time to visit with the passengers. "We'll follow the Platte most of the way to Denver, tracing a big arc that swings from northwest to southwest until we get there."

Their train rolled into Denver the next morning well after sunrise. Both were so travel-weary they sat numbly until the car was nearly empty before they picked up their luggage and stumbled into the station.

Sam Barker greeted them cordially when they walked slowly into the lobby of the Drovers' House.

Ted's grin was lopsided. "Don't even think of letting anyone wake us. They're apt to get themselves shot if they do."

Sheer exhaustion and the lower temperature worked wonders. Sue was asleep almost instantly on the cool sheets. Much later, she was shocked when she awoke to see the midmorning sunshine of another day. She turned over, stretching stiffened muscles to find herself alone in the bed.

Her heart was light, humming to herself as she freshened up. She dressed as usual and headed downstairs.

The desk clerk looked up and smiled when he saw her. "Good morning. Ted asked me to tell you he'd be in the dining room. That wasn't too long ago, so I'm sure that you'll find him there now."

She found Ted in the dining room where he gave her a discrete caress as she slid into the booth beside him. "I can't believe we slept as long as we did."

"I couldn't believe it either. I must've been more tired than I thought."

Other diners stopped to greet them, offering best wishes for their marriage and congratulations for their achievements in Washington D.C. Both looked at the other, mystified.

Claire Gray explained. "Senator Hill sent copies of the Washington papers to The Denver Post every time you were featured. They reprinted every article, so most of Colorado knows what you did."

Sue blushed, and Ted rolled his eyes. "Don't believe even half of what you read," she sighed.

When they had finished breakfast, they walked the short distance to the Federal Court House. They were immediately ushered into Leonard Simpson's private office where he met them with a wide smile.

"I've been expecting you. I heard last night you got back to town during the day." He grinned. "All I asked you to do was to make a delivery but you accomplished far more. Senator Hill sent me reports, both while you were in Washington and after you left. The Marshal Service is one of the very few agencies that didn't have their budgets cut. It's the senator's opinion your testimony was a significant factor. We didn't get any more money, but we didn't lose any either, which is a major positive. The committee was forcefully reminded that protection of the population is one of government's primary obligations."

Sue flushed as she fell speechless.

"I know. You don't think you did anything out of the ordinary but most of the rest of the world does," he chuckled. "I know most of what you did, but why don't you give me a full report in case I missed something?"

The morning slipped by while they took turns telling of their trip. They had just finished their report when there was a knock on the door.

A clerk entered. "I hate to interrupt, but there's a young man out here who says he has a message for Missus Storm. He claims it's a matter of her life and death."

The levity in the room vanished. Sue and Ted sprang to their feet and faced the door with hands near their holsters.

Sue's voice was brittle. "Send him in."

Her body was taut as a bowstring as the door opened wide. An unarmed stranger entered, his hands pointedly held chest high. His face was hidden by a neatly trimmed beard. She stared, trying to remember where she had seen him. Recognition suddenly dawned. Her hand dropped even closer to the butt of her revolver as the face of Theodore Preston Junior crystallized from her memory.

His voice was flat with no sign of the arrogance she remembered. "I see you remember me. Whether you believe it or not, I'm not the one who's out to kill you."

Her vigilance relaxed not a whit. "Ted. Leonard. I don't believe either of you have been introduced to Theodore Preston."

"I never have." Ted's voice crackled with menace. "I think he'd better give us an explanation."

"Why don't all of us sit down? I'll tell you why I'm here," he offered calmly. "After that, you can do whatever you want, but I'm leaving on the next train."

Sue and Ted sat down far apart, giving them an open field of fire. Their faces showed their clear suspicion.

"I know you don't have any reason to trust me," he admitted. "After what my father did, I don't blame you. My father is a member of an organized gang of criminals who will stop at nothing to get what they want. You wrecked their plans and they now want revenge. They'll go to any means to get even, so they sent a hired killer to Saint Louis to assassinate you on your way home. I know you didn't go through there because I went there myself to warn you. I asked around, but no one had seen you since you left D.C." His voice was bitter.

Her body began to tremble softly.

"I know about the hired killers because they told me their plans for you and were going to kill me too. The only reason I'm still alive is because they wanted me to squirm until they caught up with me." His voice strengthened. "I had nothing to live for back there, so I took what money I could scrape together and ran. I hate your guts and ain't a model citizen, but what conscience I have wouldn't let them gun you down with no warning. I decided to warn you before I disappeared."

Sue met his eyes. "Do you know if they sent more than one killer?"

He snorted in disgust, "There's only one. They think he's perfect, so why clutter things up or pay for more than one. Before you ask, I don't know what he looks like. I can't help you with a description," he sighed.

Sue turned her gaze to Ted to meet his for a moment. He was thoughtful as he considered for several moments before nodding in agreement.

"I believe you. We're indebted to you, and you can leave with a clear conscience." Ted extended his hand.

Theodore stared in disbelief for a moment before he offered his own hand in return.

Sue offered her hand, but he hesitated for a moment. Rather, he bowed with a courtly gesture and kissed the back of her hand. "Missus Storm, I hope you can forgive me. May both of you live long and happy lives." He turned on his heel and walked out without a backward glance.

They stared after him in silence until he disappeared. Sue broke the silence. "I certainly misjudged the man. He's not the worthless trash I thought he was. He has guts and honor."

Leonard grunted agreement and called his secretary from the door. "Hoyt. Go talk to the officer in charge at our usual precinct house. Tell him we need him here for a war council as soon as possible."

Hoyt nodded and left straight away.

Leonard turned back to Sue and Ted. "We have to assume a few things. One, the killer knows you are back in town. Two, he knows you will only be here for a few days. Three, he'll have to strike quickly. We can't assume anything else because he could be a bum or an aristocrat. In hiding or in plain sight."

Ted grimaced.

Leonard sighed and returned to his chair. "The two of you are going to have to be extremely careful. Hopefully, he isn't aware we've been warned. I think it's time for me to call in some favors... I know a few rats who'll sell their own mothers for a price. There must be whispers going around, and a stranger is going to be noticed sooner or later. If it's Captain Knudsen on duty, he can probably give us a list of newcomers at the upper end of society for his men to check out as well."

***

Captain Knudsen was in Leonard's office within the hour. He listened quietly while the situation was explained before asking one question. "What's this Theodore character look like?" Sue described him and the captain nodded. "I've seen him. I walked through the station on the way here. He was just getting on the train for Cheyenne. That's one less newcomer from the East, so we can concentrate on others."

"There are other Easterners in town?" Ted asked.

"Yeah. There are a dozen or so I personally know of that have drifted into town over the last month or so because of the new mines that have opened up. I mean the ones working in the general area of my precinct because our suspect would need to be sure of your return to Denver. I wouldn't think we'd have to worry about anyone that's been here longer than that. The problem is that the dozen are about evenly divided between trash and quality folk." He frowned. "Do we eliminate any with families with them? There are two with family that don't have jobs."

The room was silent for a moment as they exchanged glances. "I'm no expert," Sue began, "But I'd think that even though it would be a perfect cover, it would make it hard for a quick getaway."

Ted nodded his agreement.

Leonard said, "I'd have to agree. It's not likely that our assassin is a family man."

With that, their meeting broke up. Sue and Ted were to act as though they suspected nothing while remaining especially alert. Meanwhile, Leonard and Captain Knudsen would pressure all of their undercover sources for any hint as to the identity of the suspected killer.

CHAPTER 33

Midday had passed and they were hungry. There were many eating places near the court house, and Ted selected one of his favorites. They were still scanning the menu when friends and acquaintances began stopping by their table to offer congratulations.

Not wanting to attract too much attention, they ate quickly and went back to the streets where they were hailed again and again. Each meeting kept Sue on edge until Ted acknowledged the greeter by name. They were asked frequently how long they would be in Denver and one or the other would answer vaguely. "We'll only be here a few days."

After the first several queries, Sue whispered. "That should help smoke him out. He'll have to try for us here because he would really stand out if he were to follow us to Wilford."

They spent the last of the day going from one familiar business to another while covertly trying to gather a list of possible suspects, always being greeted warmly. While Ted carried most of the conversation, Sue watched unobtrusively for any unusual reaction to their presence.

They met in Leonard's office after full darkness fell to review every scrap of information anyone had collected.   Leonard gloomily summed up their efforts. "We don't have any prime suspects, but at least, we managed to eliminate a few possibilities. I guess that's progress of a sort. Anybody have anything to add before we go home?" He grimaced.

Sue cleared her throat. "I don't have anything other than a feeling, but I saw a couple of men I don't feel good about." She shook her head to forestall questions. "No. I don't have any specific reason. Call it intuition, if you will. We can check on them again tomorrow to see if they've done anything odd."

The meeting broke up a few minutes later. Sue and Ted headed back to the Drovers' House and a late supper in the dining room. The room was nearly empty, so they were able to discuss the day's events in some privacy. They reviewed everything again.

Ted asked, "I know you said that you didn't have anything specific to zero in on any suspects. Who are they, and what made you uneasy about the two?'

Sue thought for a second. "One of the clerks at West's General Store was real civil when we were talking to him face to face. After we turned to leave, I saw his face reflected in the front window. If looks could kill, we wouldn't have lived long enough to get out of there."

Ted reflected for a moment. "I don't recall the man at all. He hasn't been working there very long because he wasn't there the last time I was in the store. We'll check him out tomorrow." He was lost in thought. "And number two?"

"I'm afraid it's just a feeling. The clerk with the beard in Jackson's Mercantile was just too smooth a talker. I'd feel better if we knew when he started working there and where he came from."

Ted chewed on the idea for a while before he grinned mischievously. "I won't even tease you about a woman's intuition. I didn't notice anything unusual about them other than they're both newly hired. I do know someone we can ask about them but he's gone home by now. We can ask him in the morning."

The dining room was empty when they finished their meal. They picked up their room key and went through the lobby, climbing the three flights of stairs. The hall was dimly lit, adding to her sense of foreboding. When they reached their door, Ted signaled Sue to wait as he turned the key in the lock.

She nodded and flattened herself against the wall, unsurprised when he shoved the door open with the barrel of his revolver. They waited for several seconds, the silence oozing from the empty room like that of a tomb. Ted slipped inside and confirmed the room was empty.

He turned and dropped below the level of the window sill before tiptoeing back to the hallway. He closed the door, cutting off the dim light flowing into their room. Sue followed when he moved silently down the hall to the third door on the other side. Ted produced another key from his pocket and opened the door into a much smaller room overlooking the street. He waved her inside before locking the door behind them.

He whispered, "I spoke to Sam this afternoon. He didn't rent out any rooms on this floor for tonight. He put dummies in our bed and moved us here for the night... just in case we were to have unwanted visitors in our old room. This way, we don't have to be on watch all night."

***

They were sound asleep when a sudden roar of gunfire thundered through the hotel, shocking them awake. They dressed hastily. Ted took the lead, silently opening the door and scanning the dimly-lit hall with his Colt ready in his hand. His eyes met Sue's in the dim light spilling through the door. He slipped through the door and she followed with her own Colt at the ready. Both could hear a cacophony of voices coming from the lower floors.

They were almost at their old room when Ted pointed with his revolver. A ragged line of bullet holes were strung knee high along the wall. He leaped diagonally across the hallway, his shoulder smashing into the door, splintering the lock. His dive turned into a roll, and he was back on his feet, with his gun ready as Sue covered him from the hallway.

"He's gone. Wait in the hall until the crowd from downstairs gets here."

The night clerk arrived less than a minute later, brandishing a gun. His grim expression eased when he saw her standing at the door.

She said, "Whoever it was is gone. Can you get us a lamp? Ted needs it to look for evidence."

The stairway was jammed with curious onlookers who had followed the clerk up the stairs. Word was passed down the stairway. Moments later, a lamp from the lower floor was handed from one man to another. When the lamp reached Sue, she called to Ted.

"Are you ready for some light?"

"Yeah. He's long gone. I haven't been able to see anything out the window."

Sue held the lamp high while the clerk followed her into the room. Her throat tightened as she looked at the bed they would have been sharing. She shifted her eyes to meet Ted's grim scowl, both staring at two dummies riddled with bullet holes.

Her first reaction was fear. If they hadn't been warned and moved to a different room, they would've been dead. Fear erupted into white-hot rage. "Enough of this! We're going to settle this one way or another!"

Ted turned from the window where he had used the lamp to examine the exterior of the hotel. He saw the play of emotions on her face and echoed her. "We'll get him. He slid down from the roof on a rope. I didn't see any marks on the window sill, so he must've fired through the open window before sliding the rest of the way to the ground. The rope is about ten feet short, so it's possible he landed hard. Dawn's not far away, so the first thing we'll do is check on your two possible suspects."

At that moment, the crowd in the hallway grudgingly opened to allow the nightshift captain from the local precinct through. His quick glance swept the room. "Find anything yet?"

Ted was far more furious at the attempt on Sue's life than his own. He snapped, "No, but we're going to go question the two suspects Sue had reservations about yesterday."

***

Devon West was a deep sleeper and was still groggy when he responded to the heavy pounding on his door. He swore with gusto upon hearing the reason for his being awakened, unaware of Sue's presence, which would have embarrassed him if he had known.

He growled, "Yeah. Alfredo has only worked for me for about a month. Told me he was from Oregon and was working his way east. You can find him at Missus Akins' flophouse over on Oak Street."

Two officers staked out the back of the flophouse while Sue and Ted went to the door of Missus Akins' small apartment. They waited silently, hearing small sounds of someone stirring in response to their hearty knock.

A sleepy voice asked through the closed door, "Who is it?"

Ted hovered in the background while Sue answered. "I'm Marshal Sue Storm. I'd like to ask you some questions about one of your roomers."

Reassured by the sound of a female voice, the old woman opened the door slightly. The faint light of dawn illuminated a sleep-rumpled face. Her expression sharpened when Sue asked, "What can you tell me about the whereabouts of Alfredo Doria? Where is he now? Where was he last night?"

Missus Akins was snappish because of having been awakened. She snarled, "His room is the first one at the head of the stairs. He always pays his rent on time. As far as I know, he was in all night. Now, leave me alone!"

Sue murmured, "Thanks."

Her word was cut off by the closing door. She turned and headed for the stairs as Ted followed. The risers creaked slightly as they ascended. They stopped on a small landing in front of a flimsy wooden door. Ted pulled their room key from his pocket and examined it in the faint dawn light before inserting it in the lock. He turned the key very slowly and the lock opened with a faint click. He dropped his left hand to the doorknob as his revolver appeared in his right. He then nodded silently.

He shoved hard. The hinges squeaked shrilly in protest as the door swung open. He stepped inside with his gun covering the occupants of the bed. "Freeze! You're under arrest!"

Sue followed and flinched as the man ignored the command and tried to protect the body of the young boy beside him with his own. Silence returned except for whimpers of fear from the bed.

She said softly, "Ted. We have the wrong suspect."

She holstered her revolver and Ted did likewise. She stepped to the bedside and gently touched the man on the shoulder with her left hand, apologizing. "Please sit up. We made a mistake and I'm sorry. We mean you no harm and I'd like to explain."

The man's face turned toward her, radiating a wealth of emotions as fear, rage, and despair were replaced by hope. She shoved her Stetson back and dropped to one knee by the bed. Her right hand gently raised the frightened face of the boy to the light, comparing their features.

Sue's voice wavered as the fear on the boy's face slowly faded. "I'm sorry we scared you so badly. We were almost murdered in our bed tonight by a hired killer. After seeing your face reflected in the window yesterday as we were leaving, you were a prime suspect. You don't have to tell me, but why do you hate me so?"

The man's face and voice softened as he explained in the thick accent of a recent immigrant, "I do not hate you. Yesterday, I thought you were the same as the policeman in Oregon who accused my dear Rosa of being a thief before he murdered her. That is why we left Oregon and started back to the Old Country."

Sue stood up slowly. The eyes of father and son widened in alarm when her hands went to her wide gun belt, but both relaxed when the fingers of one hand slipped into the hidden pocket. She fumbled for a moment before withdrawing two objects that she placed in the father's hand.

Her voice was barely more than a whisper. "This is not charity, but a gift from one motherless child to another. Use it well for your son and yourself." Ted had already retreated and she turned to go. She whispered as she drew the door shut behind her, "Our apologies. You're free to go. I wish you luck."

The father and son stared at the closed door in shock as the footsteps retreated down the stairs. The father opened his clenched fingers, both gasping as the first full light of dawn reflected from two shiny gold double-eagles. His eyes misted as he whispered, "We have seen an angel. God is with us."

***

The two officers who'd been watching the alley headed on foot back to their precinct while Sue and Ted headed for the business district. They were still some distance from Jackson's when the imposing store front became easily visible. Two stories high, false front and porch extended the length of the building for much of a block. Several doorways allowed entry for customers... the horses of several early customers were tied to the hitch rail, waiting for their owners to conduct their business.

"Sure is a busy place for so early in the morning," Sue commented.

"Yeah. Jackson claims to be the biggest in Denver. I don't think he's exaggerating."

When they entered, their gun hands were ready for action but their suspect was nowhere to be seen. Ted hailed the owner and Sue described their quarry.

"That's Tex. He's usually late, but he's so good with figures I put up with it."

Sue's eyebrows rose. "Tex?"

"Yeah. He claims to be from Texas by way of Durango." *Not very likely* was left unsaid. "Started working for me about three weeks ago. You want to talk to him?"

"We sure would! Mind if we wait?"

"Not at all. It won't be long because I just saw him turn the corner down a block." Jackson pointed at a solitary figure some distance away.

Sue and Ted traded quick glances and headed for the door, waiting at the windows while each automatically checked the revolver in their holster. Their quarry sauntered up to the door, turning his head to greet an approaching customer. He stepped inside and stopped abruptly, his face turning white with disbelief.

"Hands up! You're under arrest!"

The suspect ignored the order and spun on his heel, leaping through the open door. The unsuspecting customer was knocked off his feet by the collision, but the suspect bounced away and ran for the horses at the hitch rail. He grabbed the reins of the first horse and tried to mount, but the horse shied away, kicking viciously at the rider and knocking him to the ground.

The fleeing man had drawn a Derringer but the impact of the kick knocked it from his hand. Stunned and blinded by dust, he groped desperately for the gun. His hand closed over it but he screamed in pain when Ted's boot heel landed hard.

Despite the early hour, spectators appeared from all directions. The suspect raised his head and saw two gun muzzles pointed at his head from inches away. He slumped in surrender. Ted lifted his boot and claimed the Derringer in the dust. A crowd gathered as the suspect sat up, dejection and resignation on his face.

Sue glared at him contemptuously until his eyes dropped. "Tex, a real Westerner knows that you mount a horse from the left side."

***

Their train was late because of a broken rail. Eric Thompson, Wilford's station agent, greeted them cheerily while they waited for their luggage to be unloaded.

"It's good to see you back again. Everybody's been following your adventures 'cause Jack's been printing them in the Messenger." He snickered. "You sure showed those stuck-up Easterners a thing or two."

The sun was brushing the mountains to the west while they walked the short distance to Manlick's Boarding House. Normally only a few minutes' journey, this time it took far longer as everyone stopped to ask questions and welcome them home.

When they finally reached the dining room, they were greeted with a hearty round of applause. Sue blushed crimson when Missus Manlick greeted her with a hug and said to Ted, "Sue sure got a keeper when she landed you."

Doc Madison and Jack Ames arrived together a few minutes later. The editor made a bee-line for their table. "I talked to a peddler who was in Denver last night. What's the story about the guy who tried to kill you?"

Sue grimaced. "I hoped you wouldn't hear about it. You've already told too many tall tales about us."

They tried to evade the question but were pelted with demands from everyone in the dining room. Ted surrendered for them both, relating how the suspect had broken under police questioning and revealed a plot extending all the way to Washington, D.C.

"The gang back East will probably never be charged for trying to kill us," he concluded. "But the law there now has their names and can dig for other evidence. They shot themselves in the foot when they sent their hired killer out here."

***

When they rode out of Wilford the next day, it was late and approaching midday. They rode into the ranch yard late in the afternoon as the shadows were lengthening. Sue dismounted at the porch and turned toward the ranch house, halting suddenly.

"What in the world is that?" She asked, pointing at the mountain behind the house.

A new stone structure squatted next to the stream of spring water that tumbled toward them. A trail of freshly-dug earth led from there to the ranch house.

"Oh. That. I'll have to show you." Ted's devilish grin lit his face.

He dropped his horse's reins and took her hand in his, leading her inside. Her eyes grew wide when he led her into the kitchen where she found a large tank mounted on the back of the stove. Two new faucets were poised above the sink... when he turned both water gushed out. He smiled to split his face. "Cold. And hot. When there's a fire in the stove, that is."

She followed in a daze as he led her down the hall to what had been a bedroom. She looked through the doorway and gawked at the new plumbing fixtures in astonishment. He grinned. "Indoor plumbing, no less."

Sue stumbled over her words in astonishment. "How did you do it?"

"I talked to old man Horwick before we left and told him to go ahead."

She was still stunned and he laughed at her discomfiture. "I know it's backwards compared to most marriages. Usually dowry is paid before, not after the wedding."

She laughed through tears of joy and kissed him as he wrapped her in his arms.

***

Sundown was fast approaching while they stood side by side, watching the western horizon.

They admired the muted colors of a glorious sunset in silence until Sue broke the silence. "I said it before, but the sunsets here sure don't last as long as they did back in Iowa."

"Without mountains, it does take quite a while for full darkness to fall," he acknowledged.

She snuggled against his shoulder in silent contentment.

"I'm glad we're finally home with our sudden sunsets," he said softly.

Sue turned to face him with her eyes sparkling in the afterglow of sunset. "Tonight and tomorrow, and for all of our tomorrows, the three of us can watch."

Ted froze with his arms wrapped around her as his voice turned incredulous. "The three of us?"

"We're going to have a baby." She bubbled happily.

His wild cowboy yell of joy half deafened her before it echoed back from the surrounding mountains. Startled wildlife broke into flight as the Marshals Storm kissed.

www.ingramcontent.com/pod-product-compliance
Lightning Source LLC
Chambersburg PA
CBHW070740190726
48292CB00002B/348